FAITHLESS

VENGEFUL GODS MC
BOOK 1

CRYSTAL ASH

VENGEFUL GODS MC PLAYLIST

Rise Against - The Violence
Me First and the Gimme Gimmes - Straight Up
Halestorm - Heathens
Mushroomhead - Holes in the Void
Stone Sour - Song #3
The Civil Wars - Devil's Backbone
Egypt Central - White Rabbit
STARSET - Monster
Thrice - Black Honey
Cilver - I'm America
Linkin Park - Burn it Down
Dorothy - Gun in my Hand
Atmosphere - Graffiti
Badflower - Animal
Nirvana - Rape Me

Listen on Spotify: crystalashbooks.com/VGMC

GLOSSARY & PRONOUNCIATIONS

- **Tezcatlipoca** (Tess-CAHT-lee-POKE-ah): An Aztec deity of the night sky, hurricanes, sorcery and divination, jaguars, war, and more.
- **Astarte** (As-STAR-tay): A Canaanite and Phoenician goddess of war, love, healing and hunting
- **Jandro** (HAN-dro): Short for Alejandro, one of Rori's fathers
- **Mija/Mijita** (MEE-ha/MEE-hee-tah): My daughter, derived from *mi hija*
- **Viejito** (Vee-HEE-toe): Old man, diminutive form
- **Callate** (CAH-yah-teh): Shut up
- **Paloma** (pah-LO-mah): Dove

CONTENT WARNING

This series takes place in a dystopian world and contains graphic violence, foul language, and sexually explicit scenes.

This book also contains people who are enslaved (gladiators/sex workers).

The epilogue contains blatant misogyny, as well as references of violence against women, and implied sexual assault of a male character.

I had never seen anything like it before. Blood and carnage covered the sands. Audience members in the colosseum were standing, yelling and pumping their fists at the grisly scene below. My fellow gladiators stood at my sides, shoulders stiff with tense grips on their weapons.

None of this was unusual. But the violence happening right then on the sands was unprecedented, at least in my four years as a gladiator.

The pitmasters had unleashed a black jaguar, its spots in the glossy coat visible only at certain angles in the harsh sunlight. That in itself wasn't usual either. They loved to throw large animals into the fights. I'd fought jaguars before, and they weren't even the biggest of cats. They'd set loose lions, bears, bulls...even full-grown elephants.

It took fifteen gladiators to take down the last elephant, a male in his prime. Five men had been either crushed to death or gored on those massive tusks. But eventually, the big beast fell. The animals always did, often taking a few gladiators with them.

But this one. This black jaguar that may have even been

small for its species, killed everything in its path. Nobody could even scratch it.

It darted like a shadow across the sands, leaving blood and detached limbs and entrails behind. When it slowed or paused, all I saw were its bloody teeth before it became a blur again.

At first, the pitmasters threw a few gladiators at it, one by one. Then they sent two at a time. Then three. Then five.

The last one in the group of five was running away, dragging a bloody, maimed leg behind him. The cat followed at a leisurely pace, then crouched down and wiggled its rear end before pouncing on the man.

This creature was playing with us.

"They're gonna run out of gladiators," the Ghost muttered to my left.

I tightened my grip on my twin machetes in response, hoping that wouldn't be the case. We were easily replaceable, sure. All they had to do was enslave more able-bodied men, put a weapon in their hands, and throw them out into the pit.

But being short on gladiators meant fewer fights, which was bad for business. They already had to replenish our numbers at a steady rate, considering a handful of us died every single day.

I was banking on them calling this fight soon. Sending fighters out to this demon of a jaguar might as well have been putting live men through a wood chipper. We were dropping like flies, and no one stood a chance.

But the crowd was going nuts over it. So this could potentially get dragged out for the sheer entertainment value.

The jaguar dragged the last man by the throat to the center of the pit, leaving a trail of blood behind. It released the body, letting it fall limply into the sand, then turned to face the rest of us behind the gate.

Something happened the moment the animal's eyes met mine.

A sensation overtook me that nearly brought me to my knees. This jaguar was no animal or person but...*more*. It was time and history, bloodshed and the purest devotion. It had seen the rise and fall of empires, centuries of colonization and genocide. This thing was timeless, ageless. And all of this perspective happened to be contained in a snarling, four-legged package that walked straight toward me.

Tezcatlipoca.

The word ran across my brain, making me shiver in the hundred-degree heat, and I knew it was this entity's name.

"Butcher." The pitmaster called for me and angled his head. Before I could even process what was happening, the gate in front of me opened, and I was shoved forward. I heard Ghost hiss out a protest, but there was nothing he could do. If I was picked to fight, I couldn't refuse. None of us could. Nor could I turn around, to try getting away from the fight. Cowardly gladiators were captured and corralled separately for the bare-knuckles fights, in which a mob of five other men were tasked with beating him to death.

Now, nothing stood between me and whatever this thing parading as a jaguar was. I stepped out from under the awning of the building into the harsh sunlight. The crowd reinvigorated itself, the noise elevating to a roar when they saw me.

I was a crowd favorite. It was them who had named me the Butcher, after all.

Normally, I liked to play it up for the audience and give them a good show. Not because I enjoyed it, but it kept me alive and made me valuable as a fighter. The resort even sold charms of my twin machete blades in the gift shops.

But right then, showmanship was the last thing on my mind. I could actually die today.

I held those blades out to the sides, forcing my feet toward the cat-shaped shadow in the pale white sand when all I wanted to do was fall to my knees before this creature.

I was human and unworthy. A sack of flesh, only 28 years old. A slave, and barely even a person. I hadn't made a single decision for myself in four long years. What was I to this thing that could take my life with one bite to my windpipe?

When I was nearly ten feet away from the jaguar, it sat down.

It just calmly planted its hindquarters on the ground and tilted its head at me like a curious housecat. My breath felt stuck in my chest, and I circled my wrists to make my blades dance. The weight of them was comforting, a natural extension of my arms, but the last half hour of watching this animal slaughter grown men could not be erased from my mind.

Don't be afraid, Santos. I will not harm you. The voice was vast and deep, penetrating my ears while also rolling over my skin; as comforting as a hug, and powerful as a building collapsing on top of me.

"What?" I whispered, then I really did fall to my knees. I hadn't heard my given name spoken to me in years, even before my time as a gladiator. The Ghost was the only one who knew it, but he couldn't call me that name here. Anything that gave us identities and humanity was forbidden.

You are under my protection, my dear son.

The voice was just as ancient and timeless as the energy I felt from this being. I was humbled in the presence of someone, or something, great but no idea what.

"Who are you?" I said, lowering my eyes to the sand. If the crowd was still going, I couldn't hear it past the pounding of blood in my ears.

In the simplest terms for you to understand, I am a god. You know one of my names.

"Tezcatlipoca." The strange word that had stamped onto my

brain now rolled off my tongue, despite it being in a language I'd never spoken before. "The Smoking Mirror. Ruler of the North." I dared to lift my gaze to the golden eyes of the feline in front of me. "Have you come to free us?"

It is not that simple, Santos. There is much to be done. Many pieces must come together at the right place. The right time. The jaguar's tail flicked as he regarded me. *I have two primary roles in this manifestation. One is as your protection. I will be your guard and invisible shadow, Santos. Follow my guidance, and you will reach the freedom you seek.*

I released a shaking breath, unable to believe this was happening, that this nightmare I lived every day could actually come to an end.

"And your other role?" I asked.

A wave of scorching heat passed over me, oppressive and painful. It constricted my throat and forced my palms down to the burning sand. The weight of something impossibly heavy, like the entire colosseum filled with people, seemed to press down on my back.

I realized this was the weight of Tezcatlipoca's anger.

Vengeance, the god answered.

"Whew!" I slammed the shot glass facedown, tilting my head back to savor the burn of liquor down my throat until it turned to warmth in my belly. Releasing the glass, I pointed to Lily across the table. "One more shot for the birthday girl!"

Flushed and giggling, my friend shook her head. 'No, I'm done!' she mouthed while her hands moved in fluid sign language.

"Aw come on, Lil!" I was proficient in signing but at the moment, was too drunk to move my hands in any eloquent way, let alone remember the gestures. She got my meaning, though. Plus, I was loud enough that she could probably hear me with her hearing aids. "Is your birthday," I slurred. "You gotta go all out."

Lily's boyfriend, my twin brother Daren, pushed a tall glass of water toward her. "Stay hydrated," he reminded her in a warm, gentle tone that reminded me of the way our fathers spoke. "I'll share the last shot with you," he added with a smile. His sign language was just as fluid and effortless as Lily's, which made sense considering they'd known each other since they were five years old.

Lily accepted the water and gulped it down, a coy look on her face while Daren and I waited for her verdict. "Okay, fine. One more, only if you'll share it with me," she relented.

I slapped my palm down on our table as I slid out of the barstool. "I'll make it a double, then."

But the happy couple were too wrapped up in each other to catch what I'd said. Lily leaned against Daren's shoulder and his arms went around her with a kiss on her forehead. I headed for the bar, shoving down the pang of longing in my gut.

I loved them both dearly, but sometimes I envied that they had found each other so easily. Lily had been new in Daren's kindergarten class at school, which wasn't equipped to accommodate her needs right away. She didn't know anyone yet, and my shy twin was determined to be friends with her. They'd been inseparable ever since.

Lily spent so much time at our house that our parents learned as much sign language as they could to communicate with her. To no one's surprise, she and my brother started dating in high school.

Fast-forward to now; we were all twenty-three. Daren and Lily had an apartment together and were planning a wedding. He was the head mechanic at our dad Jandro's auto shop and was set to take over the business when dad retired. Lily was now an ASL teacher and interpreter.

In both love and life, the two of them just seemed to have it so...easy.

I shook the thought from my head as I pushed my way through the crush of bodies in the bar. I was drunk and in my feelings. No one deserved forever love and success more than those two. They were my best friends, my family. I wanted only the best things for them, honestly.

As for me? I was a hot mess by comparison. Daren and I might've been born minutes apart, but we couldn't be more different. He had always been quiet, calm, and studious. I was loud, boisterous, and impulsive. A tornado of sunshine, as my mother called me.

And unlike my twin, no prospects for love or career had fallen into my lap. It wasn't for lack of trying. Just nothing, so far, had seemed to work out. I wasn't all that bitter about it, but some guidance from the universe would be nice. I wouldn't say no to a clearly laid out path with a neon sign that said, *Here, Rori. Do this, and you'll live happily ever after.*

I knew life didn't work that way, but again, I was currently in my feelings.

I eventually made it to the bar, coming face-to-face with Bryce, the owner. He was a man in his fifties, hair and beard streaked with gray, and a longtime family friend, practically a fifth father to me. Some of my earliest memories were of him and my dad, Reaper, teaching me to ride a bike and later, a motorcycle.

Bryce peered at me shrewdly, lifting a bushy caterpillar eyebrow at my approach. He could probably smell how drunk I was.

"One more round," I said, circling my index finger in the air. "On my tab."

"You're cut off after this, Rori," Bryce grunted as he set up the shot glasses on the bartop.

"Yeah, yeah. I get it."

"How you gettin' home, young lady?"

"Walkin'," I answered, throwing a thumb over my shoulder. "I'm crashing on the lovebirds' couch." Daren and Lily's apartment was just a couple blocks from the bar. I'd parked my motorcycle at their place earlier, and we'd all walked over here together.

Bryce seemed satisfied with that and poured our drinks without comment. He hesitated over the fourth shot though, and lifted his head to look around. "Where's the fourth member of your merry band?"

"Dunno." I wanted to resist looking around myself, but I had no self-control while drunk. I craned my head to scan over the crowd, head swiveling. I was tall for a woman, just under five foot ten, but it was a busy night, and I couldn't see Torrance anywhere. He was probably fucking some girl in the bathroom.

Oops. My drunk ass said that out loud, and Bryce gave me a disapproving look. "He better not be getting up to that in *my* establishment," he grumbled.

"Hey, Daren's the only one with a leash on him. Don't look at me." I had actually been able to *not* think about Torr for an hour or so. But now the mental image of him thrusting into some girl propped up on the bathroom sink turned my stomach.

"You kids kill me." Bryce shoved the shots toward me, but I caught the smile under his beard. He and his wife didn't have kids of their own, so he was like an honorary uncle to me, my siblings, and all the other kids in town we grew up with.

"But you *love* us." I gave him my cheekiest smile as I gathered up the shot glasses in my hands. "Thanks, Bryce."

He waved a hand, shooing me away from the bar as he turned to serve another patron. It took all of my drunken concentration to not only hold the drinks but sidle my way through the crowd back to our table. I went slowly, careful not to spill the precious liquid that numbed both my heartache and general lack of clarity about my life.

I spotted Torrance finally, about halfway back on my journey. A beautiful brunette clung to the sleeve of his leather jacket, brows drawn together and lips frowning like she was upset. Torr seemed to be pulling away, his free hand gesticulating as he talked to her. I couldn't make out their conversation, but it looked like an argument.

Typical Torr. Breaking hearts and vaginas, sometimes in the same night. A lot of people didn't understand how he, a capital-P player, and my brother Daren, utterly devoted to one girl since he was *five*, came to be best friends.

The thing was, Torr didn't hide that finding love was the absolute last thing on his mind. He was at least honest with every girl he hooked up with. His utter lack of commitment wasn't his best personality trait, sure. But playboy tendencies aside, he actually was a solid friend and a really good guy.

Which made it really, really hard for any woman not to develop feelings for him. My pathetic ass included.

But I would never let myself become one of Torrance Knight's many flings or one-night stands. So I kept my trap shut and hid it all behind a numbing waterfall of booze. Although, I probably gave myself too much credit. We'd known each other for thirteen years, and in all that time, he'd never looked at me that way. To him, I was nothing but his best buddy's sister.

Astarte.

The strange word entered my brain out of nowhere, like someone had planted it directly in there. I stopped in my tracks, drawing my gaze to the window where a white dove sat perched on a tree branch outside. It just stared at me with its beady bird eyes, looking ghostly with its white feathers against the night sky.

The fuck?

I closed my eyes and shook my head. Okay, maybe I should have stopped drinking at that last round. But I knew my limits. My parents had allowed me tiny sips of booze since I was a toddler. Right then I felt good-drunk, but not sloppy-drunk. And I'd definitely never drank to the point where I was hallucinating.

"Hey, Ror!" someone yelled through the noise.

I opened my eyes to see Torr coming toward me, the pretty brunette gone. He cut through the crowd like a shark through water, everyone subtly ebbing away to give him room. His towering height certainly gave him that power, but there was also just something about *him* that made people want to stay out of his way.

He wasn't scary, but intimating? To those who didn't know him, absolutely. Torr had a hell of a glow-up in high school, muscles filling out his skinny frame and a cool, detached confidence taking over the haunted skittishness he'd portrayed as a child. Shit, I thought he was mute when I first met him. He didn't speak for a week, and even when he was safe, he had the demeanor of a wild animal that had been caged and abused.

People used to think Torr and Daren were twins. They both had that quiet, dark-eyed broody thing going on. My brother was a total sweetheart underneath, but Torr was hard to sum up in one word. And that word was definitely not *sweet*.

I'd known him for years and still found it hard to describe him. In school, he was known for protecting kids from bullies. But he'd beat the bullies so badly, they spent weeks in the hospital. Some of those fights resulted in battery charges and short stints in jail. He had a lot of anger, a lot of violence churning within him. He'd always been a good friend to Daren, Lily, and I, not to mention warm and respectful to our parents. But I still didn't feel like I really *knew* him.

And yet, he was the subject of all my dirtiest fantasies.

Fuck my stupid heart. And my vagina.

"Good, you didn't drown in pussy," I said when he got closer.

"Unfortunately," he sighed dramatically.

"Take a couple of these, will you?" I thrust the shot glasses at him. "I'm worried about spilling."

"I wondered why you stopped suddenly like a ghost possessed you." His hands were warm, but thankfully dry, as they brushed mine. I didn't want to think about who or what they touched tonight.

"So who did you send away crying this time?" I asked, both because I was a masochist and because I didn't want to dwell on that weird moment with the bird in the window.

"She didn't cry, thank fuck," he grumbled. "But that was Kay. She works in the governor's office."

"Trying to get those arrests scrubbed off your record?" I teased as we made our way back to the table together. "Probably shot yourself in the foot there."

"Nah, I don't give a shit about that. But she's a single mom, told me she was down for the casual thing because her kids come first and all. Tonight, she can't stop talking about how they need a strong father figure and that I would be so good for them. So, I ended it."

"Would it really kill you to settle down with a nice ready-made family?" The words hurt as they left my chest, but as soon as I downed this shot, I knew it wouldn't hurt as much.

"First of all, I knew her for all of three weeks. Second of all..." We reached the table and set the drinks down. Torr turned to me, smirking, with his shot still in his hand. "You're one to talk, Aurora Wilder."

"Touche." I rolled my eyes and raised my drink, turning toward Daren and Lily.

I knew he was only teasing, but I still hated how much Torr's words stung. He wasn't wrong. I had a bit of a reputation for being the female version of him. But for me, it was different. I genuinely *wanted* love—the constant, passionate kind that my parents had.

The only kicker was, I wanted it with multiple men. My mother, with her four devoted, loving husbands was exactly what I dreamed of for myself. They had essentially raised me to not settle for one partner, so why would I?

But their arrangement was still an unusual one in our fairly small town. And my attempts at dating multiple people had been met with derogatory remarks and heartache. It sucked, and I hated the double standard that made people respect Torr for playing around, while treating me as a warning sign.

Today was not about me, however. I put on a big smile as the four of us toasted our drinks and said happy birthday to Lily once again. Last call was made soon after, and I decided not to push my luck with Bryce and try for another round.

We chatted about work and mundane things while nursing waters until the crowd started to thin. Daren, ever the helpful one, started bussing tables until Bryce shooed us all out. Once we left the bar and hit the sidewalk, I realized that I needed a little extra concentration to walk, but I was otherwise fine. Daren and Lily walked ahead, arms around each other while Torr and I trailed behind.

"Smoke?" Torr held his pack out in my direction, a cigarette already dangling from his full lips.

"Yesss." I took the cigarette greedily. Smoking was not my usual thing, and I was certain I'd regret it in the morning. But the nicotine buzz hit so much harder after a few drinks, and I really wanted to float away on a high right then.

I expected Torr to just hand me his lighter like normal, but instead he turned and stepped in front of me, forcing me to stop walking or else I'd crash into him. His dark eyes were shadowed in the dim streetlights. When he held up the lighter, flicking the spark wheel, the flame's light danced over his cheekbones and nose, highlighting all the sharp features of his handsome face.

Our gazes remained locked as I leaned forward a few inches to light my cigarette. I sucked in a long drag, our staring contest continuing as he lit his own. The flame's light disappeared and his face was cast in shadow again. We released our smoke in unison, the toxic clouds mingling in the air between us, molding into one before dissipating into the night sky.

Then I broke the spell with a snort. "What the fuck was that? Your latest seduction technique?"

"You wish." He smirked before turning to walk alongside me again.

"Yeah, right," I scoffed, maybe a little too loudly.

He let out a dry chuckle, more smoke exhaling from his nostrils. "It's just fun to mess with you, Ror."

I know, I thought but only grunted in reply. That was just Torr. He flirted with everything that had a pulse. I was the fool for reading into it.

Something bright caught my eye. I glanced up, thinking it was the moon or an especially bright star, but no.

It was that fucking bird.

The same creepy white dove that had stared at me though the window of the bar was now perched on a tree branch hanging over the sidewalk. I stopped walking but not because I wanted to. Something seemed to hold me in place, something outside of my control.

"What the fuck are you?" I muttered under my breath.

It answered me, with the same ancient, omnipresent voice I'd heard earlier. *I am called Astarte, and I am your destiny, Aurora Wilder.*

2

____

RORI

The neck pain woke me up first.

I rolled over with a groan, then promptly rolled back at the sensation of teetering on the edge of a cliff.

Ah, that's right. It was coming back to me now. Torr ended up crashing at Daren and Lily's place too, so he got the big couch while I squashed myself onto this tiny-ass loveseat. I vaguely remembered complaining drunkenly that Daren and Lily needed more bedrooms for us to crash comfortably. Daren said something about us paying rent, then I said something along the lines of, "Fuck you, but I love you," and that was the last I remembered.

I stretched my arms and legs, which meant throwing them over the arms of the loveseat. My throat was dry as a bone and a little scratchy. I knew I shouldn't have had that cigarette.

The memory of Torr lighting it for me came to the forefront of my mind and replayed like a movie. I knew I'd be recalling that moment again and again—the way his dark eyes bore into me, how the light and shadow played across his face, the smoke swirling around his silhouette like he was some mysterious figure in the night.

I would think back to it while daydreaming, because I was that pathetic. I was no better than the girls orbiting around him, desperate for a scrap of his attention.

I rubbed my forehead, keeping my eyes closed. He was across the room right now, his long frame stretched out over the couch. It was kind of unusual that he didn't find some other girl to take home. His place was only a few blocks up from here. But I suppose even players had their off days.

Slowly, I lowered one leg to the floor, then the other, pushing myself up to sitting. Whispers and gentle sounds of movement came from the kitchen, which meant Lily and Daren were already up. Damn early birds.

Ugh, no. Don't think about birds.

That whole shit with the dove was so weird and had never happened to me before. As I padded to the kitchen, I wondered if maybe I should cut down on drinking. I liked to party; I mean hell, my whole family did. But anything to do with hallucinations freaked me out, which was why I wasn't a hard-drug type of girl.

Lily signed a cheerful, "Good morning!" to me as I shuffled over to their breakfast bar.

I gave a small wave and said as I signed back, "Good morning, birthday girl. Thank you," and accepted the mug of coffee she held out to me.

Daren had his back turned, tending to something sizzling on the stove. Some kind of breakfast sausage from how it smelled. "Hey Ror, next time you come over," he said over his shoulder, lazily signing one-handed so Lily wouldn't be left out of the loop, "can you bring another carton of eggs? We're getting low."

"Sure, but text me later to remind me." My ASL wasn't at the level where I could say everything one-handed, so I set my coffee down to answer. "You know I can't remember shit first thing in the morning."

Lily chuckled as she brought plates down from a cabinet. "How are you feeling?" she asked.

"Thirsty and a little sore from your loveseat, but I'm otherwise fine," I told her, knowing she would want the honest answer.

She shook her head as if in disbelief, then playfully bumped Daren with her hip. "I'm always amazed at the alcohol tolerance of you two. I had half the amount of drinks and still needed headache medicine when I got up this morning."

"That's our biker tolerance," Daren said with a laugh, then kissed her temple. "Steel Demon genes, whatever you want to call it. It's a blessing and a curse."

"Why a curse?" Lily asked before handing him a plate.

"Because we don't always know when to stop," I answered for my brother while his hands were busy plating up food.

Our dads didn't make it a secret that they had used drinking as a crutch, though that was mostly in the past. Shadow had been especially careful about his intake for as long as I could remember.

Probably the most important thing about growing up in a family of bikers was that they didn't hide bad shit about the world from us. Me, Daren, and our younger siblings all knew that our parents had been outlaws when the world was in turmoil. The Collapse of the United States over thirty years ago meant territories were unstable, with laws and order going completely out the window.

Wars over territory and resources were constant back then. My parents' accounts were backed up by our history classes in school.

There had been a big war just outside of our territory before I was born, with all of my parents playing key roles, that ended in victory. They had become heroes, local celebrities. To this day, everyone in our town, Four Corners, knew who they were.

My parents left their outlaw ways behind and started legitimate businesses when the territory was still young and had been here ever since.

Even though Daren and I had grown up happily, with a loving, supportive family, our parents didn't hide that the past war and turmoil left lasting damage. Reaper didn't have full use of his left hand. Jandro, Gunner, and even our mom had scars from gunshots and stab wounds. Shadow was covered in scars, including a large one on his face that cut through his eye. He was the "scariest" of my dads, but what most people didn't know was that he was one of the kindest, most loving people on earth.

Daren and I were fully aware of the sacrifices they'd made so that our lives could be better. Right then it made me feel a little guilty for my pity-party feelings last night. So what if I didn't have four hot boyfriends, or even one? Who cared if I didn't have my life fully figured out at twenty-three? At least I'd never seen a day of war in my life.

I tried to hold on to that sentiment as Torrance noisily rose from the dead, groaning as he stretched and then the loud thump as he rolled from the couch to the floor. He still looked half-asleep as he stood, following the smell of food to join us in the kitchen.

Wearing nothing but his boxer shorts, of course.

"Fuck, smells amazing," he mumbled, dropping into the chair next to me.

"Make yourself at home, why don'tcha?" Daren dropped a plate of eggs and breakfast sausage in front of his best friend, then playfully smacked his shoulder. "I told you, Lil. We should be charging both of these losers rent."

"Hey man, you're lucky I left my chonies on. I'd be buck-ass naked if I was at home. Can't sleep with clothes on." Torr grabbed my coffee and slurped it loudly.

"Excuse you!" I swiped it back from him mid-slurp.

"I was actually thinking we should swap out the loveseat for a futon," Lily signed to Daren, a smile pulling at her lips. "So it could be folded down and overnight guests would be more comfortable."

"Nooo, don't encourage them," he pretended to whine as he pulled her into a hug, laughing as he cradled her head in the center of his chest.

"Love you too, bro," I muttered into my coffee mug.

"Look at these two. It's too early in the morning for so much damn cuteness." Torr made a gagging sound as Lily hugged around Daren's waist. She looked up at my brother, and their smiles of love and adoration matched perfectly before they kissed.

"Absolutely disgusting," I said, playing along with Torr.

"Hey, you want to keep sleeping on the loveseat or not?" Daren shot back.

"I'm perfectly good with the couch. Mr. Sleeps Naked over here just needs to find his naked ass in some damsel's bed more often. Or I dunno, his own."

Torr turned to me, stretching up so the full length of his abs and torso were on display. "And deprive you of this stunning view? I could never be so cruel, Rori."

"I dunno, you're looking a little squishy here." I reached out and pinched some skin on his stomach. Of course, there wasn't much to grab because he was wrought with muscle, and I was full of shit. "Been slacking in the gym?"

He shrugged, completely unaffected by my teasing. "Just doing some *new* workouts," he said with a salacious grin. "Lots of hip thrusts, if you get my drift."

"Ew. You're grosser than them." I angled my gaze back toward Daren and Lily, though something bright caught my eye in the kitchen window. The sight nearly had me dropping my coffee cup. "Mother-*fuck!*"

The white dove was right there, perched on the windowsill and staring at me.

You cannot ignore me out of existence, Aurora. The voice raked over my brain and skin, taunting me.

Oh shit. Shit. Shit. This was bad. I wasn't drunk anymore. Why was I still hallucinating?

"Hey, Ror? You okay?" The voice sounded far away, like it was coming from the opposite end of a tunnel.

My chest felt tight, and it was hard to get a breath. The rapid pace of my own heartbeat seemed like it was trying to choke me. What the fuck was happening to me?

"Rori, hey!"

The weight of a hand fell to my shoulder, fingers gently squeezing to bring my attention back. It worked, a little. Torr was leaning in close to me, the scent of him calming. It was his hand on my shoulder; his warm, dark eyes searching mine with concern.

"You're shaking like a leaf," he said, his brows pinching together. "What's wrong?"

"You need to lie down, sis?" Daren asked me, his expression also concerned. "You went really pale all of a sudden."

"No, no. I, uh..." I brought my hands to my face, rubbing my eyes like that would make the hallucination go away. When I looked again, the dove was still there, preening its feathers. Mocking me.

"I need to go home." I stood abruptly, nearly making my chair fall backwards but Torr caught it. "I just...yeah, not feeling great. Want to lie down in my own bed, you know?"

"Are you sure you're okay to ride your motorcycle?" Lily's hands moved swiftly as she asked the question, chewing her lip in concern.

"Yeah, yeah. I'm good." I was so frazzled that I forgot to sign, so I repeated the words with my hands. "I'm sober, just maybe a little more hungover than I thought." I forced a smile, trying to lighten the mood. "Steel Demon blood isn't invincible."

Torr's hand went around my forearm in a gentle but commanding hold. "Let me take you home."

"No." I pulled my arm loose. "I'm fine, Torr. Really." He was the last person I wanted in close proximity while...whatever this was was happening. Was this a psychotic break? Would I need to be committed to a mental hospital? As if it would hide my frantic thoughts, I walked away from everyone's stares to find my shoes.

Nobody said a word while I laced up my boots, not even the stupid bird, thankfully. I purposely kept my gaze away from any of the windows as I grabbed my keys from the bowl on the side table.

"Text me when you're home, Rori," Daren said as I headed for the door.

"Me too," Torr piped up.

"What, do I have six fathers now?" I grumbled.

"Pull over and call me if you're not able to ride safely," Torr added. "I'll pick you up and take you the rest of the way."

"Fucking hell, it's a ten-minute ride! And I'm sober, like I said. No need for all the hand-wringing."

"Just check in with us anyway," Torr said. He was using that bossy tone that all the girls hanging off of him melted over. Well, it wouldn't work on me.

I mean, I knew it came from a place of caring, so I'd do it. But it was still annoying. I'd been riding since my toes could reach the footpegs. I didn't *need* to check in with them like a child.

"Fine, whatever." I swung the door open, calling out over my shoulder, "See you guys later," before I closed it behind me.

Once away from their worried faces, I hurried to my bike and instantly felt a sense of comfort when I sat in the familiar seat. My parents got me this bike for my eighteenth birthday, and it was my greatest treasure. Jandro custom-built it, along with Daren's bike, since we shared the same birthday, while Gunner had everyone else helping him source the parts for our gifts. I can only imagine it took months, maybe even close to a year, to piece together both bikes.

I turned the key and welcomed the roar of my machine coming to life. Riding was the only thing I knew I wanted to do for the rest of my life. It was freedom and exhilaration unlike anything else in the world. My bike and the road were always there for me whenever life kicked me down, like when guys decided I was too slutty to be a serious girlfriend.

Riding was healing, and I needed it right now more than ever.

I pulled out of Daren and Lily's driveway, not looking at my mirrors until I was out on the main road.

Sure enough, I saw a white dove flying behind me.

3

———————

TORRANCE

The white dove flew away from the windowsill just as Rori left the apartment. Daren and Lily watched it too, all three of us puzzled as to why it spooked her so much.

"Do you think Rori's okay?" Lily signed to Daren, worrying her lip between her teeth.

"I dunno," he admitted, pulling his girlfriend into an embrace when she started leaning into him. "I've never seen her act like that before."

I could only nod, chin in my hand as I pondered her behavior. As her twin, Daren knew Rori best. If he'd never seen her in that state before, that was really alarming.

Something we could all agree on though, was that Rori was fearless.

In all the years I'd known her, I'd seen her enraged, heartbroken, or hurt over some douchebag who didn't deserve her. She was at times moody and sarcastic, with an especially sharp tongue that came out when she drank. But I'd never seen her *afraid*.

This was the first time I'd seen Aurora Wilder, the daughter of the bikers who'd once ruled the lawless southwest, express genuine, unabashed fear.

My mind was made up in an instant. "I'm gonna follow her."

I went to the couch for my clothes and turned when I heard a soft snort behind me. Lily grinned as she signed at me, "Good luck. She'll have your balls in a vice if she finds out."

"She won't find out. I'll stay far enough behind."

"Like usual," Daren muttered under his breath, the words not meant for my ears, but I heard them anyway.

"What was that, D?" I finished getting my pants on and shook out my shirt before putting it on. "If you're gonna say something, say it with your whole chest."

"I said, like usual," he repeated in a normal voice. Next to him, Lily sucked her cheeks in and widened her eyes in a, *oh shit, here it comes,* kind of look.

"And what's that supposed to mean?"

"Means you'll keep watching her like a hawk but be too chickenshit to actually date her."

A tense silence fell, and Lily took the opportunity to leave the kitchen, which I was grateful for. Daren always signed when she was around so she wouldn't be excluded from conversations, which was fine under normal circumstances. But I didn't want an audience for *this* talk.

"Rori doesn't want to date *me,*" I reminded him. "And besides, she's your sister, bro."

Daren held up an index finger. "One, of course she doesn't, not with the way you're acting now. And two, you know I don't give a shit about that. The four of us hang out all the time anyway. You two are always squabbling like a married couple as it is."

I did *not* want to get into this with him. The sound of Rori's motorcycle was already fading, and I needed to have eyes on her to make sure she was okay.

"Daren," I sighed, shrugging my leather jacket on. " No offense, bro, but you're a terrible fucking matchmaker if you think me and your sister would be good together."

"If both of you pulled your heads out of your asses, maybe it could work." He whipped a dish towel in my direction. "But what do I know? I've never run away from the person I fell in love with."

"Yeah, good for you." I got my shoes on and headed for the door. "I'll see you later. Tell Lily I said 'happy birthday'."

"Yup. Later."

I headed for my motorcycle, parked alone now that Rori's was gone. She'd said our rides matched one time a few years ago, so we always made the effort to park next to each other. Two peas in a fuckin' pod.

"When I'm president of a club, you can be my VP," Rori had teased. "Only the best bikes get to ride next to mine."

"And what if I want to become president?" I'd asked her.

"You'd have to kill me for it." She'd laughed. "Rules of the road."

Once my steed roared to life, I eased onto the road, deciding to loop around and take a different route to her family home. Even if she didn't see me behind her, there was a chance she would hear my bike. It wouldn't be as obvious that I was following if I spotted her from a different direction.

Rori. Gorgeous, infuriating Rori.

I hated that Daren was right. It pissed me off how perceptive he was sometimes. Like he had a sixth sense for the things I tried to bury in a vault.

Everyone asked me why I could never keep the same girl around, why I couldn't just settle down and commit to someone nice. The excuse I gave was always accompanied by a smirk and a shrug. "I'm twenty-five, not forty-five."

I'd never spoken a word of the truth to anyone, but Daren had apparently caught on somehow. Every girl I hooked up with was a poor attempt at a distraction. A means to get Rori fucking Wilder out of my head.

Newsflash: it never fucking worked.

When I closed my eyes at night, it was always the wild, fiery biker princess with the short bob of blonde hair that I saw. Instead of being excited to see whoever I was fucking at the time, I always looked forward to hanging out with Daren or the parties at the Steel Demons' house because she was always there.

Shit, I got half of my tattoos from her dad Shadow's shop because she worked the front desk part-time. I'd schedule my appointments for when she was there, and we'd talk while her dad or one of the apprentices worked on me. It was just convenient that Shadow was the best artist around for hundreds of miles.

I'd known for years that Rori was the only one I could see myself with long term. But Daren was wrong about one thing. She truly did *not* feel the same way about me. If she did, I would know.

Rori was bold. Ever since we were teens, she was never shy about making her interest in a guy known. At parties, I'd seen her walk right up to a guy, kiss him, turn around and kiss his friend, then lead both guys to a bedroom and close the door.

Yeah, she wasn't shy about wanting multiple men either. And honestly? She deserved it. I'd have no qualms about sharing her with a guy or a few, as long as they were good to her and she was mine too. I knew deep in my marrow that I'd never so much as look at another woman again if I had her.

But I was never one of the guys she kissed and dragged to a bedroom. I was the guy she treated like, well, a brother.

We were friends, sure. Close enough and trusting enough that we could rely on each other in times of need. But our relationship rarely went beyond a surface level—partying or riding together, cracking jokes and giving each other shit. And every day I tried to be satisfied with that while I buried my cock in someone else.

I came to a four-way intersection and slowed to a stop. Looking to my left, I saw a glint of short blonde hair in the sunlight before Rori turned another corner. She appeared to be driving fine, which was a relief to see. When it was my turn to go, I continued on straight, hoping to catch sight of her again at the next block.

My strategy worked, and Rori had no idea I was following her. Lily was right in saying she'd be pissed if she knew, but, well, Rori didn't have to know.

If the chumps she dated couldn't appreciate her enough to stick around and actually watch out for her, it might as well be me.

As she crossed the bridge over the long, skinny lake that cut through our town, I maneuvered onto a side street to make sure she wouldn't spot me. This side of Four Corners was older and not as condensed as the downtown area where Daren's apartment was. The lots here were bigger with more land per household, especially on the other side of the bridge where Rori and her family lived.

She'd be safely in her own driveway moments after crossing, so once she made it, I turned my bike around, satisfied that she was okay. My phone buzzed with a text a few minutes later, and I checked it at a stoplight.

Rori: Made it home, Dad #5. Satisfied?

Torrance: Good girl ;)

Rori: Ew, don't be weird.

I STARTED TYPING out a joke about spanking her, then quickly erased it. Rori and I liked to push each other's buttons. We flirted, sometimes said raunchy shit, but always as a joke, always in front of other people. But a text was private. For some reason, that felt a step too far. Too intimate. The last thing I wanted to do was accidentally make my real feelings known. That would only make shit awkward. So I replied with a quick, "hope you feel better" and shoved my phone back in my pocket.

RORI

I parked in the driveway next to my parents' motorcycles and paused for a moment after turning the engine off. My mom's bike was here, thank fuck. She was the one I really needed to talk to.

I didn't know if the hallucination had continued during my ride. I was too freaked out to look in my mirrors after the first time.

Smoothing out my hair, I took a deep breath and retrieved my phone to text Daren and Torr that I'd made it. Daren replied instantly with a simple thumbs-up emoji. Torr's reply came when I reached the front door, calling me a good girl.

I snorted and told him not to be weird. That whole praise kink shit was never my thing. At least, the guys I'd been with had never done a convincing job of it. Getting them to talk dirty, whether it was praise, degradation, or just telling me what the fuck they liked, was like pulling teeth more often than not. I was lucky if I got a quiet moan most of the time.

I bet Torr's good at it, though.

Ugh, I needed to focus.

I went inside, the familiarity of the home where I grew up

instantly comforting me. With five parents, me, Daren, and my two younger siblings, it was always a full house. Torr had even lived with us for a few months back when Daren and I first met him at ten years old. Plus, Lily has been hanging out with us since we were five. I could only imagine how exhausted my mom was, looking after *six* children in the house while also balancing her demanding career as a doctor.

I never remembered her being especially tired or stressed out though, and that was probably due to the fact that my dads were always present and involved. They took many burdens off her shoulders and were happy to do so. When Mom came home from a long day and us kids were still at peak energy, she'd say hi to us quickly, then one of my dads would put a glass of wine in her hand, send her to the bathroom with an already-filled tub, and shut the door behind her.

Our household was chaotic at times but always loving and happy. A family with multiple husbands just made sense to me. I didn't understand why other people thought it was so strange.

It was quiet when I walked in. My dad Gunner sat next to my youngest brother, Nolan, at the kitchen table, the two of them poring over what looked like math homework. Nolan was fifteen and a lot like Daren in that he was perceptive and enjoyed figuring out all kinds of puzzles. Whereas Daren preferred hands-on puzzles like cars, motorcycles, and sign language, Nolan excelled with numbers.

"Hey, Ror." Gunner looked up at me with an easygoing smile. He was the least outwardly threatening of my biker fathers with his friendly smile and cool, relaxed demeanor. Few people knew he was also one of the deadliest. He taught me everything I knew about weapons and self-defense. Before he retired, he worked as a military strategist, often with my grandfather, who had also been the general of the Four Corners Army.

Not that it mattered but Gunner was also my bio-dad. Pretty obvious when only the two of us had blonde hair in the family. His was pulled back in a ponytail, still lush and full with only a few wisps of gray in it. I could never stand the texture of our hair—not quite straight but not curly either, some weird wavy thing in the middle. My waves had a mind of their own, so I kept my hair chopped in a short bob no longer than my chin.

"Hey." I approached the table and rested my hands on the back of a chair. "Where is everyone?"

"Lucia was at a sleepover last night. She'll be home later," Gunner said, referring to my seventeen-year-old sister. Lucia was *gorgeous*, the spitting image of our mother, and incredibly popular. She had a large circle of friends and was always out somewhere with them. I had no doubt she'd find multiple men to adore her one day.

"Shadow had a tattoo client today," Gunner went on. "Your mom, Jandro, and Reaper are out back. How was Lily's birthday?"

"Good!" My voice went high with false cheer. "It was good, we had fun."

Gunner's face darkened. My parents always knew when something was off. "Everything okay, Ror?"

"Yeah. Just, you know, tired. A little hungover even though Bryce cut me off." I tried to make my voice normal, but I knew I couldn't hide everything from him. "I do want to talk to Mom about something, though."

That was code for I needed her for women-only-business, and my dad nodded with understanding. The whole while, Nolan kept his head down, punching things into his calculator or scribbling on his homework page. I wasn't offended though. My baby brother sometimes got hyper focused when he was deep in a complex puzzle.

Gunner stood as I rounded the table, heading for the sliding door that led to the backyard. He pressed a kiss to my temple as I passed him. "Here if you need anything, okay?"

I gave him a grateful smile. "Thanks, Dad."

Outside, Reaper and Jandro looked to be repairing part of the chicken coop while my mom watched them, holding a sleeping chicken in her arms. Mom was the first to spot me, shielding her eyes from the sun as I approached. "There she is! How were the birthday celebrations?"

"Good." I repeated what I told Gunner inside, putting on a smile, but it dropped the instant I saw the white dove settle on the fence behind everyone.

"Just good?" Jandro hadn't seen my face yet, since he was stretching a roll of chicken wire across some posts which Reaper held steady. "Did you get Lily to dance on the bartop? Get Bryce to flash his titties?"

Reaper grimaced. "Ugh, God. Why, Jandro? Nobody wants to see that."

Mom was the only one who noticed my expression, and she pinned me with her knowing doctor's stare. "Rori, is something wrong?"

My dads instantly stopped what they were doing and whipped around to face me.

"I'm fine!" That annoying, fake squeak entered my voice again as I fought to keep my eyes away from the fence. "I just wanted to talk to Mom real quick."

"Ah, girl stuff?" Jandro's worried face relaxed with the question, though Reaper was still scowling.

"Yes, girl stuff," I confirmed. Mom was a gynecologist, so I'd talked to her privately about "girl stuff" plenty of times in my life. Of course, that had nothing to do with hallucinations of birds following me everywhere, but as a medical professional, she would know what steps to take, at least.

"Here." Mom handed the chicken she'd been holding to Reaper. "Take Mimi while us girls chat."

He grunted in protest but cradled the chicken to his chest, who had woken up from the commotion with a few annoyed clucks. I knew he didn't care for raising them, that was mostly Jandro's domain, with some help from Mom. But like everyone else in our household, Reaper loved fresh eggs for breakfast, so he didn't complain. Much.

"Oh, before I forget." I snapped my fingers, turning to Jandro. "Daren wants another carton of eggs."

My father made a dismissive noise while rolling up the excess chicken wire and putting his tools away. "Tell that boy to come get them himself. He never comes over anymore."

"Let him be." Reaper slapped Jandro's back with his free hand. "Daren's a man, about to get married. Let him enjoy his independence." He kissed my forehead and squeezed my shoulder as he walked by me. "Love you, sugar cube. Hope everything's alright."

"He can enjoy his independence and still come over to see his dads once in a while! Sheesh," Jandro kept grumbling as they went into the house.

Once it was just me and my mother, my defenses immediately began to crumble. "Mom..." I choked out. It was getting harder to breathe. My chest and throat seemed to tighten and close up with panic.

She was right there, as she'd always been. Her arms went around me in a protective embrace. Because I was a few inches taller, she pulled my head to shoulder and petted my hair, kissing my forehead. "Let's sit down, sweetheart. Everything's going to be fine."

I allowed her to lead me to a bench, feeling like a child again as she soothed me. Everything seemed to be hitting me right then. I was so confused, so scared.

"Take a deep breath. Slowly," she said, gently rocking me. "You're breathing. You're healthy. You're not dying. I'm right here. No matter what's going on, you will be fine, Rori." When I calmed down enough to finally speak, she said, "Whenever you're ready, I'm listening."

"I'm...I think I might be schizophrenic or something," I blurted out. Not the most eloquent thing to say, but my mind was all kinds of jumbled. "Mom, I'm really scared."

The powerful, calming tone of her voice didn't change. "What makes you think that, sweetheart?" Her palm passed up and down my back in soothing, repetitive patterns.

"I've been having hallucinations. It started last night, and I thought I drank too much. But it kept happening this morning." I lifted my head from her shoulder, staring into my mother's bright hazel eyes. "Mom, am I gonna have to be committed?"

"One thing at a time, love." She cupped my cheeks, holding my gaze on her. "Have these been visual hallucinations? Auditory?"

"Both," I said.

"Are you hallucinating right now?"

I shifted my gaze to look past her, where the white dove now stared at me from atop the chicken coop. "Yes. I keep seeing the same white dove since last night. It followed me from the bar to Daren's house, then from there to here." I closed my eyes, wishing my brain would stop fucking with me. "I know it's not real. I just want it to stop."

My mom was silent for a long time. I just knew she was trying to tell me in the gentlest way she could that I *would* have to be committed and likely on a cocktail of medications for the rest of my life. Of course, she couldn't diagnose me herself since it wasn't her field, but one of her colleagues would.

The worst part was knowing that it probably wouldn't be safe for me to ride, and that was absolutely heartbreaking. I was only twenty-three, for fuck's sake! I didn't know *what* exactly, but there was so much I wanted to do with my life.

Eventually, my mom said, "Are you talking about the white dove on top of the chicken coop?"

My eyes snapped open in shock. "You see it too?"

"Yes." Her voice hardened to one I didn't recognize. "I can see it, Rori."

I felt a huge rush of relief and then more confusion. If she could see it too, then I wasn't hallucinating! But then...what the fuck?

Mom's head snapped around to face me. "The dove has talked to you? Has it told you its name?"

"I...what?"

"Answer me, Rori. What has it said to you?"

I'd never heard my mom speak so harshly before. Now it was her breath coming out in short, panicked puffs. My fearless mother, Mariposa Wilder, motorcycle club queen and battle medic of wars past, didn't just look afraid. She looked terrified.

I swallowed, but there was no moisture left in my mouth. "Its name is Astarte," I said. "And it said it was my destiny."

"Oh no..." Mom whispered with the smallest shake of her head. Then she turned to face the dove, anger coursing through her words. "Listen, you will *not* take my daughter! Not after everything *we* did! Do you hear me?"

An odd sensation rumbled over my skin, and I somehow knew it was an amused reaction. Something like laughter.

Mariposa, child of Freyja, the voice chuckled. I felt it in my head, on my skin, everywhere. *You know how this works. Your daughter is already mine.*

5

RORI

I was so fucking confused.

Over the next twenty minutes, my mother refused to explain another word. She only said that all my fathers needed to be here for a family meeting. She called Shadow at the tattoo shop, telling him something in a hushed whisper before hanging up the phone after a few seconds.

The next thing she did was send Nolan to our grandparents' house down the street, which confused me even more. Rather than a family meeting, it seemed more like some kind of parental intervention.

Shadow must have left his shop immediately after getting off the phone with Mom, because his loud motorcycle rumbled up the driveway just as my other parents and I settled into the living room. I sat cross-legged in the big armchair, hugging a pillow to my chest as he came through the door. A looming, scarred figure with black hair to his broad shoulders, Shadow made grown men swallow and step back when he entered a room.

He also worshiped the ground my mother walked on and

was the first to hold me whenever I had a meltdown as a kid, whether from a nightmare or a scraped knee.

I didn't know exactly what he did for the Steel Demons back in the day. Everyone said he was an enforcer, which could have been anything from slitting throats to making sure people were loyal to the president, Reaper.

I knew in my gut that he had killed people. All my dads and probably even my mom had. Their softer sides were private, reserved for at home with our family and friends. The public only knew their deadly sides, and Shadow was said to be the deadliest of all of them.

"Rori," he grunted out softly, crossing the room to my armchair in two long strides.

"Hey, Dad—uh, hi." To my surprise, he dropped to his knees in front of the chair and hauled me to his chest in a protective bear hug. He even bowed over me, as if the house were caving in and he was trying to shield me from a collapsing roof. My family and I were close, but it had probably been a decade since he hugged me like this, if not longer.

He held me like I was a little girl, using his size and strength to protect me like I was tiny and vulnerable again. And that was what clued me in to how serious this really was. I was a grown woman, one that had learned to hold my own and take care of myself, and my most protective father wanted to shield me from it all.

I gripped the edge of his cut at his shoulder, allowing myself to burrow into his embrace for a moment. "Dad, what's going on?"

Shadow lifted his head. "Have you filled her in?"

"Not yet," Mom answered. "We wanted everyone to be here."

"Yes, please, fill her in whenever you're ready," I snapped, annoyed with all the secrecy.

Shadow released me and went to sit on the couch next to Jandro while my mom opened the sliding door all the way. "You might as well come in. We all know what you are," she yelled outside.

The dove flew in moments later, perching on the stair banister while I felt myself curl up into a ball again.

"Astarte," my mother said in a clipped tone. "Tell us what you want with our daughter."

That is between Aurora and I. It does not involve you, daughter of Freyja.

Everyone else in the room flinched as if something unseen had touched them all at the same time. "Shit, been a while since I heard a god inside my head," Gunner said, rubbing his temple.

Something clicked into place, a missing piece of my parents' past that made the big picture much more clearer.

"What did you say?" I demanded. "A *god?*"

An oversimplification but one that will do, Astarte commented.

"You're a god?" Shadow looked like he wanted to wring the dove's neck and serve it up on a barbecue. "And you've chosen *our* daughter?"

That is correct.

It was so strange to hear a voice inside my head, especially knowing now that it wasn't a product of my own brain.

"Why? We did our part," Jandro growled, also staring murderously at the bird. "Why are the gods coming for our children now?"

Times change. Situations change. There is unrest that must be quelled, and I need a human. This *human.*

Reaper stood up, and everyone's eyes swayed to him. He'd been quiet since the whole thing started, observant and calculating. As the Steel Demons president, his word was once law. If anyone could make this situation go away, it would be him.

"Our children are not sacrificial lambs for your causes," he told Astarte with a deceptive amount of calm. "Our sacrifices to the gods have already been made, ten times over. You have no right to come in and use our daughter for whatever game you're playing. *We* accepted our bonds and did our duties so that our children would be safe. The war is over, and like Jandro said, we did our part."

Your war is over, yes. But this is no game. Another war is brewing under all of your mortal noses. It grows out of control, day by day. If I wait as long as your gods did, it will be too late for humanity.

Your gods? What the hell did she mean by that?

Before I could ask for clarification, Shadow jumped to his feet. "Then let us go instead. Rori, she..." he trailed off, gaze falling to me. "She doesn't know about all of this."

Obviously, I thought, still feeling completely in the dark while everyone else argued with this bird-god.

Your time has passed, Astarte said. *You've had your days to prove yourself, Son of the Sisterhood. A new generation must step up to the mantle.*

Shadow froze, his whole body going rigid like a block of wood. "What the fuck did you call me?" he demanded, a viciousness in his voice I'd never heard before.

Next to him, my mother wrapped an arm around his bicep and her lips went to his shoulder, as if to comfort him. That or to prevent him from actually killing this bird, which he seemed intent on doing.

Aurora doesn't know about that either, does she? The dove made a soft cooing sound. *Leaving children in the dark does them no favors. Humans always seem to forget this.*

Reaper stepped closer to the dove, his nose mere inches away from its beak. "Rori was never supposed to meet gods. You were never supposed to interfere with our lives again. Hades, Horus, and Freyja said they wouldn't!"

None of this seemed real. I felt like I was watching some strange alternate reality, my life playing out in a bizarre, fictitious version of the real thing. Hades and Freyja were a dog and cat we had when Daren and I were kids. Horus was a trained falcon that belonged to Gunner around the same time. I knew they were named after gods in ancient myths, but they weren't actual...

A memory hit me so hard it took my breath away. No, it was a dream. A memory of a dream I hadn't thought about in years. But it crashed to the forefront of my mind as vividly as ever.

I was around twelve years old and dreamed I was in a desert. There was nothing but dry, sandy earth and scattered bushes around me. There were mountains far away in the distance, and I remembered feeling hot. A scorching, dry, oppressive heat like I was inside an oven. Each breath felt like I was inhaling sand.

"Miserable, isn't it?"

I turned around to find a man standing a few feet away, when I had been alone moments before. He looked like a younger version of my dad Reaper, with brown hair, green eyes, and a warm smile.

"Who are you?" I had asked him.

"I'm Daren," he'd said. "It's nice to meet you, Rori."

"That's my brother's name."

"Yeah, you kinda got my brother's name too." He'd smirked, charming and teasing.

It clicked for me right away. I had seen flashes of him in dreams before, but never photographs or anything. My parents had told plenty of stories about him, though.

"You're my *uncle* Daren."

"That's right, kiddo."

He was Reaper's younger brother and had died years before I was born. Reaper's real name was Rory, which he hated and never went by. My nickname was a means to tease him at first, but it stuck, and he'd always said it was much better as a girl's name.

"What is this place?" I had asked my uncle's ghost.

"When you come here in a few years, it'll be called the Great Wasteland. Back when your dad and I used to ride through it? It was the Nevada desert."

"When *I* come here?"

"The gods will lead you here," he'd said, nodding at the mountains like they were the ones telling him this. "It will be dangerous and the most difficult thing you'll ever do in your life. But you're the only one who can, Rori."

"I don't *want* to be here. I want to go home."

Uncle Daren had turned to me then with a kind smile and knelt to talk at my eye-level. "I know, kiddo. It won't be for a while. Sometimes grown-ups have to do really difficult things. But it's okay. You won't be alone." He gave an affectionate squeeze to my shoulder and there, the dream ended.

I'd had dreams of my uncle for as long as I could remember, and I always believed *he* was real. Something like an angel, guiding and protecting me. Reaper told me that he dreamed of his little brother too, at times. But I had completely forgotten his cryptic message about gods until now.

In the present, my parents were still arguing with Astarte, one of the gods who I could only assume would lead me through the Great Wasteland as my uncle had told me.

Hades, Horus, and Freyja finished their business with you, Astarte was saying. *They are not part of this.*

"They wouldn't allow this," Gunner said. "They won't interfere, but they said they would remain present to watch over and protect our family."

I'm sure your trinity gods will continue to do so, but that does not mean they will interfere now.

"They never were just animals, were they?" I piped up.

Everyone seemed to have forgotten about me, despite the conversation being *about* me. A hush fell over the room as my parents exchanged glances, as if deciding telepathically what they should tell me.

"By the time you came along, they were just our pets," Reaper said. "But before that, during the war, no." His gaze slid to my mom, who gave him a subtle nod. "Hades, Horus, and Freyja *were* gods in animal vessels. Just like Astarte here."

"They bonded to us," Gunner added. "They gave us…gifts which enabled us to win the war."

"Humanity would have been headed for extinction if we had lost," Jandro said. "So we were prepared to make sacrifices and fight with everything we had. But…" He turned a narrow-eyed glare to Astarte. "The human population has been increasing. Territories are stabilizing. It's been twenty-six years of peace and progress. So can you understand us losing our shit over a god coming back after all this time and demanding our oldest daughter?"

The threat that looms is in its infancy, but its power is continuously growing. If another decade passes with it going unchecked, all your sacrifice will have been for nothing. All the progress of the past twenty-six years will be undone.

"What exactly would I be going up against?" I asked. "Another god?"

Other humans, for now.

"So why are gods getting involved if it's a human issue?" Mom asked.

It always starts with humans, Astarte answered cryptically. *But it may not end up that way. It seems you forget, Mariposa. Gods are human concepts given personification. When you give those concepts power, you deify them. War, love, fertility, prosperity. Each of these ideas have gods attached because humans gave power and personhood to them.*

"None of us have forgotten," Reaper snarled. "But why does it have to be Rori? Why *our* daughter?"

The dove fluffed up its feathers and promptly smoothed them down, looking directly at me. *This is simply the path she is meant to take.*

6

RORI

Astarte flew away soon after dropping that bombshell, but I knew the dove would return. Reaper came to kneel in front of me, taking one of my hands in the silence that followed. "Sugar cube, you don't have to do this. No matter what that god tells you, you have free will, and you can say no."

"Love." Mom came up behind him and placed her hands on his shoulders. "You know that's not true. I know you want to protect Rori, but please don't lie to her."

Reaper let out an angry huff of breath, staring at her hand like it offended him. "We didn't do everything we did just so the gods could come back and take our kids from us, Mari."

"Rori, what are you thinking?" Jandro leaned forward from his place on the couch, the side of his face coming to rest against my mom's hip. "You've been quiet, mija. Do you have any questions?"

"I don't...I don't know." I ran my fingers over my scalp, still unnerved by the sensation on my brain that came from a god speaking to me. "I'm glad I'm not hallucinating, I guess."

No one laughed. At this point, I was starting to wonder if mental illness would've been an easier outcome.

"What...do I even have to do?" I scanned the room, looking at each of my five parents. "What did you guys do?"

They all exchanged looks again, that silent communication between partners that had known each other for over twenty years. With a pat on his shoulder from my mom, Reaper got up from the floor and returned to the couch. My mom squeezed in between him and Shadow.

"The gods we had bonded to us in different ways," Reaper began. "Hades, a god of death, chose me. He came to me in the form of a Doberman." My father paused and laced his hands together before continuing. "And I...reaped for him. I carried out kills on his command. In exchange, he protected me from death. Even though there were times where I got *very* close."

"He protected all of us," Jandro added. "Our bonds to him were different, but I'm certain he had a hand in all of our survival."

"Freyja bonded to your mother." Reaper angled his head toward her.

"I heard a kitten crying," Mom said, just above a whisper. "And I found myself tied to this beautiful black cat in ways I couldn't explain."

"What did you get out of it?" I asked.

"Freyja is a goddess of love, healing, and fertility. All of us, and every patient I worked on, healed rapidly from their injuries. I had some skills back then, but Freyja's guidance was... intuitive. I just *knew* what to do." She gave a small smile to Shadow next to her, who returned the look. "I think she was a bit of a matchmaker for us too."

"She was," he confirmed. "But Freyja was also a goddess of death. I don't know how exactly, but she worked with Hades in some sense."

"She did," Jandro confirmed with a nod, his eyes unfocused, his mind somewhere else.

"Horus is a sky god. He never talked to me much." Gunner had his elbow propped up on the arm of the loveseat, his gaze out the window. "Not until later, but I could see through his eyes. Falcons have binocular vision, and it was great for battlefield tactics." His smile in my direction was almost sad. "If I miss one thing about those days, it's the sensation of flying."

"Horus also gave me my sight back." Shadow absently scratched the long scar cutting through his brow, eyelid, and cheek. His eye underneath the scar was white, while the uninjured eye was dark brown. "Even improved my vision so I could see better in the dark."

"Is that how you always caught me sneaking to get cookies out of the kitchen at night?" I asked.

He grinned. "Yes."

"You got the dad-vision turned up," Jandro added.

Soft chuckles rose from everyone, but the humor was short-lived. We all fell back into a pensive silence. The situation felt too grave for cracking jokes.

"So Astarte is going to give me...some special ability?" I asked. "It doesn't even sound like this god likes me very much."

"Seems like it, but we don't know what that'll be," Mom said. "Everything we had was slightly different."

"What kind of animal vessel is that anyway?" Jandro muttered. "A pigeon? What a shit bird. If our girl's gotta go out there, she deserves an eagle or some shit."

"It's a dove," Shadow informed him dryly. "There's lots of symbolism attached to them."

"Whatever. Same thing as a pigeon. Fucking rats with wings."

"Says the guy who calls his chickens *magnificent swans*," Reaper muttered.

"My girls *are* magnificent!"

"Guys, can we focus?" Mom cut in before looking at me. "What else can we answer for you, sweetheart?"

Silence fell again as they all waited. It almost felt like they were expecting something from me.

"I don't know, like…" I spread my hands, shaking my head as I looked toward the ceiling. "What do I do? How do I deal with being chosen by a god? I don't even know what to ask!"

"It's a lot to take in," Mom said. "But it will become clear to you." The answer felt placating. Patronizing. It was a non-answer, and that only made me more frustrated.

"So I *have* to do this?" I asked in the silence that followed. "Like Astarte said. It's the path I'm supposed to be on?"

Reaper was the one that answered. "Every time I resisted Hades, he made a point of reminding me just how…*human* I was. And that he was something more. Humans may have brought gods into existence, but they are *more* than us. They exist outside of the bounds of time and physical space. They know things we don't, and everything they have us do is for a reason." The look on his face was pained, like it killed him to say it. "So yes, sugar cube. Your mom is right. There is no getting out of this once you're chosen."

My chin went up and down in a nod, even though I didn't feel like I was *really* understanding. I had all this information coming in but none of it was processing. I knew the words, but the meaning, the gravity of the situation wasn't sinking in.

I was still the same directionless woman from last night, drinking and partying my feelings away for the town's heartbreaker. Like tons of others born after the Collapse, I was trying to find purpose in a world that was still recovering from irreparable damage. There was no reason why a god should choose me.

Only one thing was clear to me, a persistent need itched under my skin.

"I'm going for a ride," I said, standing abruptly.

I loved my family more than anything, but I was sick of them staring at me like this. Like they were waiting for me to accept this mission proudly, the prodigal daughter finding her purpose at long last.

I needed the road to clear my head.

"Helmet," Shadow barked as I walked past the couch.

"Yeah, yeah," I grumbled back.

* * *

I TORE through town on my motorcycle, then turned onto the winding road that would lead to a secluded pond just outside our borders. The location must have been a park for families and children before the Collapse. Rusted metal play structures were in a fenced-off area next to the pond, which was shallow and little more than a mud hole.

Daren, Lily, Torr, and I used to come here as teens to drink and just be dumbasses. My brother once stole one of Reaper's clove cigarettes that he liked to hide, and all four of us nearly choked on the intensity of it. When Reaper found out, he was so pissed that he told Daren and I to finish smoking it. We tried, both threw up before we could, and never stole from our parents again.

I eased back on my bike, reducing my speed once I left town and let the curving road guide and sway me through the landscape. The wind in my hair was cool at this time of year, but it would start warming up soon. It never got too cold in this region, not that I'd really spent much time anywhere else.

My family and I went on rides, sure. We camped and went on road trips every summer. I'd seen much of the land that was once a single country, before the central government fell apart and it became a bunch of warring territories. I'd never lived anywhere but in Four Corners though, and I'd never gone on a multi-day ride alone.

Would this mission from a god really be so terrible if it took me somewhere new? My parents were all worried, even angry. I knew they'd suffered in the war and didn't want the same for me, but it didn't sound like that was what I'd be walking into. But then again, Astarte hadn't revealed much.

The only thing that seemed certain was my lack of choice in the matter. And that in itself made me want to dig my heels in and tell that bird to fuck off. I was perfectly content in my small town life—riding motorcycles, working part-time at the tattoo shop, drinking the night away while pining over a man I couldn't have.

Perfectly fucking content.

The ride ended too quickly, and I pulled up to the gravel area next to the pond while my thoughts still churned. I sat atop my bike for a minute, just looking at the place where my friends and I had once been blissfully ignorant troublemakers. It felt different than I remembered. None of us had come here in years, to my knowledge.

I turned off the bike and swung my leg over to dismount. My boots crunched over the gravel as I headed for the playground, hopping the short, barely-standing fence with ease. I sat in one of the rusted, creaking swings, my legs stretched out in front of me and dragging along the ground. Bending my knees to pull my body forward, I allowed myself to gently swing.

The rumbling of a bike pulling up next to mine moments later wasn't surprising in the least. Neither was the tall rider with tousled dark hair walking toward me after he'd parked. My gaze remained impassive as he approached, watching songbirds and dragonflies fly over the surface of the pond.

Torr sat in the swing next to me without a word. He offered me a cigarette, which I accepted, again, without a word. He lit mine for me and then his own. We swung lazily back and forth, taking drags with no conversation for a few minutes.

"Stalking me now?" I asked him when my smoke was halfway done.

He made a small huff of laughter, the corner of his mouth pulling up. "I was running errands in town when you tore through like a bat out of hell. I'm sure the next ten blocks could hear your bike. Didn't know what to think, especially since you'd just texted that you got home."

Yeah, speeding through town probably wasn't the best idea. In a place like Four Corners, people would likely ask my parents what the hell that was about. We weren't the only biker family, but we were the most well-known.

"Everything okay, Ror?" Torr asked when I didn't respond.

"Not really," I admitted, my chest clenching painfully. How much could I even tell him?

"Well, what's up?" Torr tossed his cigarette butt and scraped his boot over it as he swung forward. "Who do I gotta put in the hospital?"

I snorted out a laugh. Typical Torr, solving problems with his fists or his dick. "It's nothing like that. My parents just kinda...dumped some news on me."

"Like what, they kicking you out or something? You need a place to stay?"

"No." I stared at him, a little unnerved by his prying. He'd never been this...protective over me before. "It's...I dunno. Family stuff."

I regretted the words once I said them. While *I* never thought of Torr as a brother, he and Daren were as close as brothers, their bond forged during that time he lived with us. My parents essentially considered Torr to be another son. Even after he was placed in a foster home, my parents made it known that he could stay with us at any time. Which he often did. In every way that mattered, he *was* family.

If my words bothered him, he didn't show it. He just nodded and kept swinging lazily next to me.

"Thanks for the smoke, but you don't have to stay with me," I told him.

"Would you rather be alone?" he asked.

It took a while for me to answer. "No," I admitted. That was the last thing I wanted. I didn't feel prepared to handle this on my own. My thoughts would just end up spinning in circles. I wanted someone to tell me what I should do. Or at the very least, provide an outside perspective.

"Then I'll stay," Torr answered, like it was the most simple matter in the world.

My knee-jerk reaction was to crack a joke about him having somewhere better to be, like hitting up one of his many booty calls. But in reality, I was grateful for him being there. I'd never have him in the way my chest ached for him, but he'd always been a solid friend.

And friends trusted each other. They gave each other support and guidance. Torr was fairly closed off when it came to his own feelings, but he'd never made me feel bad for wearing my heart on my sleeve. Hell, my heart was on every single stitch of clothing I wore when I was drunk. Whenever I cried into a bottle about a guy cheating on me or dumping me because I was "easy", Torr and Lily would take turns holding me in equal measure. I'd lost count of how many times I'd woken up, hungover and puffy-faced, with my head in his lap, his calloused fingers stroking gently through my hair.

The only thing I kept to myself was how I really felt about him, because we all knew that would end disastrously.

So I couldn't keep quiet about *this*. He'd go around and start asking questions if I suddenly up and disappeared, anyway. My dads were hardasses, but Torr was just as stubborn. He'd get to the bottom of it eventually.

Torr offered me another smoke and chuckled in surprise when I accepted. "Something must be really fucked for you to be smoking this much," he observed.

I took a deep drag, letting the nicotine hit all the right neural pathways before I answered him.

"Do you believe in gods, Torr?"

TORRANCE

"Gods?" I repeated. "Like, more than one?"

Rori shrugged, flicking the end of her cigarette with a delicate finger. "Anything bigger than us, really. Higher powers, that sort of thing."

I paused to light up and inhale. "Yeah, I guess so."

She looked surprised at that, eyebrows lifting. "Really?"

"Yeah. Not in a religious sense, but I've always believed in something bigger than us. Why would humans have evolved to search for greater meaning if it's not there? Looking for those answers has always been a part of us, since we've lived in caves and shit. Maybe it's the searching itself that matters, and not the answer, but we all have that drive to find things that aren't right in front of our face. It's imprinted in our DNA."

Rori's lips curled with a soft smile. "I didn't know you had such a philosophical outlook on things."

"You never asked." I tried to soften the words with a smirk, taking another pull of my cigarette. I wished she'd ask me what I'd imagined that mouth doing, especially as her lips pursed to drag on her own cigarette.

"I've never believed in anything." She looked almost embarrassed by the admission, her amber eyes flicking away. "Like, sure, I don't know all the answers. But I've never really cared either, you know? I'm just one person. Who am I to figure out how the universe works? There are people way smarter than me who can't agree on what it all means, so why should I worry about shit beyond my own day-to-day life?"

"Nothing wrong with that either," I said.

Rori glanced back at me. "You don't think that sounds bitchy and self-centered?"

"Nah. But I feel like it's more personal than that, though. If something makes sense to *you* and makes *your* life feel meaningful, then who gives a fuck what so-called experts say? And by the same token, if you *don't* feel like you're missing anything by not having gods or something bigger in your life, that's cool too."

Rori sighed and tilted her head back, stretching the long, pretty column of her throat. "What if I didn't think I was missing anything until a god literally flew into my life?"

"Um." I braced my feet on the ground to stop my swinging and look at her more shrewdly. "What do you mean, Ror?"

"I left Daren's this morning all out of whack because I thought I was going crazy." She tossed her cigarette down almost violently and scraped over it with her shoe. "If I tell you, you'll probably think the same thing."

"I already know you're not crazy," I said. "But I can tell something's weighing on you, and you're thinking about it really hard. If it's family shit, like you said, I'll stay out of it. I'm here for you though, Ror. Just say the word, and I'll shut the fuck up while you get whatever it is off your chest."

She pushed back a wave of thick, blonde hair. "I mean, you are basically family."

I tried not to outwardly cringe at that. Sure, Daren and I

were as thick as thieves, practically brothers ourselves, but I never saw *her* as my little sister. She had a point though. Her family was really the only family I ever knew.

I barely remembered my life before I ended up in Four Corners. The clearest memories were how badly my feet hurt. The soles of my shoes had worn out, and my blisters were bleeding. I remembered how hungry I was after walking for what had felt like days. The skin on my nose, ears, and neck had been made raw and red from the sun.

Night was falling as I happened upon Four Corners for the first time at twelve years old. After trekking alone through the desert for who knows how long, thinking I would surely die, I'd never been so happy to see civilization again. Even so, I had remembered a vague warning as I entered the town. Something about not trusting people, not letting anyone find me.

I wasn't ready to die yet, so I took that to heart. I snuck into a building with large roll-up doors and hid in a dark corner behind a large, metal contraption. There was just enough room for me to curl up between the big metal thing and the wall, where my exhausted body finally fell asleep.

I slept so hard that I didn't hear the roll-up door open the next morning, but I felt the stabbing rays of sunlight and roused just in time to hear a man say, "Que mierda? Who— what the fuck?"

Now jolted awake, I went to scramble away, but the man had me cornered. He crouched low, eying me with confusion but not anger or malice. "Easy, son. You're alright," he said in a gentler tone. Not removing his eyes from me, he yelled over his shoulder, "Hey, Lark. Call Mari. Tell her it's an emergency."

"Yeah! Everything okay, Jandro?" a voice called back.

"Found a kid sleeping next to the Mustang's V-8." To me, he said, "You got a name?"

I just shook my head, curling up to make myself smaller.

"That's okay. Looks like you had a rough night." He tilted his head, inspecting me from the painful, blistering sunburn on my face to the holes at the bottoms of my shoes. "Rough several nights, by the looks of it."

"Papi?" A boy about my age came up to him then, wrapping his arms around the man's neck as he looked at me curiously. "Who's that?"

"Do me a favor, mijo." The man hugged around the boy's waist and kissed his mop of dark hair. "Get a cup of water from the sink in the break room, okay? He needs our help."

The boy took off running, his father watching him for a moment before returning his gaze back to me. "I'm Jandro, and you're in my shop, kid." He smiled at me, warm and at ease. "My boy is Daren. He's ten, looks about your age."

The sound of running water in a nearby room made me realize how thirsty I was, how much everything hurt, and that I didn't want to be alone anymore. The warnings kept going off in my head, memories of some faceless person yelling and shaking my shoulders. My mother, maybe?

Don't trust anyone, you hear me? You can't let any of them find you. Promise me, Torrance. Say it back to me. Again, promise me.

I was made to repeat my promise over and over, but I couldn't remember by who. Even now, it was a blank hole in my memory. I repeated my promise over and over, miles after I'd been told to start walking. The muscle memory of the words on my lips was probably the only reason I remembered it at all.

It was important to whoever had sent me off. But fuck, I was so tired and so fucking thirsty. And this guy seemed nice. Like, he took care of his kid rather than send him on a death march in the middle of nowhere.

"I'm Torrance," I whispered through my parched, aching throat. "I'm twelve."

"Well, Torrance." Jandro rubbed his jaw, still looking over me with that curious but kind gaze. "I don't know what you've been through, but you're going to be okay from now on."

Jandro did more for me in that moment than any parental figure ever had until that point, I knew that much.

Next to me in the present, Rori was silent for a while after calling me family. She chewed her lip, staring at the ground as she swung back and forth.

"So?" I prompted. "If I'm family, you gonna bring out the skeletons in the closet or what?"

She stopped swinging and met my eyes again. "They're some serious fucking skeletons. I'm still processing it all. And like I said, it sounds crazy."

I took a stab in the dark. "Because it has to do with...gods?"

"Yes." She sighed and held out her palm. "I'm gonna need another cigarette."

* * *

Rori and I had killed off my pack by the time she finished explaining it all to me. Once she fell quiet and I sat back to just process all of the information, my fingers itched for another smoke to help me sift through it. Because she was right. It was a fucking lot.

"That's not at all what I expected to hear," I admitted, raking a hand through my hair. "I thought one of your dads had a spiritual awakening or some shit and wanted to go off and live on a mountaintop by himself."

"None of them would do that," she snorted. "Okay, maybe Shadow."

"Nah, he's too devoted to you all."

Shadow was the scariest motherfucker I'd ever seen in my life. He made Jandro look like a puppy. He hadn't said much to me when I first came to live with the Steel Demons. It wasn't until maybe two weeks later, after I started school and came home with a black eye from some bigger kids, that Shadow approached me.

"Do you want it to stop?" he'd asked me. When I'd barely nodded, trying my best to keep my tears at bay, he said, "Follow me."

I followed him out to the backyard gym area where he pointed at a large dumbbell on the ground. "Pick that up."

I did as he said, imagining crashing the weight into my bullies' faces.

"Lift it over your head," he instructed. "Arm straight."

It took some grunting and effort, but I got it up, holding the dumbbell aloft like a trophy.

"Good. Now put it back down on the ground."

I did so with a confused frown.

"Pick it up."

I did as I was told, the weight feeling heavier this time.

"Lift it over your head."

My arm trembled as I raised it this time.

"Good job. Now put it down. With control, don't drop it." He pinned me with that scarred, pale eye as I released the weight, panting for breath. "I know you feel weak right now, Torr, but keep doing that over and over, and you *will* get stronger. Not just here." He tapped one finger to my shoulder. "But up here." He touched that same finger to the side of my head. "Daren works out with me three days a week if you'd like to join us."

I'd hit the weights every single fucking day since then.

It was an outlet I didn't know I'd needed. Every time I questioned why my birth parents didn't want me, why they left me out in the desert to die, I added more plates to a barbell and let the pain be my answer.

To this day, even though I was in my prime and Shadow was in his fifties, I never could beat that guy's deadlift or his bench press.

"You're right," Rori said, drawing me out of the memory. "Maybe Shadow would've done that before he met my mom though. Everyone teases him about how he was too shy to talk to her and that she pretty much had to pursue him herself." Rori's smile faded, her hands twisting on the chains of the swing on either side of her. "But no, it's gods. They helped my parents win the war years ago, and now one of them has come for me."

"Yeah, that's...a lot."

Silence fell over us again until Rori asked, "What are you thinking?" Like she couldn't stand the quiet any longer.

"Honestly?"

She swallowed. "Yeah."

"I'm thinking there's no way in hell I'm letting you do this alone."

Rori blinked, then shifted in her swing to face me directly. "Wait, hold on. You believe me, though?"

"Of course I believe you." I couldn't help the laugh that escaped. "Why would you lie about something like this?"

"I wouldn't, but I mean, this sounds nuts, doesn't it?"

I shrugged and reached for another cigarette before remembering they were all gone. "The whole world has been pretty fuckin' nuts for while, Ror. Since before we were born. It actually doesn't surprise me to hear that something else is brewing."

"Me neither, but come on, *gods*?"

"Why not?" I countered. "We fucked up pretty badly to have had a Collapse in the first place. Maybe some things are still out of the cosmic balance or whatever."

"I swear, Torr." She rubbed her forehead with a groan. "I could tell you unicorns flew over my house and we need to race them on a rainbow track, and you'd be like, 'Cool, when do we start?'"

"Hell yeah, I would. That sounds dope." I let her roll her eyes before continuing. "But really, it makes sense for me to come with you. Your parents have fought their fight. Daren and Lily got each other to think about, so they shouldn't go. I know you can handle yourself, but it only makes sense for you to have backup."

Rori shook her head, the worry clear on her face. "I *don't* feel like I can handle this, I'm way the fuck out of my element here. But that doesn't mean you need to get involved, Torr."

"Actually, that's even more reason for me to get involved," I pointed out. "If you're not prepared, who else is gonna save your damsel ass?"

Rori laughed so hard, she nearly fell off her swing. She hated being referred to as a damsel, so I teased her with it as often as I could. For all of her confidence and boldness, I could see the insecurities she tried to brush off. Always comparing herself to her twin brother. Stepping out of her parents' tall shadows. She truly was the brash, take-no-shit biker chick everyone knew, but sometimes she played it up to hide some of those fears.

You could be a damsel, I thought. *Just for me. I'll keep your secret safe.*

"Fuck you," she threw at me once she recovered. "How are you gonna live without pussy on tap, huh? It's gonna be slim pickings out in the desert. Unless you're into fucking cacti and tumbleweeds."

I was used to her throwing that in my face, but it still cut me every time. A repeated reminder that she would never want me.

"I'll live," I answered dryly.

"Sure," she scoffed, turning to rock back and forth in her swing again. "I won't see you for months when we get back because you're gonna be buried in an avalanche of ass." She paused, tilting her head. "*If* we get back, that is."

"We will," I said. "Besides, I'm Daren's best man. I'm gonna have to come up for air sometimes."

"Ew."

"You're the one who said 'avalanche of ass', not me."

"And I already have regrets," she sighed. We sat in silence again for a few moments until she nudged the toe of her boot against mine. "So you're really coming with me?" Her voice went quiet, almost a whisper.

"Hell yeah." It wasn't even a question in my mind. As if I'd last a single minute sitting on my ass here in Four Corners while she rode off into the great unknown by herself. Even if she'd never told me, I'd still find out and chase her down. "What's a damsel in distress without her Knight in shining chrome?"

"Torr!" Rori palmed her forehead. "You did *not* just make a pun with your last name."

"I sure as fuck did."

"I'm gonna kill you before this is over," she groaned, covering her face with both hands.

"Well, until then, I'll be your backup. Your right hand, whatever you need."

She peeked over her fingers and her eyes crinkled with a tiny, but genuine smile. "Thanks, Torr."

I nodded as I stood from the swing, immediately stamping down the fluttering in my chest. "We should probably tell your folks, huh?"

"Yeah." She rose from her swing as well. "Let's get this show on the road, I guess."

A white dove settled on the fence surrounding the playground as we headed toward our bikes. I glanced at Rori, but she had no reaction. There was no fear or confusion in her eyes now, only resigned acceptance.

Well, now.

The voice in my head made all my hairs stand on end. It felt ancient and everywhere, in my head and on the surface of my skin like a breeze. Possibly feminine, but it was hard to tell. I stared at the dove, who just cooed at me impassively.

This will certainly be interesting, the god said.

8

RORI

"Torr's going too?" Gunner raked his hands back through his hair, gripping it like he wanted to rip the strands out.

"I am," Torr confirmed, standing next to me.

"And he knows...?" Mom trailed off, looking between the two of us.

"All of it," I said. "The present god, the past gods. I told him everything you all told me."

We were in the kitchen, the two of us having come back just as my parents were having lunch.

"So you're just accepting this?" Shadow leaned back in his seat, his arm draped over the back of my mother's chair. "Both of you?"

"It doesn't seem like I have a choice," I said.

"It's true. You don't." Jandro was stone-faced, all the humor gone as he regarded us from across the table. "And I fucking hate that." He brought a fist down on the table, startling everyone. "I hate that *we* gave up so much, and it wasn't enough. We *still* couldn't keep you safe from this. I'm sorry, mijita."

"Papi," I breathed, using the name I called him as a little girl. "It's okay. It's not your fault."

"She's right." Reaper leaned over and squeezed his shoulder. "We can't blame ourselves. We had no way of knowing this would happen."

"But the gods probably did," Gunner pointed out. "And they couldn't have warned us? I hate this too. It's fucking bullshit."

"We *all* hate it," my mom said, raising a hand. "None of us wanted this for our kids. But that doesn't change the fact that it's happening. And," she hesitated, lowering her palm, "Astarte is probably right in the sense that Rori is better equipped to handle such a threat than anyone else of her generation."

"Because she was raised by us," Reaper said, his chin lifting with pride.

"Yes, exactly."

I swallowed heavily, hoping no one noticed. I didn't feel like I was equipped with a goddamn thing. For all I knew, I was going against a tank with a slingshot.

"We've taught Torr well too," Gunner said, eyes falling to the man at my side. "You still shooting at the range?"

Torr nodded. "Couple times a week."

"Still lifting?" Shadow asked with a small smile. Anyone could tell Torr was ripped just by looking at him. He and Daren hit the gym together every morning.

"Shit, I gotta beat your deadlift one of these days," Torr answered.

"Hm. Not likely, kid," Shadow said coolly.

"If there's one thing I can feel comfort in, it's that he'll be with you," my mom said to me before turning a grateful glance to Torr. "Thank you for doing this. We love you like one of our kids, so my mothering side is in pieces over this, but at the end of the day, I'm glad it's you with her, Torr."

I noticed Torr standing a little straighter, his chest puffing out slightly. "You're all the closest thing to a family I've ever had, so when Rori told me about this, it was a no-brainer. I know you'd never ask this of me, but she also shouldn't be out there alone. I promise she'll be safe and back home in one piece."

"If it was any other kid giving me that speech, I'd send him out the front door with my foot up his ass." Reaper glowered. "But you're not just any other kid, Torr. You *are* our family too." My father stood, extending his hand. When Torr went to take it, Reaper grabbed his forearm and pulled him into his chest, clasping his other arm around Torr's back in a rough hug. "I know you'll take care of Rori. But get yourself home safe too. You hear me, kid?"

"Yes, sir."

They released each other and Torr glanced back at me, his expression a little dazed. That often happened when someone got close to Reaper. Bryce once joked that he never knew if Reaper was going to hug him or stab him.

I met Torr's gaze and nodded with another hard swallow. The inevitable couldn't be delayed any longer. "Guess we should start packing."

* * *

I MANAGED to go a whole half hour of picking out the lightest, but most usable items from my wardrobe for the trip before my fathers started hovering. One of them barely knocked at my bedroom door before all four of them crowded their way in.

"Jesus, you guys can still knock!" I shoved the underwear I'd laid out into a side pocket of my saddle bag.

Jandro paid no mind to my panty selection and immediately assaulted me with a bear hug. Unsurprising, since he was easily the clingiest of my dads. He'd be happy to have me live under his roof until I was well into my forties.

"We're not gonna see you for shit knows how long," he murmured into my hair. "So don't get mad that we want to spend every last second we can with you."

A painful twinge pulled at my chest, and I melted, returning his hug. "I don't know what I'm doing, Papi," I whispered into his chest.

He let out a shuddering breath as he rubbed my back. "You don't know yet, but you will. I promise you will. Trust in your god. Astarte won't lead you astray."

"But I don't *know* that," I protested. "I've never trusted in anything like this."

"I know, mijita. Believe me, I know how terrifying this is."

"You'll have Torr," Reaper reminded me from where he stood a few feet away. "He'll have your back, no matter what. I believe you can trust Astarte, but other gods...they may try to manipulate you. So don't trust *all* gods, only the one bonded to you."

"Great. I can't wait to hear about where that piece of advice came from."

Reaper smiled but it didn't reach his eyes. "I'll tell you the story another time."

"If all else fails, trust in yourself," Gunner said. He stood tall, eyes sharp and alert like a general on a battlefield. "Your instincts, your reflexes. I didn't train you to shoot left-handed for no reason. We've taught you everything you need to know, Rori. You just need to believe in it."

I nodded, wishing I could steal his cool, controlled demeanor for myself. "Thanks, Dad."

Gunner softened immediately, his lips quirking into a lopsided smile as he held his arms out. "Come here."

I released Jandro and went to him, slipping into his solid

hug. He was my father by blood, and while all four men played equal roles in raising me, my bond with Gunner was just a little unique, a little different. Not closer necessarily, but different. I'd never hoped so strongly that I inherited his instincts for weapons and strategy. They just might save my life on this trip.

I looked at Shadow, who'd remained silent since walking into my room. He wasn't even looking at me but glowered at the clothes and supplies strewn on my bed. I had a feeling he wasn't looking *at* my stuff though, but that his mind was somewhere else far away.

"Any sage advice for me, Dadow?" Like with Jandro, I used the name I called him as a child.

His gaze snapped to me, and the look in his eyes actually made me jolt in fear. I'd never seen it before in my life. This giant of a man had always made me, my mother, and my siblings feel safe and loved, but I barely recognized him at that moment.

"Don't ever trust anyone who says they're with the Sisterhood of Bathory. You got that?" The words came out harsh and biting, like he was scolding me.

"Yeah, Dad." I could feel myself shrinking in Gunner's arms.

"I fucking mean it, Ror. You see someone who claims that, you get the hell away. Keep Torr away from them too. They'll use you to get to him."

My eyes narrowed with confusion. He was making zero sense. "Use me how?"

"Doesn't matter. Just stay far fucking away. I'm talking if they're in the same town as you, go to another town. Don't even let them *talk* to you, Ror. I—"

"Hey, hey." Reaper approached him, settling a hand on the other man's chest. "Take it easy. You're getting worked up."

Shadow turned his gaze on him, his jaw clenching and pupils like pin pricks. "Reap, you know I'm not exaggerating."

"I know, man. But it's upsetting you, and that's not helping Rori. She's smart, she'll know what to do."

"Aurora, *promise* me." Shadow returned his gaze to me, serious enough to ignore Reaper and use my proper name. "Promise me right now you won't have anything to do with them."

"I promise, Dad. I swear." Eager to reassure him, the words tumbled out of me quickly. "Sisterhood of Bathory, got it. I'll avoid them completely."

Only then did Shadow relax, his fists unclenching at his sides as a heavy breath escaped his chest. "I love you, Ror. I just don't want a fraction of what happened to me, to us," he glanced at Reaper, "to touch you. There's rotten, evil shit out there that shouldn't exist, but it does. And if I could prevent you from being exposed to any of it, I'd do it in a heartbeat."

"I know, Dad. I love you too." Sliding out of Gunner's embrace, I went to him. "But I gotta be a big girl too and fight my own battles."

"Nooo," Jandro whined, rubbing his face.

"Yeah," Shadow huffed in agreement with him. "That part, you fighting battles, scares the shit out of me."

"All of us," Reaper chimed in. "We were all just saying earlier, your mom too, that *this* is the hardest thing we've ever done. Letting you go."

"What the fuck, guys?" I blinked rapidly and wiped at my eyelashes before moisture could collect on them. "You're getting all sappy on me."

"Don't tell anyone," Reaper chuckled, kissing my brow. "Or we'll lock you in the garage."

"Not a bad plan." Jandro rubbed his chin. "She'll be safe in there, so will our reputation."

Gunner laughed. "You say that like she won't take a hammer to the walls to escape. Remember that?"

Like I could forget. He brought up my epic tantrum from eight years old at every opportunity. "That was an *accident!*" I reminded him. "I just really didn't want to be in time-out; I didn't know it would go *through* the wall."

"A lesson in repairing drywall that I never want to repeat," Shadow sighed, but he smiled at me. "We know you'll kick ass out there, Ror. Your dads are just always gonna worry about you."

"I know." I leaned against him and let him wrap me in a tight hug. My chest ached already, knowing how much I would miss them all.

* * *

TORRANCE ARRIVED EARLY the next morning, just as the sun rose. Everyone in my house was up and about except for Nolan and Lucia. My parents talked in hushed whispers so as to not wake them. I guzzled down coffee and forced eggs down my throat despite not feeling hungry. I would need the energy for the ride.

Torr immediately got roped into breakfast too—no one escaped being fed when the Steel Demons served up a meal.

"Did you say anything to Daren?" he asked, sitting across the table from me.

I nodded. "On the phone last night. He was...weirdly calm about it. When we hung up, he was just like, 'See you when you get back, sis. Love you.'"

My forkful of eggs paused on its way to my mouth. I wondered then if he had similar prophetic gifts to his namesake, our uncle Daren who passed and visited me in dreams. It never occurred to me until then, but it made sense. My twin had always been the wise, quiet one, while I'd always been a doofus.

"He expects us to be back in time for the wedding, I bet."

Torr looked up and smiled as my mom placed a cup of coffee next to his plate. "Thank you, Mari."

"I mean, the wedding's six months away. How long do you think this will take?" I asked.

We both looked toward the kitchen window, where Astarte peered at us from atop the chicken coop again. *As long as it needs to take*, she answered cryptically.

"And where exactly are we going?" Torr asked.

Somewhere far and not on any map.

"Fantastic," I grumbled. "Somewhere in the Great Wasteland, I take it?"

On the northern side of it, yes.

"Even better."

Torr and I ate until we couldn't anymore and my parents couldn't pretend to be occupied with other things.

"Rori?" Mom cleared her throat while two of my dads squeezed her shoulders. "Did you want to say goodbye to the littles?"

I nodded, swallowing the dry lump in my throat as I got up from the table. Even though they were teens now, Lucia and Nolan were respectively six and eight years behind Daren and I. We knew they looked up to us, and we felt our own share of responsibility in raising them.

I went to Lucia's room first, finding her fast asleep on her stomach. Like a typical seventeen-year-old, clothes were tossed in piles all over her room and pictures of hot male celebrities were haphazardly taped to her walls. She was sprawled out on her bed, all arms, legs, and long, dark hair.

Pushing back a lock of her hair, I bent to kiss Lucia's cheek and whispered, "I love you, baby sister. I won't be gone for long."

Her brows pinched together, and she stirred with a soft groan but didn't wake up. I stood from her bedside and left the room quickly, knowing that if I stayed, I'd be tempted to slide under the covers and sleep next to her like we used to. Sister sleepovers, we had called them.

Nolan's room, on the other hand, was meticulously clean and organized. He was very particular about how and where things were placed. My baby brother was barely older than a toddler when he started making his own bed in the morning because he didn't like how our mom did it.

Unlike Lucia, he was also a light sleeper and roused the moment I stepped into his room.

"What time is it?" he groaned, rubbing his eyes.

"Early," I said. "You don't have to get up, I just came to see you."

He blinked, confusion etched into his features. Like my other siblings, it was unclear which dad he came from. I saw a lot of Reaper in him but also some Jandro. "See me for what?"

I pointed to his bedside. "Can I sit?"

He nodded, sitting up higher.

I crossed the room and sat down on his comforter, completely at a loss of what to tell him. I'd half-hoped to just kiss him and say goodbye like with Lucia. I figured our parents would tell him the most difficult parts, if they felt he was ready.

"I have to go away for a little while," was what eventually came out. "But I'll be back."

"Go where?" Nolan's eyes narrowed. "For how long?"

"I'm not sure about either of those things," I admitted. "There's a lot I don't know other than that this is an important job that I have to do."

"Is it, like, dangerous?"

"Maybe." I couldn't find it in me to lie to him. "But Torr's coming with me. So I'll be okay." I brushed my knuckles against his jaw in an effort to wipe away his frown. "Don't worry. Your big sis can handle it."

"What aren't you telling me?" he demanded. The poor kid couldn't stand *not* knowing things, and I felt for him. I hated keeping him in the dark, but I also wasn't his parent. I didn't even fully know what I was getting into, so I had no idea how much was safe to tell him.

"A lot. And I'm sorry for that." I ruffled his hair, and he slapped my hand away in annoyance. "Mom and Dads will be able to tell you more."

"Yeah, right." Nolan grunted, flopping back down in bed. "They never tell me anything."

"They will," I said. "When you're older." Our parents hadn't really opened up to Daren and I about their war stories until we were eighteen, going into our early twenties. Looking back now, I understood why. Those weren't stories for kids, not even smart teenagers.

"But you're leaving now, right?" Nolan asked. "Why do I have to be older to know why my big sister is leaving right now?"

Tears sprung to my eyes, and I quickly blinked them away. Fuck, this was hard. I knew where he was coming from. Shit, I could still remember being fifteen myself and feeling like everything was so unfair. He was frustrated, and that wasn't his fault. As badly as I wanted to alleviate that for him, I knew protecting him was more important.

Maybe the battles my parents fought couldn't fully protect me. But if *my* battles could protect Nolan and Lucia, then I would do whatever it took.

"Listen, big guy." I fought to keep my voice steady. "I love you, okay? And this will all make sense one day, I promise. But right now, all you need to know is that this is something that *I* need to do. For you and Luce."

Nolan just made an annoyed noise, turning to face the wall away from me. I tried not to take offense to it. He didn't know how serious this was, what Torr and I would be risking. All he was thinking about was that he was being left out of the loop. And he wasn't wrong.

Steeling myself, I stood up from the bed and repeated the words Daren had said to me over the phone. "See you when I get back."

When I left his room, Torr and my parents were already gathered outside. Torr sat on his motorcycle next to mine, his engine already humming gently. One by one, each of my fathers walked up to hug me and offer final words of wisdom.

"Eat good, mijita. Don't take shit from nobody," Jandro said. "And remember to change your fucking oil. Don't let your bike suffer, okay?"

I snorted. "I will, viejito."

"Call us for help if you need it," Reaper told me next. "For anything, sugar cube. Even if we're not hovering over you, we're right here. You're *never* alone, understand?"

"Thanks, Dad." I nodded, my throat drying out again.

Shadow came up to me next and said nothing for a long moment, just held me against his broad chest until he pulled away, his hands still on my shoulders. "You're stronger than you think you are," he said. "There will be times when you want to give up, but you won't. You're going to hold on, because you have it in you. Trust me on that."

There was so much experience and personal meaning layered into those words, like he'd said them to himself hundreds of times before. I only nodded, meeting his gaze to show that I understood. Then I turned to my last father.

"Trust your instincts, Rori. Your aim is true, you know why?" Gunner whispered into my ear as he hugged me. "Because you're *my* fucking daughter."

I was already getting swept over by emotion, but that last sentence did me in. My eyes squeezed shut as I took a shuddering breath, clinging to his shoulders.

"We love you," Gunner said, gently rocking me from side to side. "And we're so fucking proud of you."

"I haven't even done anything," I whispered back. "I don't know *what* to do."

"You're taking the first steps. You've accepted the responsibility. That's huge." He pulled away, hands cupping my shoulders as he looked at me. "No matter what happens, we're so fucking proud." His hands dropped away as he stepped back with a lopsided smile. "Just come back to your old dads, alright?"

"Will do," I said shakily, forcing a smile. With another deep breath to center myself, I turned to my mother.

She stood off to the side while my fathers had fussed at me and now smiled as I approached. "You remind me of myself," she said, pulling me into a hug.

"Clueless, scared shitless, and in way over my head?" I asked, holding onto her tightly.

"Yes, exactly. All of that." She pushed her fingers through my hair. "Those feelings are normal, Rori. They don't mean you're not ready for this. You know what else I see?" Mom pulled back and held my face in her hands. "Someone a lot braver and more prepared than I was. I know you don't feel like it, but you *are*, my love. You were a warrior the day you came out of my womb, screaming bloody murder and kicking your brother in the head."

I let out a very undignified snort, but my mom's words did the trick and eased a little bit of my tightly wound fear. "Thank you, Mom. You don't know how much it means to know you believe in me."

Now she blinked back tears right before bringing my face down to kiss my forehead. "Always, my daughter."

When we separated, I still felt clueless, scared shitless, and in over my head. But also a little steadier. A little more determined to see this through, if only to return to my amazing family again that much sooner.

I went to my bike and climbed on, my tentative steadiness turning rock solid the moment I sat on that machine. The world was mine when I rode, gods or no. This was freedom, and this was power. As I turned the key and felt the engine roar to life, I couldn't imagine arriving at my destiny any other way.

With a quick nod to Torr, I shot out of the driveway. Together, we followed the dove flying just ahead.

Astarte led us northwest, toward the Great Wasteland.

9
____

TORRANCE

We followed Astarte through miles and miles and *miles* of desert. With the exception of a couple of pit stops, Rori and I rode nearly the entire day. I'd never admit it to her, but my ass and balls were aching like crazy by the time night started to fall. She'd been riding years longer than I had and probably never got sore from riding anymore.

Around dusk, Astarte perched on a rusted sign, which teetered dangerously to one side and was riddled with bullet holes. I had to tilt my head and squint to read, *Welcome to Carvers, Nevada.* Damn, so this was a pre-Collapse place. No one my age ever called it Nevada, only the older folks did.

You will rest here for the night. I shuddered at the sensation of Astarte's voice. It felt like fingertips dragging over my brain. Rori didn't seem to have the same reaction. I wondered if she'd gotten used to it.

"Where?" Rori looked around, and she had a point. There wasn't much to see.

In the tavern, child. In the morning, you will meet your first contact in that same location.

"*That* place?" Rori sounded incredulous as she nodded

toward a building that had seen better days. Dust caked the windows and exterior walls. The siding was warped with age and some parts were tagged with faded graffiti. Neon signs in the windows advertised liquor and food, although their illumination of all the dust made the offers feel a little suspicious.

Windows covered the second and third stories of the building, and I could only assume those were rooms for the overnight travelers like us.

"Come on, it's not so bad." I nudged Rori with an elbow. "Imagine if Bryce's place was also a motel. That's what this is."

She rolled her eyes toward me, her expression dripping with disapproval. "Don't insult Bryce's like that."

"I mean, sure, it'd probably be less dusty, but Bryce isn't exactly a clean freak."

"We can't stay anywhere else?" Rori looked at the dove.

The answer came with a straightforward, *No.*

"Alright," Rori huffed, not sounding convinced as she popped up her kickstand.

We drove up the short distance to park in front of the building, and I waited until we turned the bikes off to keep ribbing her. "I thought you loved roughing it on camping trips," I said, following her to the front door. "This is just like that."

"I know my sleeping bags are clean and where my food comes from on those trips," she shot back. "This...I don't know anything about this."

"It's an adventure." I reached in front and pulled the door open for her. "And remember, I've got your back."

She glared at me on her way inside, but her mouth tipped up with playfulness. "Your eternal optimism is already exhausting."

"Sounds like a stamina problem for you, not me." I stepped in behind her, head swiveling around the dark room as I allowed the door to close behind me.

We'd walked right into the small bar-slash-restaurant area. Only a few wooden tables with benches lined the walls, most of them empty. The long bar at the far end, backed with rows of dusty liquor bottles, was similarly empty.

The bartender, a woman in her sixties with salt and pepper hair, looked up and squinted at us as we entered. "Can I help y'all?" she called across the room.

The few people, maybe eight in total, occupying benches and barstools turned to look at us as we crossed over to the bar. Rori paid them no mind, but I glared at the men who blatantly ogled her.

"Hi," Rori said cheerily to the bartender. "We'd like a couple of rooms for the night, please."

There was a pause as the bartender eyed us. "Separate rooms?"

"Yes, please."

I ignored the uncomfortable little prickling in my chest as I planted my feet wide, crossing my arms and meeting the eyes of everyone who stared at us until they looked away. While the bartender flipped through some pages in a logbook, Rori glanced over her shoulder at me, her brows drawn in confusion. I was standing close to her, probably hovering. But none of these perverts were about to get an unobstructed view of her ass in leathers. Absolutely the fuck not.

"Sorry, miss." The bartender looked up. "Only got the one room available. Will that work?"

"One room?" Rori repeated, looking around the bar. "Are you sure? It doesn't seem very busy tonight."

"We're doing some renovations," the bartender clipped out. "You want it or not?"

Rori pushed a hand back through her hair, her fingers landing on her bare nape. "Well, does it have two beds?"

Damn. Just twist the knife and announce to the whole world that you don't want me, I thought.

The bartender's eyes slid to me once before answering. "I think so. I'm not sure, though."

"You're not sure?"

The woman held up her logbook, the pages of which had been copied and recopied so many times, the room information was barely visible. "We don't have computers up here yet. We're all working with what we've got, miss."

Rori sighed. "Well, I guess we'll take it then."

While she filled out our information in the book, I went out to get our saddlebags from the bikes. When I returned, Rori had our key and angled her head toward a rickety-looking staircase. I followed her up, floorboards creaking with each step I took. The landing brought us to a short hallway with doors on either side.

"This is us." Rori went to a door with the number six and inserted the key. I wondered if we were both holding our breath as she turned the knob and swung it open.

"Fuck," she hissed.

I barked out a laugh.

There was only one fucking bed.

"Where the fuck is that bird?" Rori crossed the room and opened the window, sticking her head out to night air, supposedly looking for Astarte.

"Relax, it's no big deal." I slid the bags from my shoulders and placed them on the bench at the foot of the bed. "They have cots in these places, right? I'll sleep on that." I went to the closet and found it empty aside from a few wire hangers. "Or the floor, I guess."

"You're not sleeping on the floor." Rori pulled her head back in and shut the window. She turned toward the bed hesitantly, like she didn't want to look at it. "Looks like a queen, so there should be plenty of room."

"Aside from my feet hanging off the edge, sure." I sat in the single, small armchair and started to take my boots off. A queen bed was actually pretty small for a guy my size, and Rori was a tall woman too. My bed back home was a king, not only because it was long enough to support my whole frame, but it was spacious enough to feel like I was still sleeping alone when anyone spent the night.

A queen bed would put enough space between Rori and I, but just barely.

"Do you snore?" Rori asked, perching on one side of the frayed quilt covering the mattress.

I snorted. "How many times have we both crashed at Daren and Lily's place and you still don't know the answer to that?"

She wrinkled her nose. "Well, I sleep pretty hard when I'm fucked up." With a sigh, she tilted her head back to look around at the walls and ceiling. "But I don't think I'm sleeping a wink in here, regardless."

"You can kick me if I snore." I slipped my fingers into the collar of my shirt. "Also, uh."

"Oh God damnit, I forgot." Rori stood from the bed with a groan. "You sleep naked. Maybe you should take the floor, I don't want any cooties."

"Sure, if you want." I shrugged, pushing down the jab like I always did. "But I'll keep my boxers on, I just get really hot. And I use protection and get tested regularly, by the way." I hated everything about that last sentence that came out of my mouth and wished I could take it back. Maybe it was the ride and the long day, but she had me feeling so damn defensive.

Rori's mouth wobbled. "Sorry. I was just poking fun, but that was mean. I'm sorry, Torr. I'm an asshole when I'm tired and stressed."

"It's nothing. Here, just give me a sheet and a pillow."

"You're not sleeping on the floor," she insisted. "Just don't strangle me like an anaconda, and we'll be good."

"My anaconda is far gentler than that, I assure you."

"*Okay!*" She made a sound halfway between a groan and a laugh as she came to rummage through her bags. "I'm taking a shower, unless you wanted to get in first?"

"Nah, go ahead."

When she disappeared into the small bathroom and closed the door, I flopped back onto the bed with a sigh and pulled out my phone.

No reception, which was pretty much what I expected. Cellular service was spotty in most places, except for well-established territories and only if there were peace treaties between those territories. At least Sevier, a neighboring territory to Four Corners, was finally in the process of manufacturing new phones now. Everything we used now were relics from before the Collapse.

Rori's parents, Bryce, and all the other old timers talked about how technology used to advance so quickly. Before the Collapse, they had powerful computers that were so sleek, fast, and could perform all kinds of functions. Electric vehicles and the automated machines that built them. Speakers that you could talk to and order things that were delivered straight to your house.

That kind of growth happened at a snail's pace for Rori and my generation. There were just fewer opportunities to learn the things of the past, and those who knew enough to teach it were dying off.

I played some puzzle game on my phone until I heard the shower shut off. Then I tried and failed to focus on my game instead of imagining Rori step out of the shower, her bare skin glossy with water as she swiped a towel over herself. The mental image of her naked was too much to bear, and I dropped my phone, palming my erection with an annoyed grunt.

Maybe I'd wait until she was asleep, then slip out of bed to sleep on the floor after all. The fact that she insisted on two rooms, and then her utter disappointment at the lack of two beds, got under my skin more than her usual jabs.

We partied together, crashed together, told dirty jokes, and flirted all the time. We'd known each other for years, and yet had never been in the position to share a bed. I'd be a gentleman and not touch her, of course. But for some reason, her repulsion of me bothered me to the point where I'd rather take the floor than force her to share a mattress with me. She'd never outright tell me that it made her uncomfortable, but I knew she'd be relieved to wake up in bed alone.

The bathroom door opened, and Rori stepped out in a cloud of steam. She was dressed in sleeping shorts and an oversized T-shirt, thankfully saving me from seeing the impression of her nipples against anything tighter, like a tank top. Her hair was brushed back, the wet strands sticking to each other and ending at chin-length. Normally her hair was so voluminous, hovering around her face like golden clouds, but I liked the slicked back look on her too.

Who was I kidding? I liked everything on her.

"No lead poisoning?" I asked, watching her rub a towel over her hair in the mirror.

"Not enough to croak yet, at least," she chuckled. "The water's hot, which was a pleasant surprise."

"That's good."

She turned, hanging the towel on a hook as she came toward me with a thoughtful expression. "Do you remember what else Astarte said? Something about a contact tomorrow?"

"We'll meet our first contact in the morning here," I said.

"You think this place serves breakfast?" I laughed when she wrinkled her nose. "I'll taste-test everything for you, princess."

"It's not that, dick." She gave a playful shove to my shoulder before flopping down on the bed next to me. "The word *first* has me worried. Like this is some kind of top secret covert mission in those old spy movies. How many contacts are there going to be? And are they humans or...?"

Gods was the unspoken word she left hanging on the end of that sentence.

"I dunno, Ror. We'll find out when we meet them, I guess."

She grabbed a pillow and hugged it to her chest as she turned to face me on the bed, drawing her long legs up to sit cross-legged. Funny how she called me an anaconda when I'd love nothing more than those legs to wrap around my hips and squeeze the life out of me.

"What do you think this whole mission is going to entail?" Rori's chin rested on top of the pillow, brows knitted together as she thought out loud. "Are we just receiving instructions from various mysterious contacts? What if they tell us to, I dunno, hurt people without any clarifying details?" She jerked her head up abruptly, pinning me with a wide-eyed stare. "What if we're on the wrong side of this, Torr?"

I snatched the pillow from her and softly whacked her over the head with it. "Don't *what-if* yourself to death. That's not gonna help us. We'll find out more tomorrow. And if shit looks fishy, we'll plan accordingly."

"You ass!" Rori dove for the pillow, but I swung it out of her reach. With nothing to hold on to, she barreled forward into my lap. I half expected her to scramble away, but to my surprise, she pressed her palms into the tops of my thighs, pushing herself up until we were eye-to-eye.

"How are you so calm and collected about this?" Our faces were inches apart, and I could feel the warm puffs of air from her lips as she spoke. "How does your mind *not* race with all the worst possible outcomes, Torr? Whatever you've got, I want some, because I wish my brain worked like that."

I shrugged, practically sitting on my free hand so I wouldn't be tempted to run my fingers up one of those arms braced on my thighs. "Being left for dead taught me pretty quickly that it's not worth worrying about things I can't control."

Rori blinked those forest green eyes and eased back slowly, her fingers dragging a few inches down my legs before her hands returned to her lap.

"You deserved better than what your parents did to you, Torr. I don't know if I, Daren, or my parents ever told you that, but it's true."

I shrugged again. "The point I'm trying to make is that you can't run through scenarios in your head, trying to predict an outcome, because it'll never turn out the way you think it might. You'll just get yourself worked up for no reason."

"My dad Gunner would disagree," she argued.

"He made predictions as a tactician with the knowledge he had available to him. His battle strategies were based on his expertise in the field, not wild guesses. Your predictions are based on your anxiety."

"Well, shit. Ouch."

"All I'm saying is, it's better to hear what the facts are and then plan accordingly."

Rori sighed before she snatched the pillow back from me. I saw it coming, but I let her take it anyway. "You're right," she sighed, hugging the pillow to her chest again. "I know you're right. I just...can't turn my brain off."

"I know." I leaned forward and tickled the bottom of her foot, something I always did to distract her from an anxious meltdown when we were kids. "I'm here for that too."

"Stop!" She laughed, flinging her foot out and narrowly

missing kicking me in the chin. With all the times she had kicked me when I tickled her, I was surprised I still had all my teeth.

"Try to sleep," I told her. "And when your mind starts racing, imagine kicking me in the face. I'm sure those thoughts will be a lot more satisfying."

She scoffed, tossing the pillow back up to the headboard. "Thanks, Torr."

Rori scooted across the bed to her side and reached for the lamp on the nightstand. I stripped down to my boxers and climbed in, careful to stay close to my edge so I wouldn't accidentally touch her. Once I pulled the sheets up to my chest, Rori clicked off the light, and the room plunged into darkness.

"Goodnight," I heard her whisper softly from across the bed. "Night, Ror."

I adjusted my pillow, settled in, and waited, listening for when her gentle breathing deepened so I could move to the floor.

10

—

RORI

I woke up exhausted, feeling like I needed another eight hours just to feel normal. I had fallen asleep faster than expected, probably because we'd ridden all day and it was my first long ride in several months. My body's weariness made up for the fact that my mind ran like a hamster wheel.

Groaning, I rubbed the sand from my eyes. Why did my body feel so heavy? Oh wait, there was an arm thrown over my waist.

Torr's arm.

I noticed the dark lines of his tattoos first, the half-sleeve of swirling gray smoke that solidified into a snow-capped mountain on the top of his shoulder. His forearm was a golden tan from the sun, visible veins and corded muscles stretching down to a strong hand with long fingers.

My breath paused in my chest, and I laid there for a few seconds, frozen. I became aware of his deep, even breathing directly behind my head. Not snoring, thankfully. His chest wasn't quite pressed against my back, but I could sense the solidness and heat of him all the same.

Unfortunately, I needed air to live, so I started breathing

again, forcing the inhales to be as slow as possible so as to not disturb him. So I could make this last a little longer, before he realized what he'd done.

Or had *I* instigated this? A quick look told me no, I was still on my side. Torr had been the one to cross the invisible boundary in our bed, and it secretly thrilled me.

He slept on, breathing deep and steady, so I began turning over as slowly and quietly as humanly possible. The sight of his sleeping face nearly made me gasp. He was *so* beautiful. Did he always have those freckles? I'd never noticed them before. But of course, I'd never woken up in bed next to him either.

Tons of women must have gotten this view and woken up the same way I did. But I couldn't bring myself to be jealous right then. He was here with me, not with any of them.

The thought brought a cold dose of reality, like icy water to the face. He wasn't *with* me, not really. He hadn't even wanted to sleep in the same bed. If I hadn't insisted on it, he would probably be on the floor now.

I wanted to touch him and curled my hand into a fist just so I wouldn't be tempted. He wouldn't welcome that, not from me. The only reason he came on this ride with me was because there was no one else. Lily needed Daren more than I did. My parents weren't fighters in their prime anymore. Torr put aside his own wants and was being an incredible friend by doing this. I had to be grateful for that and not hope for anything more. To do so was selfish.

Torr pulled in a deep breath and stirred, rolling to his back with a soft groan. That arm lifted away from me as he rubbed his eyes.

"Mornin', sunshine," I greeted.

"Hm?" He lifted his head and squinted one eye at me. "Aw, damn it."

"What?"

"It's nothin'," he croaked, his voice rough and groggy with sleep.

I pushed back my blanket and began to slide from the bed. "Sorry I'm not the chick you were dreaming about." The words came out harsher than I intended.

Torr groaned, scrubbing his palms down his face. "S'not that, Ror."

"I'm kidding." I walked around the bed, grabbing my leathers and a fresh shirt.

"I was gonna move to the floor after you fell asleep," he said, lacing his hands behind his head so that his biceps and the wide expanse of his chest were on display. "But I guess I conked out before that happened."

"Why? I told you the bed was fine." I went to the vanity just outside the bathroom and pulled a brush through my hair, trying to distract myself from the little stab of rejection in my chest.

"Just to give you some space. Make you more comfortable."

I could almost believe the sweet sentiment in his words. Torr was masterful at letting a girl down easy.

"Well, all turned out fine." He must not have realized he was practically spooning me moments ago, so I wasn't about to mention it. "You sleep well?"

In the mirror, I watched Torr bring one hand down to rest on his chest. "Yeah, better than I thought I would. Guess it was a pretty grueling day. You?"

"Yeah, same. You ready to meet this mysterious first contact?"

"Yeah, let me get a quick shower in."

He pushed back the cover and I busied myself with my toiletries as he gathered up some clothes, wearing nothing but his snug boxer briefs. I kept avoiding eye contact as he approached me, all the way until he squeezed into the tiny bathroom and shut the door. Then I tilted my head back and let out a long sigh before looking at myself in the mirror again.

"Get a grip, bitch," I told my reflection. "You're just making this harder on yourself."

I got dressed while Torr showered, then after he was decent, we headed down the rickety stairs together.

"Did the all-knowing Astarte tell you anything this morning?" he asked as we entered the main room with the bar and tables.

"Nope. Not a peep." The room was even emptier than last night, with only the bartender, one grizzled older man sitting at the bar, and one table occupied by a group of three men.

"Want to take our chances with breakfast?" I asked Torr.

"Hell yeah, I'm starving."

He grabbed us a table while I went up to the bartender. The breakfast selection was simple but plentiful. Eggs, sausage, toast, and country potatoes for five Territory Credits, or TCs as they were most often called.

TCs were a relatively new currency, only put out into circulation about ten years ago. Six of the most stable allied territories came together and forged an agreement to make TCs their de-facto currency. This was to encourage more trade between the territories and make it easier for their traveling citizens to buy and sell goods across each other's borders. Many of the smaller territories and neutral zones had also adopted TCs for everyday use.

The days of bartering goods and services were something my parents' generation had been accustomed to for years, so a standardized currency had received some pushback from them. Especially Gunner, who prided himself in negotiating good deals.

"You can keep the eggs, my homie's chickens lay much better ones," I could imagine him saying with that charming grin. "And I'll give you two TCs for the rest of the spread, what do you say?"

I went to sit across from Torr at a table once I put our food order in. For a moment, we just stared at each other, saying nothing.

"So now what?" My anxious ass couldn't help but break the silence first.

Torr shrugged, propping his elbow on the table and then resting his cheek on his fist. "Guess we wait. We didn't get a description or a code word or anything, right?"

I leaned back while the bartender came over and dropped a pot of coffee and two mugs on the table, waiting until she left to speak. "Nope. We are well-equipped spies for this mission, clearly."

Torr only chuckled as he poured coffee for both of us. Our food came out a short while later and we dug in, mostly quiet as we ate. None of it was terrible, but my dads definitely wouldn't approve of the eggs. They were small, and the yolks were pale. I could imagine Jandro walking back to the kitchen himself with a lecture on how to raise chickens properly so they gave you large, nutritionally-dense eggs.

The activity in the room didn't change much as we ate. The guy sitting at the bar left halfway through our meal. The three men at the table talked quietly among themselves as they nursed cups of coffee.

We finished our food and the whole pot of coffee without incident. Torr and I locked eyes when the bartender cleared our plates.

"Don't say it," Torr warned.

"Now what?" I said at the same time.

"Damn it." He laughed and playfully kicked me under the table.

"It's nearly noon, right? Morning's almost over. What do we—"

The front door opened, spilling light into the room. The brightness of the outside was quickly blocked off though, by the dark figure stepping into the room.

And by the massive black wolf at their side.

Holy shit. I was too stunned to let the words leave my mouth, especially as the figure and their wolf turned toward us and headed straight for our table.

Neither Torr or I moved when the two of them paused in front of us. The figure lowered their hood, revealing herself to be a dark-haired woman. She looked to be a few years older than me, possibly in her early thirties.

"May I sit?" the woman asked in a soft voice.

"Um, sure." She could only be the one we were waiting on, so what else could I say?

Before I could scoot on the bench to make room for her, Torr got up and gestured to his bench, offering her his seat. "You can talk to both of us easier this way." He slid in next to me, and I was grateful for his presence at my side.

"Thank you," the woman said politely, sliding into the free seat with all the grace and poise of a princess. Her wolf jumped onto the bench beside her and rested its head in her lap.

Looking straight at her now, it dawned on me that she was really pretty. Naturally so, yes, but she also made herself that way. Her eyebrows were perfectly shaped and filled in, and her long, curling lashes were clearly extensions. Aside from her lashes and brows, there was no hair on her face, like she even removed the soft peach fuzz that every human being had. She wore no makeup, but her face was a smooth, pristine canvas.

"My name is Gwen," she said in that soft, polite voice. "And this is Lupa."

The wolf lifted her head at the sound of her name, looking

at her human expectantly for a moment before laying her head back down.

"I'm Aurora. I go by Rori," I said. "This is Torrance."

"Torr," he said with a small wave.

"So you're our, um, contact?" I broached.

"I suppose I am," Gwen said with a small shrug. "Lupa brought me here. She said I would find the woman who is the light and the man who is her guard."

Torr glanced at me, his brow furrowed in confusion and I laughed softly. "Aurora is a type of light," I told him. "You know, like the aurora borealis?"

"The what now?"

"You know, the northern lights. Those greenish-blue lights in the sky that happen near the north pole? Those are auroras."

"Huh," he mused. "I never knew that."

Aurora is also a goddess of dawn. The ancient, feminine voice trailing gently over my brain was not Astarte's. It took me a second to realize it was Lupa, the wolf. She propped her head on the table and gave us a sweet, doggy smile. *You're touched by gods not only through your parents, child, but in your name.*

Torr and I looked at each other first before glancing at Gwen across the table. "Well, I'm glad we're not the only ones who can hear that."

Gwen smiled, her shoulders relaxing. She'd been so poised since the moment she walked in, I hadn't realized she'd also been stiff as well. "It's a trip, isn't it, when you first hear them in your head."

"I actually believed I was hallucinating," I admitted. "Until my mom let me know that the same thing happened to her and my dads."

"My parents were called on by gods too," Gwen said.

I rocked forward, bracing my palms on the table. "Are you serious?"

She nodded. "Lupa first came to me a few years ago. My mission has been ongoing." Her dark brown eyes traveled over us curiously. "And now it seems to have intersected with yours."

"We don't even know what it is," Torr said. "We just followed Astarte here and were told to wait for you."

"Ah, yes." Gwen tilted her head, her smile growing. "It's fun when you're only given information in bits and pieces, isn't it?"

"A fucking blast," I deadpanned.

"I wish I could tell you more about your own path." My heart sank when she said that. "But all I know is what I've been tasked to give you." Her eyes darted between us again. "Pardon me for asking, but are you two a couple?"

"No," Torr and I answered in unison. "No, we're just friends," I added to clarify.

Gwen narrowed her eyes, her lips pursing into a frown. "Are you two...close?"

"I mean..." Torr and I shared another look, and my hands folded nervously on the table. "We've known each other for thirteen years. He's basically a member of my family so, yes, you could say we're close. Platonically."

"I see." Gwen's eyes slid to Lupa, who licked her muzzle and opened her jaws in another doggy smile. "Well, I'm meant to help you get somewhere, and the place you're going has very strict rules for entry. Depending how uh, truly *platonic* your friendship is, you may have some difficulty gaining access. Or you may not, I don't know you well enough to speculate."

Now it was my turn to narrow my eyes at her. "What exactly are you saying?"

Gwen's shoulders stiffened again, her ramrod posture returning. "You will have to convince the staff at this establishment that you are a married couple."

11

RORI

"Excuse me?" Torr sputtered. "Married?"

"Not *just* married, but happily so," Gwen went on. "This place is a resort that appears to cater to honeymooning newlyweds."

"What the hell are we looking for in a place like that?" I demanded.

"I don't know," Gwen said. "I'm sorry, I wish I could tell you. What I can tell you is that this place is very mysterious and exclusive. They don't publicly say what any of their amenities or attractions are. You have to apply to be a guest, and they've never outright said what the requirements are. But the pattern we've noticed is that only married couples and single women have had their applications accepted."

Torr and I fell quiet. "That *is* strange," he mused.

"Let me rephrase." Gwen placed the edges of her hands on the table so that her palms faced each other. "Married couples and single women who can afford it. The other catch is that the cost is very high. Even the application fee is exorbitant and nonrefundable."

"I have a good nest egg of TCs saved up," I said.

"Whatever you have won't be enough," Gwen said while I tried not to feel insulted. "That's where I come in. I'm going to sponsor your application and attendance fees. But you two also need to look the part, and I don't just mean acting like you're married." She leaned back, pulling her hands into her lap. "You two need to act and look like you come from wealth. And I mean *serious* wealth."

Torr leaned forward, placing one elbow on the table as he rubbed his jaw. "And who are *you*, again? How exactly do you know all this, let alone have the funds to get us in?"

Gwen's dark eyes hardened. Her perfect posture didn't crumble under his stare, and my respect for her only increased. It took serious balls to stand up to Torr when he was trying to be intimidating.

"I'm the publicist for a Blakeworth family," she said. "One of the Elite Eight."

Ah, so now the perfectly groomed brows and eyelash extensions made sense. The Blakeworth territory was known for having an obscenely wealthy elite class whose favorite past times included flaunting that wealth and crushing anyone beneath them into the dirt. Many of the citizens in Four Corners had been Blakeworth refugees, fleeing the outrageous laws and human rights violations that applied to everyone *but* the elite class.

I knew they were briefly involved in the war my parents had been in. One of my favorite stories was about how Shadow, his brother—my uncle Grudge and his club—and my mom, were wanted fugitives in Blakeworth. The Blakeworth governor had kidnapped my aunt Kyrie, the woman who would become the wife of Grudge, T-Bone, and Dyno, who ran the Sons of Odin MC. They all rescued her on that mission but knew they would be shot on sight if they ever returned.

"So you're a Blakeworth bootlicker, huh?" Torr's mouth twisted disdainfully.

"No. That's just my day job." To her credit, Gwen kept calm and not at all defensive. "What I'm actually doing, with Lupa," her gaze slid to the now-sleeping wolf next to her, "is providing resources and escape routes to those carrying all of the elite's bloat. The *real* citizens." Her eyes blazed with a passion I hadn't seen up until that point. "And from the inside, I'm dismantling the elite class, brick by brick."

Silence fell over our table while the pieces slowly began to click together in my head. "So this resort," I said. "Who runs it? The elite Blakeworth families?"

Gwen shook her head and spread her hands. "There's lots of speculation being thrown around, but no one knows for sure. My employers don't have any involvement, but they have been guests. Their friends claim no involvement either, though a son of *that* family claims to know an investor but apparently has been sworn to secrecy. It's one of those things where everyone seems to know something, but no one can locate the source."

"And probably half of them are lying," I said. I sure as hell didn't trust people with an obscene amount of wealth and power.

"Yes," Gwen agreed. "That's also a likely factor."

"How long has the resort been around?" Torr asked.

"About five years ago was when invitations to apply began circulating. I never heard anything before that, so construction must have been top-secret."

"And no one knows *anything* about what goes on in there?" I asked.

"That's correct. And those that have been guests in the past aren't saying a word. Apparently, they lose the privilege of returning if they divulge anything."

"Well, if that doesn't sound fucking shady, I don't know

what does." I drummed my fingertips on the table and looked at Torr, but his focus was across the table.

"Sorry I called you a bootlicker," he mumbled.

"That's alright." Gwen smiled gently. "I've been called worse."

"It's admirable that you're doing this," I said. "I can't imagine the anxiety of working for a rich asshole family who would do terrible things to me and my family if they knew—" My mouth slammed shut, but I realized my misstep too late. "Sorry, I wasn't thinking."

"It's okay. My family is fine." Gwen raised a palm. "They're safe and far away in another territory. One of my dads is actually an accomplished hacker, so the false emergency contact information I gave to my employer cleared with no issues. They have no idea where my family is."

"Good. Still, that can't be easy." I smiled, feeling an odd sort of kinship with her. "How many dads do you have?"

"I have three."

"That's nice. My cousin has three. I have four."

Gwen's polite smile went into a full-on grin. "Our lucky mothers."

"Uh, so." Torr cleared his throat. "What's next? We tell everyone we're...married? Get ourselves some colored contacts and rich people shit?"

"Right." Gwen's expression went serious again. "You need suitable transportation too. How did you two arrive here?"

"Motorcycles," I said.

Gwen shook her head. I expected as much but still felt myself deflating inside. There was no other ride I preferred over my bike.

"I can store your vehicles in one of my employer's garages. They'll never notice. And I'll lend you one of their cars to take to the resort. Actually." She paused, tapping a finger on her chin. "I'll come with you in a separate vehicle. Your stay will likely be a month long, so I'll bring along changes of clothes and things you'll need. I just need to take your measurements, because everything has to fit like a glove."

"A *month?*" Torr balked. "People really go on honeymoons for a month?"

"In my employer's circle, three week vacations of any kind are the minimum," Gwen explained. "Any shorter than that and you will be looked down upon as frugal. Four weeks to three months are more typical."

"Jesus." Torr rubbed his forehead.

"What do we need for this application?" I asked.

"I'll handle all of that." Gwen waved her hand. "It's sent electronically, so when I finalize today, we should have an answer by tomorrow." She looked at Torr. "You asked about colored contacts. Yes, I'll get you both several pairs. When you're at the resort, you'll want to change them out regularly. It'll be expected of you to coordinate your eye colors with your outfits or jewelry."

"Jesus," Torr said again. "Fucking rich people."

"Aww, honey!" I wrapped my arms around his bicep, leaning my head on his shoulder and batting my eyelashes with a cheesy smile. "We can have matching irises like a couple of psychos!"

"Do *not* ever call me honey again."

The corner of Gwen's mouth tilted up as she watched us. "Any other questions for me?"

"Is there any other reason why you're helping us?" I asked. "Aside from your god leading you here, plus sticking it to rich assholes. Is there anything personal in this for you?"

She took a moment to answer, one hand stroking through the wolf's thick fur. "People have been disappearing. People I...

knew. Worked with, in secret. Just missing, with no rhyme or reason."

Torr and I looked at each other. "You think that's related to this resort?"

"I don't have any proof, just a strong gut feeling." Gwen frowned at Lupa, like she was frustrated at the wolf goddess. "If anyone knows about the disappearances, they're not saying anything. These are not elite folks, either. Just normal people."

"So the elites don't care and aren't doing shit to find them," Torr said. When Gwen nodded, he added, "I'm sorry."

"The weirdest thing is," Gwen looked up at me, "you know how vulnerable people are usually the ones kidnapped? Women by themselves, teens, children, you know."

"Yeah?"

"That's not the case here. It's strong, able-bodied *men* going missing. Guys you'd never pick a fight with for no reason."

"Sorry to ask." Torr held up a hand. "But what makes you think they're being kidnapped? What if they're just getting the hell out of Blakeworth?"

"Because they're leaving spouses, children, and all their belongings behind." Gwen's voice hardened. "Because when the first kidnappings happened, a group of friends organized to protect their own streets since no one else would. They were gone before morning. Four men between twenty-five and thirty-five, none under six feet tall, all vanished into thin air."

Gwen's jaw clenched and her lip wobbled, her dark eyes blinking away tears. I could sense what she left unspoken—that one, maybe more, of the missing men had been especially important to her. If my deductions were correct, she was keeping together extremely well. I'd be a raging, feral animal if someone I loved was taken from me.

"I'm sorry," I said, feeling the urge to reach across the table and hold her hands. "I want to tell you that you can count on us, but I guess that's an empty promise if we don't know what we're dealing with."

"Yes. I really wish I could tell you more about what you're getting into." Gwen sniffed and quickly composed herself, folding her hands on the table. "But it's safe to say, you should probably assume the worst."

The worst being...what, exactly? I wondered. Slave labor? Human experimentation? My mind, already prone to running wild with ideas, started flipping through worst-case scenarios. In doing that, a question bubbled up, and I voiced it before getting lost in the spiral of my head.

"What's this place called?"

"Mystic Canyon Resort," Gwen answered.

We returned to our room later, where Gwen took our measurements for our rich asshole disguises, as Torr called them. If Gwen had any thoughts about two platonic friends sharing a room with one bed, she didn't say anything.

"What do you think?" Torr asked me when she'd left. "Do you trust her?"

I didn't have to think for very long. "Yeah," I said, confident in my answer. "I do. You?"

He nodded sharply, his expression determined. "I do too."

We stayed one more night at the tavern, and this time, Torr didn't bring up sleeping on the floor again.

I didn't wake up to his arm around me the second morning and got annoyed by the heavy disappointment in my chest.

At breakfast, Gwen informed us that our application had been accepted. In two days, we would arrive at Mystic Canyon Resort.

"That quick?" Torr held out a strip of bacon to Lupa, who

gulped it down with a crazily wagging tail. "I thought all our clothes and shit had to be custom-fitted."

"It's a rushed order on my employer's account," Gwen said. "The tailors know not to keep them waiting."

"Is that how you're funding this whole thing?" I asked her. "On their dime?"

A sly smile curved her lips. "Of course. I can't afford any of this on my personal earnings."

I frowned. "Is it safe for you to do that?"

"I know how to cover my tracks," she answered with a coy smile. "And this stuff is a drop in the bucket to them, so covering anything is honestly overkill. They're at the level where they still have exponentially more money coming in than going out. If I really wanted to drain them, that would take a lot more effort that would definitely raise eyebrows."

"Fucking rich people." Torr broke another bacon strip in half and gave a second piece to Lupa. "I like the Robin Hood shit, though. At least you're stealing something from them."

"Well, it's not exactly going to the poor in this case," I mused.

"It's still a worthwhile cause." He scratched Lupa's ears as she licked her lips. "Just to find out what the fuck is going on in that place."

"I agree," Gwen said. "I'm all but certain this is the only way to get in." She took in a shaky breath. "After the kidnappings started, some people went out to find Mystic Canyon. They also disappeared and never came back."

Torr leaned forward. "Is the place guarded?"

"I don't know, but I can only assume so. It's out in the middle of nowhere. The invitations have directions but no actual address. So it's possible they might have perished from heatstroke or something else along the way. I'm not sure, though."

"Whereabouts is it?" I asked.

"About three hours north of here."

I huffed out a soft laugh. "Everyone was right. The pieces are all coming together." Astarte hadn't said a word since that first night here, but she hadn't needed to. She led us right where we needed to be and no further. I was still utterly clueless, but at least I knew more now than I did before.

"If you don't mind, I'll have some of my people come and pick up your bikes today," Gwen said. "They're trustworthy and will handle your vehicles well. You have my word they'll be stored in a safe location."

"Can it wait until tomorrow?" I asked. "I'd like to go on one last ride before I'm not able to for a whole month."

"Oh, sure." Gwen tilted her head with a curious expression. "Riding is pretty important to you, isn't it?"

"It's everything to me," I admitted. "Kind of runs in the family."

She smiled lightly. "Oh, I know some people just like that."

"Yeah?"

Gwen then seemed to get a bit flustered, clearing her throat as the color in her cheeks deepened. "Enjoy your ride," she said, standing from the table abruptly. "I'll see you tomorrow."

12

RORI

Torr glared at the huge makeup kit Gwen had set down on the small desk in our room the next morning. "This is why we had to get started so early? Makeup?"

"Blakeworth's elite are always heavily made-up. You have to look the part to not arouse suspicion," Gwen explained, opening the kit to reveal a small horde of brushes, pallets, eyelashes, lipsticks, and even small gemstones. "I'm not a professional, but I can do you both up enough to get by. When you arrive, they should have makeup staff for you, since they don't allow guests to come with their own servants."

"Wait, wait." Torr held up a hand. "What do you mean you can do both of us?"

"Blakeworth men wear makeup too," I told him. "You didn't know that?"

"No! Why would I?"

"I'll do Rori first, since she'll take longer," Gwen said. "In the meantime, Torr, would you mind shaving your face? Your foundation will look patchy if you put it on over stubble."

"Ror?" The high note of desperation in his voice was hilarious.

"You heard the lady." I sat in the chair Gwen pulled out for me. "We're top-secret agents going undercover, remember?"

I held back my snicker until Torr finished stomping around in search of his shaving kit, then went grumbling into the bathroom.

"He's a good sport, he'll get over it." I closed my eyes as Gwen pinned my hair back and soon felt the gentle mist of a cleanser on my face.

"When was the last time you had a makeover?" she asked.

"Probably when my little sister wanted to use my face as a finger painting canvas. She's seventeen now."

Gwen chuckled as she wiped my skin clean and began applying a primer. "Well, lucky you are about to get one every single day for a month."

"That sounds kind of exhausting, actually."

"I hear you. As soon as I'm off the clock, the first thing I do is wash my face."

I let her work on me in silence for a few minutes before asking, "Do the makeup staff get paid over there? At the resort?"

There was a long pause before she answered. "I don't know."

My jaw went rigid. Blakeworth faced all kinds of backlash from other territories because of the supposed terrible working conditions for laughably little pay. Many even believed they used slave labor. But the territory was so secretive about their economy, always diverting attention with their flashy elite class to show how prosperous and well-off they were.

"I guess that's something we'll find out," I mused.

My ass was numb and my limbs stiff by the time I was finally done. My eyelids felt heavy, and when Gwen let me turn to the mirror, I saw she'd glued in long, wispy feathers alongside my false lashes. She'd also put in bright, crystal blue contacts in, so my normally dark green eyes were straight up freaky-looking.

Everything from my eyeshadow to my blush and highlighter shimmered with an almost blinding effect.

"Holy shit," I muttered. "Feels like I'm about to go to a costume party."

Gwen laughed. "Nope, this is an everyday look. You'll get used to it, though."

"I kind of hope not."

We dragged Torr into the chair together. He thankfully didn't put up a fight and was finished much quicker than I had been. He chose an emerald green for his eye color, and I popped the lenses in while Gwen worked on his face. When she was done, the difference was subtle but jarring.

She'd contoured his face, shaped and filled in his eyebrows, applied some neutral eyeshadow shades, and that was pretty much it. He still looked like himself but too... polished. Torr's freckles were gone, as was the rough stubble on his jaw and the small scar through his eyebrow. He'd gotten it from a fight with a playground bully, and Daren and I had taken turns applying pressure to it while we waited for the school nurse to come.

He wasn't that charmingly disheveled, rough-and-tumble guy I'd had a crush on since I was ten. Now he looked like he could put on a suit and recite the slimy words of a politician.

"That bad, huh?" He smirked, and I realized I must have been staring at him for a while.

"Uh, no, actually." I tried to recover smoothly. "You make a very convincing rich asshole."

"Great. You're not a bad rich bitch yourself."

"A match made in heaven," Gwen laughed as she put away her supplies.

Oh shit, that was right. We were supposed to act like we were married.

"Hey, don't I need a big, flashy rock or something?" I

extended my fingers, trying to imagine some obnoxiously large ring on my finger.

"Oh, right! I almost forgot." Gwen reached into her pocket and pulled out a small box. "Torr, do you want to do the honors?"

For some reason, my heart beat crazily against my ribs when he took the box and opened it. Torr let out a long whistle as he held it out to show me. "Damn. Now that's a ring."

My breath stuttered. I was not usually moved by jewelry, but this one was just *pretty*. It was a large, single black stone, cut and polished so that all its faces threw off glassy reflections like deep pools of water. It was held to the silver band with four large prongs.

"It's a black diamond," Gwen said. "They're more rare, so the elites love them. The simple setting is also fashionable right now. Of course my employer bought like ten of them in one trip, so I just snatched one that looked like it would fit you."

"Hang on. Let me do this right." Torr dropped to one knee, his eyes locked to mine as he reached for my hand.

"What? Torr, no." I pulled my hand back, my throat choking with emotion. Why? Why did he want to do this? It was just Gwen in the room. We didn't have to play pretend right *now*.

"Come on, just let me." His voice went low with that sultry, masculine growl that worked to charm all the women. Myself included, even though I knew all of this was fake.

"You don't need to commit to your character this much," I muttered, letting him take the hand I'd pulled away.

His eyes dropped to my outstretched hand, the ring finger extended like it couldn't wait to receive that rare piece of jewelry from him. Fucking traitor, that little finger.

"No matter what happens in there," Torr said, eyes returning to my face as he slid the band over my knuckle, "I'm your guard at every turn. You'll always have me."

My chest started to ache with how long I'd been holding my breath. Even my teeth started to hurt from clenching my jaw. I hoped he couldn't see how my whole body trembled with every emotion I fought to prevent from rising to the surface.

I was a swirling maelstrom inside, pissed and hurt. It felt like he was mocking me, putting on this fake display when he knew the real thing would never happen between us. It felt so painful, I wanted to scream or slap him.

But Torr would never intentionally be that cruel. He remained blissfully unaware of my feelings, so he must have thought a fake proposal would be funny. He looked so solemn though, on his knee as he carefully slid that band over my last knuckle. The ring was a perfect fit, which was just the extra, cruel cherry on top.

"We come out of this together or not at all," he said before releasing my hand and rising to his feet.

A few feet away, Gwen busied herself with putting her makeup away, acting like she totally didn't see fake marriage vows between two platonic friends. Fuck me. We hadn't even made it into the resort yet, and I was already fucking up this act.

"What next?" I asked distractedly to no one in particular. "Clothes?"

"Um, yes!" Gwen sounded relieved at the subject change. "I have your gown over here, Rori. Torr, your suit is in the garment bag hanging on the closet door."

Torr's brows pinched together, like he was confused or even insulted that I didn't acknowledge his fake vows. But his features quickly smoothed over as he crossed the room to get his clothes.

I turned to the bed where a long, flowy gown made of some satiny material was laid out before me. It was a deep, rich pink, almost burgundy in color. I wasn't big on pink in general, but the dress was pretty, and I knew Gwen would pick a flattering color for me. I brought my left hand out in front of me, staring at the ring Torr had placed just moments before. The stone's glassy surface reflected the pink hues of the dress, and I wondered how long it would take before the charade was too much for me. How long until I couldn't hold back anymore and cracked?

Closing my fist, I let my hand drop back to my side and refocused on the dress. *One day at a time,* I told myself. *One minute at a time if I have to.*

* * *

AN HOUR LATER, our bikes were being loaded into a trailer being pulled by a truck, and Gwen showed us to two luxury vehicles waiting in front of the tavern. Torr practically drooled as he approached "our" car, some kind of vintage Rolls Royce.

"I've always wanted to drive a car like this." He walked a slow, appreciative circle around the thing.

I, on the other hand, just hated that it had four walls and a roof. It might as well have been a cage. I'd always hated riding in cars ever since I was a baby. My parents complained I'd send them to an early grave because I'd always open a car door before it stopped moving. Nothing beat the freedom of a motorcycle, and a heavy stone of sadness settled in my chest knowing it would be a whole month before I rode again.

Torr seemed to sense the melancholy rolling off me, and he came around to give my shoulder a squeeze. "It won't be forever," he said, as if he knew exactly what was getting me down.

I gave him a small nod and allowed him to guide me to the passenger side with his hand on my back. He opened the door just as Gwen pulled up in front of us in her large luxury SUV, the backseats crammed with "our" things for our "honeymoon".

"Just follow me," she said before rolling up the tinted window.

Torr and I settled into the car, and he push-started the ignition. "Think she'll let me go fast in this thing a time or two?"

"Don't risk it," I said. "She has to give this back to her employer at some point."

"I know, I was just kidding."

The silence was heavy between us as we drove. I spent most of the time staring out the window at the desert rushing past us. Part of me wanted to bring up the whole business with putting the ring on my finger, mainly to ask what the fuck that was about? At the same time, I was scared of the answer I would get.

Torr didn't push for conversation, and I wondered if he was mulling over that same moment as I was. Probably not. Torr was like a mountain—everything just rolled off of him. Was it just two nights ago that he lectured me about not holding onto things I couldn't control?

Well, my control over my feelings for him was slipping. And I wasn't sure how to reel that in, especially now that we had to play the part of a married couple.

Looking upward, I was completely unsurprised at the flying speck in the sky. Astarte kept an easy pace with us in the car and apparently still had nothing to say. Would she even step in to course-correct if we fucked up? Who knew? My parents talked about bonds and abilities with their gods like there was a relationship. Gwen and Lupa certainly seemed close. But me and this dove felt like reluctant coworkers at best.

The drive was no less than three hours, but it felt like no time at all before Gwen's tail lights lit up, and we slowed behind her. I straightened in my seat, craning my neck to see what was ahead.

There was...nothing.

Only more desert stretched beyond her front bumper, and I was utterly confused as to why she stopped.

"Is something wrong?" I wondered aloud, hands going for my seatbelt.

Torr's hand stopped mine, his palm touching the ring on my finger. "Stay put. I'll check on her."

No sooner had he said that than a woman in a crisp black suit seemed to pop out of nowhere and approached the driver's side of Gwen's car. The sight made me wonder if I was hallucinating again. "Where the fuck did she come from?"

"Hang on." Torr hit a button that opened the car's panoramic sunroof and lifted up, poking his head through the top of the car. He flopped back in his seat seconds later. "Ah, I get it."

"What?" I demanded.

"There's a canyon up ahead, I could just see the edge of it just now. We're on a slight incline, so it's harder to see when you're sitting."

"Oh, so that's where the resort is?"

"Must be."

I stretched up to look myself, and he was right. A sheer drop-off was maybe thirty feet in front of Gwen's car. Across the divide, I could see just the top of the far canyon wall. The rock looked smooth, even polished, like it was carved by human machinery instead of nature.

Dropping back to my seat, I saw the suited woman talking to Gwen through her lowered window. She had to be verifying us as guests, and I hoped we were flying under the radar as well as Gwen assured us we would be.

Several long moments passed until the woman nodded definitively and looked toward us with a beaming smile. She waved and began to approach our car while Torr rolled his window down, but it was my side of the car she came to. Torr fiddled with the buttons for a moment until he got my window to lower.

"Welcome to Mystic Canyon Resort!" the woman said. "You have passed all the qualifications for entry, and we hope you enjoy your stay. I'm Nella, the guest services manager, and will be showing you around today."

"Thank you."

Nella continued before I could ask any questions. "I have staff on their way up to retrieve your things, including valet service for your vehicle. If you would like to pull up just in front of your assistant, our valet driver can take your car to the lot, and we can enter the lift to begin our tour."

"Thank you, that sounds...*lovely*." I tried my best to sound like a snooty rich person while finding it curious that she spoke exclusively to me, never glancing once at Torr.

Nella stepped away as he rolled our windows back up, and we slowly maneuvered in front of Gwen's SUV.

"I'm already creeped the fuck out," Torr muttered.

"You and me both."

"She stared at you like she wanted to eat you."

"Why wouldn't she just come to the driver's side?" I wondered.

"Shit, *I'm* glad she didn't."

"Dick." I shoved at his shoulder, but a smile never cracked his face. All of this was becoming very real.

There was a concrete pad, essentially a lone parking space, directly in front of Gwen's car, and Torr drove onto it. We were only a few feet away from the edge of the canyon now, and I stared at some kind of metal frame drilled into the side of the canyon wall nearby. It looked like a cage with only four bars making a rectangle shape, the top maybe eight feet above the lip of the canyon.

The questions in my head were answered when a glass and metal box slid up from the inside of the canyon wall and nestled into the top of the metal frame. Four people stepped out of the box, all women in the same crisp black suits as Nella.

An elevator! I realized, the word screaming out in my head. I'd never seen one in real life, much less stepped inside one. I was pretty sure Torr never had either.

Two of the women approached our car and opened the doors for us. "Welcome to Mystic Canyon Resort," they said in unison with warm, welcoming smiles. "We'll take your vehicle to the valet lot now," said the one at my door.

Torr and I stepped out, and the woman who opened his door slid into the driver's seat. The rest of the staff went to the back of Gwen's car and quickly unloaded our things. I clasped my hands in front of me, shoving down the uncomfortable feelings of someone else carrying my stuff. When you rode motorcycles, everyone was responsible for their own goods.

A whirring, grinding sound made me whip back around. "Torr!" I hissed, grabbing his arm.

"I know," he said, placing a warm palm on my back.

The concrete pad, and our car on it, was descending straight into the fucking ground.

"I apologize for the noise of our car lift," Nella said, eying her fellow staff member in the driver's seat like she was the one responsible. "We will replace the machinery immediately."

"Ah, no, that's okay," I protested, forcing a smile with a hand on my chest. "It just startled me, that's all."

"Which is unacceptable. You are our guests." Nella lowered her head in a show of humility. "Every part of your stay with us should be comfortable and pleasant."

Little dramatic, but okay. I just gave her a tight-lipped smile and a nod, unsure of how else to react. Thankfully, Gwen exited her car and came around to the front.

"This is where I leave you." She was also wearing a crisp suit, though it was an emerald green with gold trim. I assumed it was her regular work uniform. She also wore a full face of makeup, though it was more understated than mine.

"Thank you for everything," I said to her with genuine gratitude. Really, she had gotten us here. All we did was show up and do what we were told.

"See you in a month?" Torr's arm slid around my waist in a firm, possessive hold as he asked her the question.

"Yes, of course." Gwen inclined her head respectfully, as I was sure she would do for her employers. Though she glanced up quickly, catching both of our eyes. "Enjoy your honeymoon, you two."

Oh, right. That was why Torr put his arm around me.

"We will." I smiled and leaned my head against his shoulder.

One of Nella's staff slammed Gwen's trunk closed as they got the last of our things, so with a final, curt nod at us, she got back in her car.

And then we were alone at this mysterious resort with its creepy staff.

"If you would please follow me." Nella extended her arm toward the elevator before heading that way. The others had already taken a trip down with our stuff and a new, empty glass cage stood waiting for us.

I held my breath as I stepped from the natural ground into that cage, hoping I gave off the air of someone who rode in elevators all the time.

"Holy shit," I muttered under my breath, my eyes going wide at the view of the canyon.

I was quiet, but Nella heard me anyway. "Magnificent, isn't it?" The door slid closed, she pushed a button, and we began a gentle descent. "The founders wanted it to look exactly like ancient Rome, and I'd say we came pretty close."

Taking up most of the canyon, carved deep in the earth, was a giant outdoor colosseum.

13

DEVIN

Santos stood at the tiny window of our shared dorm when I came in after breakfast. His two machetes lay on the side table, freshly sharpened and gleaming in the morning sun. He stood like a statue, feet wide and hands clasped behind his back, wearing only a pair of boxer shorts.

I shamelessly admired his ass as I reclined in my bunk. He didn't do guys but wasn't bothered that I did.

"Keep standing there for another twenty minutes, if you don't mind." I groaned as I stretched, my calves and feet hanging off the ridiculously small bed.

"Why?" he asked with a soft chuckle.

"One, I have a great view of your back and your ass. Two, you're blocking out the sun, and I want to get a nap in before training."

He cast a smirk at me over his shoulder. "You might be fighting for bed space for that nap."

As if waiting for his cue, our third roommate, Santos' black jaguar, Tezcatlipoca, jumped onto the bed with me.

"Ow, Tezca!" Paws the size of my hands braced on my chest as the big cat made himself comfortable right on top of me.

The jaguar only huffed in amusement and leaned down to lick his sandpaper tongue against my jaw. He loved to groom my beard for some reason.

"Fuck, you're heavy, and your breath stinks." I shoved back against Tezca but only succeeded in sliding myself out from under him. He settled himself down on the bed, while I only got the very edge. Sighing, I brought my feet to the floor and leaned back against the big cat's flank. "What are you looking at, anyway?" I said to Santos, who'd returned to staring out the window.

"More resort guests just showed up," he answered.

"So?" I gathered my hair up and began winding it into a topknot at the crown of my head. If I wasn't going to nap, I might as well get stretched out for training.

"Something's weird about them. Come look."

I finished tying up my hair and stood to look over his shoulder. I had a few inches on Santos in height, but he had me beat in muscle mass and savage brutality that crowds loved to see in a gladiator. My talents lie in being fast and swift. My opponents always lost sight of me before I delivered the killing strike.

Hence why he was dubbed the Butcher and I, the Ghost.

Through the window and across the canyon which had been our involuntary home for the past four years, I saw the guest elevator descending with three people in it. One was Nella, the vile bitch who was the guest manager of this so-called resort. The guests were a couple in their twenties, a woman with short blonde hair and a dark-haired man. Their arms were around each other, so honeymooners probably. Their eyes were on Nella as she gestured around the canyon, no doubt giving her welcome speech filled with her cleverly woven bullshit.

"They look pretty typical to me," I said to Santos. "What's weird about them?"

"I dunno, something's off." His dark eyes narrowed, rapt on

the couple like they were a puzzle he was trying to solve. "The woman's body language is stiff. Like she doesn't want to touch him."

"They're hundreds of yards away. How can you tell?"

"Appearances are off too. Their clothing looks like Blakeworth, but they just...don't look like Blakeworth stock to me."

"So what are you thinking?" I returned to sitting on the bed, where Tezca was already asleep with a bit of his tongue poking out. "That they're the ones big kitty here says we're waiting for?" I patted the jaguar's flank. He stirred but didn't wake up.

"Maybe. I don't know, could be nothing." Santos finally turned away from the window, rubbing his eyes. "Ever since he told us that, it feels like I'm reading into every little thing."

Young gladiators often prayed for miracles. They asked their various gods to rescue them, to be kept safe in the pit, or for a quick, painless death on the sands. If they lasted a year or more, like us, they often became too jaded to have any hope left. We certainly had been. The two of us were skilled fighters, but it was also our celebrity status, our entertainment value, that kept us alive.

But for Santos and I, our answered prayers came years after we'd lost hope and in the form of a black jaguar. Or rather, a god taking on the form of a black jaguar. He was brought out for the gladiators to slaughter during an event, but the clawed, fanged shadow killed everyone who neared him instead. Everyone except us.

Tezcatlipoca had said rescue was coming. Not right away but one day. He gave us hope, but hope was a heavy burden when you had to fight for your life, day in and day out.

It was relatively easy to make Tezca our pet. He wouldn't leave our side, and we were valuable gladiators who brought income to the resort. So they just let him stay with us. It kept the pitmasters from breathing down our necks and the other gladiators from attempting to kill us in our sleep.

Yeah, the pit wasn't a place to make friends. Santos and I were somewhat of an exception in that we were already acquainted. We'd been taken from the same place—another prison, just not one where we'd been forced to fight. He and I had been housed there together, along with a third guy, Hudson, who had been left behind. Who even knew if that poor bastard was still alive?

"Has he said anything to you?" I nodded at the snoring jaguar behind me.

"Nah, nothing." Santos pulled on his pants and then secured his belt around his hips.

"So it's probably not them, right?"

"I dunno. He doesn't always tell me shit." Santos slid the machetes into their sheaths on his belt. "Sometimes it's fucking riddles, and I don't know what he means."

While both of us had heard Tezca speak, his primary bond was to Santos. An Aztec deity paired up with a Mexican guy made sense, I guess. It would be nice if a Chinese dragon would appear to save my half-Asian ass, but no luck so far.

"Well, that couple was with Nella, so you know she's gonna bring them down here to inspect the livestock," I said bitterly. "We can do some inspecting right back."

Santos sat down to lace up his boots, glancing up at me. "Which one were you inspecting more, the girl or the guy?"

"They were too far away to see clearly. But probably the girl. Guy didn't look like my type."

"Yeah, girl was cute." There was something in his voice that sounded a bit like yearning.

I held back from saying a sarcastic remark. Despite his reputation for brutality in the pit, Santos was, for lack of a better word, soft. Not in a bad way. I actually admired him a lot for holding on to that part of himself. Even after our years in captivity, he held on to that desire for a long-term partner and a family. The guy wanted love, and while I couldn't fault him for that, I wondered how he could still believe in such a thing at all.

Especially with how Nella exploited him to the guests. She was no better than a fucking street pimp, serving him up like fresh meat.

"Come on, Butcher. Let's keep you sharp." Before getting up, I gave two more pats to Tezca's flank, and that woke him up with a snort.

Santos and I both laughed at the big cat. Tezca was our sleek, prowling ray of black sunshine in this hellhole. Sometimes it was hard to believe the goofy animal was also inhabited by an ancient god.

The jaguar rolled over and slid down from the bed, now alert with ears pricked forward as he followed Santos out the door, an ever-watchful guard. I followed after the cat, already armed to the teeth like usual. Not that anyone but Santos could tell.

The pitmaster eyeballed us as we came out into the hallway, muttering under his breath as he took a headcount of all the gladiators coming out for training. The sun wouldn't be directly over the canyon for another couple of hours, so the sands were nice and cool when we entered the pit in the center of the colosseum.

Santos and I immediately separated, as was our routine. We didn't act like friends in front of the others, especially the pitmasters. Once they saw friendships, or worse, romantic or sexual relationships developing, they liked to set those fighters up against each other. Everyone knew Santos and I were roommates and had come here from the same place, but all that meant was we got along well enough to not try to kill each other outside of the pit. After four years of being here, it seemed to work. We had never once been scheduled against each other and were both still alive to show for it.

Tezca circled around Santos protectively while the guy got to hacking at a training dummy with a couple of batons. Santos had whittled down the wooden batons until they were the same weight and balance as his machetes.

My training, however, couldn't be practiced on an inanimate object.

I stuck to the shadows, slowly circling the perimeter of the sand pit while the other gladiators stretched and warmed up. The veteran fighters gave me dirty looks as I passed. They knew what to expect from me. It was a shame they didn't seem to realize my training was beneficial for them as well as myself. Only the most honed senses, the sharpest ears and reflexes, stood a chance against my attacks. And during training time, they were lucky I wasn't actively trying to kill anyone.

The newest fighters, on the other hand, would be in for a hell of a surprise.

I spotted the fresh meat from a mile away. The newest gladiators all hung out together, which was their first mistake. Alliances and friend groups only got people killed here, especially if they weren't smart enough to keep it discreet like Santos and me. The two nearest pitmasters were already leaning their heads together, talking quietly between themselves while nodding at the group with sinister smiles.

The group of four were also easy to spot because of their pasty-as-fuck skin. In time, if they survived, they'd be darkened by the brutal sun like the rest of us. After spending the first few weeks as red as lobsters, of course. This lot must have done years in solitary confinement somewhere. A couple of them squinted and shielded their eyes like they'd never been outside before.

In fewer words, they were a perfect warm-up for the day.

I continued my walk, studying them in my peripheral vision

while looking straight ahead. One of the veteran gladiators, the Animal, glared at me as I approached him.

"Don't fuck with me today, Ghost," he snarled at me through blackened teeth. "I'm not in the fuckin' mood."

"You're safe from me today, spider monkey." Just for fun, I liked to call him a different animal every time we interacted. He flew off the handle every time like clockwork, *except* for when I called him an axolotl. He only flipped me off and yelled slurs at me for a whole minute, so I think he liked that one.

Spider monkey however, did not have the same effect.

He picked up one of his clubs with a heavy grunt, bringing it back over his massive shoulder to wind up for a swing. "I fucking told you, I'm not in the fucking—"

I was behind him before he finished drawing back his arm. In the next moment, I held his wrist with one hand and had the tip of my dagger pressed into his spine with the other. The Animal froze, his body in a precarious balance. If he resisted my hold and tried to swing his arm forward, his spinal column would run straight into my blade.

I had the knife positioned between two vertebrae, and he'd seen how cleanly I severed spines during my fights. I had left people paralyzed from the waist down dozens of times. And they never figured out why, because they never saw me coming.

And if the Animal didn't resist and continued following gravity, he'd fall backwards onto my knife anyway.

"Lucky for you, titmouse," I said, "I'm not in the mood to deal with you today either."

I heard his teeth grind in anger and his furious huff of breath. But we both knew he couldn't risk moving until I released him.

Which I did, because two pitmasters were storming our way.

"What the fuck is going on?" one of them demanded, while the other rested his hand on his taser gun at his belt.

"Nothing, sirs." I stepped away from the Animal and lowered my gaze to the ground. "Just tussling a bit to warm up for training."

"Yeah," the Animal agreed, his gaze lowering like mine. "No trouble here, sirs."

The pitmasters turned around and were gone in the next moment. Scuffles were normal between gladiators during training. They just wanted to make sure no one killed each other prematurely and messed up the fight schedules. Spectators usually had a lot of money riding on those fights.

As soon as the pitmasters were out of earshot, the Animal whirled to face me. "Fuck with me again and I'll skull-fuck you right back 'til I puncture one of your lungs and you're drowning in my cum. Then I'll take your scrawny ass while you suffocate and keep going until your corpse is cold. Am I clear, Ghost?"

I kept my face expressionless as I turned to leave. "Don't threaten me with a good time. Later, alligator."

"I know where you sleep," he called after me.

It wasn't until I was a good thirty feet away that I allowed myself some deep breaths. Well that was...unsettling. Rape threats were a dime a dozen here, but that was especially graphic. He must have been really pissed. It was a good thing I slept in the same room as a jaguar whose kill record nearly matched mine.

I lifted my head and continued on my walk, bypassing the group of new gladiators. I was no longer in the mood to teach any young ones some hard lessons. Santos was by a water station, taking a quick, rationed drink under the watchful eye of more pitmasters as I continued past him.

"You alright?" he muttered under his breath, not looking at me.

"Yeah," I answered, not breaking my stride.

I would be fine, once I walked off the mental image the Animal had put in my head. That was another thing about dealing with gladiators. You could never, ever let their threats rattle you.

Once that happened, you were already dead.

14

———

RORI

"Here is the spa, where we have the most *amazing* skin treatments and massage options. There's also a nail salon and a lash, brow, and wax studio if you ever need any regular maintenance."

"Mm-hm." I held onto Torr's arm, already bored by this tour, but plastered on an *Ooh, yes! Very interesting* smile every time Nella turned to look at me.

"And right next door is the gym with all of the state-of-the-art equipment." The suited woman opened the door to let us look through.

Torr let out a low, appreciative whistle, his eyes flicking around to all of the weights, squat racks, and barbells. "Definitely gonna spend some time in here."

"Meathead," I teased with an elbow to his ribs.

He wrapped an arm around my shoulders, pulling me into his side as he dropped a kiss to my temple. "Just keeping the goods in shape for you, honey."

I gave him my best glare when Nella turned her back. He was making me pay for calling him honey before, and being

127

especially smug about it, since I couldn't tell him to eat a dick while Nella was around.

He turned me toward his chest with the arm around my shoulders, bringing me closer to talk privately. "What are your thoughts so far?"

His breath tickled my ear and the weight of his arm was comforting, grounding. Whatever fancy cologne Gwen had sprayed him with smelled amazing, and I hated that I wanted to press my face to his chest and inhale him.

"This place is fucking creepy," was what I told him instead.

The path under our feet was mosaic tile in a dazzling colorful pattern. The different areas of the resort were carved into the sides of canyons, accessible by elevators and ornate bridges. Everywhere we went had stunning views of the canyon walls and the colosseum, which was probably the whole point. Rich people paid big bucks for nice views, it seemed.

"Here's the cafe, right next to the aviary." Nella gestured to an open patio with spotless white furniture and dozens of green plants to amp up the tropical look. Beyond the patio was a large, dome-shaped cage.

"We have the largest collection of exotic birds in the world," Nella explained. "Many of these species are already extinct in the wild, but you can enjoy their songs during your morning coffee, afternoon tea, whatever suits you."

I couldn't get over how sad that was as we walked on to the sounds of many different bird calls. How hopeless would that feel to be the last of your species and caged in a desert canyon far away from home? To be nothing more than exotic background noise? My gaze lifted skyward, but I saw no sign of Astarte. It sure would be sweet, karmic justice if she dropped a little present in one of the patio guest's drink.

"You two are quiet." Nella turned to look back at us as we followed the mosaic path around the cafe and aviary. "Is everything to your liking?" She looked directly at me, still all but ignoring Torr as she had since she approached our car.

"Yes, it's beautiful!" I chirped, spreading my lips wide into another performative smile. "It's all just...I don't know where to begin."

"I've saved the best for last." Nella beamed. "The colosseum entrance is just up ahead. We can go directly to the sand pit in the center and see the gladiators perform their morning training."

My brain scratched over that last bit of information like the vinyl record player in Bryce's bar. "Did you say gladiators?"

"Of course! They're our biggest attraction. To fill up the colosseum, we sell tickets to the fights without granting access to the rest of the resort. But our resort guests, like yourselves, have private VIP boxes that offer the absolute best views of the action."

"These are *actual* gladiators?" Torr piped up. "Like, slaves that fight to the death, gladiators?"

Nella frowned at him over her shoulder. "If you have ethical concerns, sir, I assure you that these fighters are among the worst criminals in the world. We are doing humanity a favor by allowing them to release their pent-up aggression on each other rather than innocent victims."

Torr and I exchanged a look. Yeah, she sounded *way* too sure of herself. Also, what a convenient explanation for a bunch of men to have gone missing.

The ornate mosaic tile turned to concrete as we went through the colosseum's underbelly. The open, airy space of the canyon gave way to dark corridors that soon opened up into brightness again.

The sun was high, directly over the colosseum, and I had to squint against the glare on the bright sand. Across the sand pit, roughly thirty men were either sparring with practice weapons or exercising alone. Nella said something to another staff member, the first male one that I'd seen. Actually, it looked like all of the colosseum staff were men, with holsters on their belts that carried tasers, handguns, and police batons.

The uniformed man nodded sharply, then brought his fingers to his mouth to let out a shrill whistle. Immediately, all the gladiators dropped their practice weapons and came jogging across the pit toward us. When the male staff member held out his palm, they stopped.

"Line up," he barked.

The confusion must have been clear on my face as the men arranged themselves in two parallel lines, standing shoulder to shoulder. What the fuck was this about?

Torr and I, along with Nella and the male staff member, stood on a wooden platform that was elevated slightly above the sand pit like a stage. We could see all the fighters clearly from this vantage point. They stared straight ahead but didn't meet our eyes. Well, most of them didn't. A couple of younger guys in the back snuck upward glances at me. Their shoulders and nose bridges were red with sunburn, their complexions much paler than the other gladiators. Seemed they were the new guys.

"The Mystic Canyon gladiators are the best fighters you've never heard of," Nella said proudly, looking out over the men. "People come from all over to see them, and we often sell every seat in the arena. There is nothing more thrilling to watch, I can guarantee you that. If you two are the gambling types, you can place bets on the fights in the office over there."

When she looked away from them, a tall, slender Asian man glanced up at her with a death glare. There was pure murder in his dark eyes and no question that he absolutely loathed her. Just as quickly as it happened, his features smoothed over and he blankly lowered his gaze again. He was so sneaky about it, I almost missed it and wanted to smile.

"Do any of the fighters catch your interest, ma'am?" Nella's voice grew quieter, husky. A secret smile pulled at her lips.

"Interest? Uh, well..." I scanned their faces, slightly overwhelmed by it all. These weren't professional fighters. Their beaten down gazes and tattered training gear told me that. A professional boxer came into Bryce's bar once, and everyone treated him like a celebrity. He wasn't as flashy as Blakeworth elite, but he dressed well and bought rounds of drinks for everyone who was there. It was clear he had money to go along with his fame.

These men had nothing to their name.

Nella had talked about them like they were racehorses. We even stood above them like they were animals in a pen. Everything about this was wrong. Sickening, even.

Astarte, what the fuck am I supposed to be doing here?

"I mean, they all look like very capable fighters." I forced the words out through a tight throat and a boulder in my stomach. "I'm, uh, looking forward to seeing them in action."

The guy next to the Asian man glanced up, and our eyes locked for one heart-stopping moment that felt like minutes. He looked Latino, with dark hair shaved close to his scalp. The most beautiful, thick eyelashes framed his large brown eyes. He almost would have looked doe-eyed, boyish and innocent, if it weren't for his eyebrows drawn together in a scowl and his mouth pressed into a hard line. Dark stubble coated his lower jaw, and another dusting of dark hair covered the flat, sculpted planes of his chest.

Equally sculpted shoulders and biceps flared out wide, his wrapped hands resting on his hips where he had two machetes strapped. I had been mistaken, there was nothing innocent about this man. He was positively lethal.

"I don't mean as fighters," Nella continued with that secret smile. "Some of them are also very nice to look at, yes?"

My face burned. Shit, she'd caught me checking out the machete guy. I jerked my gaze away, eyes landing on the Asian man next to him. He was beautiful in an ethereal way, like those seductive fae men in fantasy stories. His glossy, black hair was long and tied up high on his head, showing off high cheekbones and a knife-sharp jawline. His muscles stretched out long on his tall frame, willowy and graceful. To be a gladiator, he must have been just as dangerous as the machete guy, but he looked almost too beautiful to be a fighter.

"Is that why women watch the fights?" Torr asked with a playful smile. "For the eye candy?"

Nella ignored him, as she usually did, and I had a passing thought to call her out on it. She knew he was my 'husband', and it was just getting rude at this point.

"Some of our gladiators also serve another purpose," she said carefully. "One that is mutually enjoyable for both the guests and the fighter."

Torr stiffened next to me and went still, as if he'd stopped breathing.

"What's that?" I had to ask before my mind went wild with ideas, because she couldn't possibly mean...

"Should you wish to sample them for sexual pleasure, we are happy to arrange it. I can point out the ones most skilled in the bedroom, if you would like."

My mind went blank, which never happened. It was like I couldn't even process what she had said. My body, however, reacted with a chill over my skin and a horrific twisting sensation in my gut. These men weren't just forced to fight... but to fuck. What kind of fucking nightmare bizzaro world had we landed in?

"Isn't that dangerous?" I asked when my brain started up again. "I thought these were the worst criminals in the world, and you let them...*sleep* with guests?"

"Not all of them are qualified, of course. And we have strict safety protocols in place for the ones who are," Nella assured. "To be honest, it was requested over and over by our guests, and who are we to say no?"

Well, you'd be exploiting them a little less, so that's something.

"But we're married." Torr's arm was a heavy weight around my waist, pulling me closer to him. "I thought this resort was for couples. Why would you offer men for a, uh, sexual service?"

Nella looked directly at him, probably for the first time since we stepped foot in this place. "Mystic Canyon accepts couples, yes, but also single women who qualify. We are a female-centered facility. Our focus is to create a relaxing, pleasurable retreat for female guests, and we're proud to be the only one of our kind. Their male partners are welcome, of course, but they are not our primary audience. Should the woman wish to sample other options, we merely provide the opportunity to do so. Her husband is welcome to participate if he so chooses."

"So there isn't a sample of lady gladiators for the men to choose from?" Torr's question was sarcastic, but it made my gut churn even harder.

"No, there isn't." Nella looked almost offended by the question. "Women have been used, degraded, and dehumanized by men for thousands of years. There is none of that here. At Mystic Canyon, women are empowered and treated like queens, as they should be."

If they can afford it, I thought bitterly.

"How altruistic of you," Torr muttered.

"So." Nella went back to ignoring him and turned to me with a pleasant smile. "Are there any you would like to try? I'm happy to give you my personal recommendations, if you like."

Fucking hell, she acted like she was talking about dresses in a clothing store. If pretending to be Torr's wife wasn't hard enough, I also had to act like I was down with sexual slavery? It was a miracle I hadn't thrown up right into the sand below. This was abhorrent on all levels. Probably one of, if not the most, evil things human beings could do to each other.

And it started to dawn on me why Astarte called on me for this. Kidnapping people. Forcing them to fight and have sex. This evil had to be rooted out. It could not be allowed to spread. This place was already obscenely wealthy from the clients it picked, so they had to be planning for even more growth. More enslavement.

But what the fuck could *I* do? A place with this much money also had power. And what kind of people were involved? Who was at the top, pulling the strings? Who hired Nella and the armed guards? They were finding these people somewhere.

I felt like a mouse going up against a wolf. I was one person, a nobody. Sure, I had Torr with me, but two people weren't an army. Not against something *this* big. Fuck, I had never wanted to ask my parents for advice so badly.

The answer is right in front of your face. You know what to do, child. Astarte's voice came through, powerful and gently chiding as a parent's would be. The white dove flew down moments later, perching on one of the empty colosseum seats a few rows away. She cooed softly and preened her feathers.

Steeling myself with a breath, I met Nella's smile with one of my own. "We can spend time with the gladiators alone? My husband doesn't have to be there?"

Torr's head whipped in my direction, staring daggers into the side of my face.

"Yes, of course," Nella said. "For safety reasons, we can only permit you one gladiator per session. If you're interested in group sex, your husband will have to be the additional person."

"No, that's alright. One is fine." I ignored Torr's stare burning into my temple while I scanned the fighters below again. No matter what, I kept coming back to the man with the shaved head and pretty eyelashes. "What's he like?" I asked with a lift of my chin. "The one with the machetes."

Nella hummed with approval. "Ah, yes. The Butcher is a popular choice among our guests. One of our best lovers, as well as one of the most brutal fighters you will ever watch. His events are not to be missed." She pulled a slim notebook from inside the pocket of her blazer and flipped through pages. "He's booked up with several appointments this week, on top of an upcoming fight, plus his training schedule. I can set you up with him next Tuesday, but no sooner than that, I'm afraid." She looked up. "Is there anyone else you would like to try? The Tormentor has availability tonight."

"That's okay. I can wait until Tuesday," I said. "In the meantime, I think we'll settle in and enjoy what else the resort has to offer." I grabbed Torr's hand, leaning into him, but nearly yelped when he squeezed my hand in a death grip. The guy was *not* happy.

"Excellent. Your session with the Butcher will be Tuesday afternoon." Nella scribbled it down in her notebook and slipped it back into her jacket. "I'll send a reminder card to your suite."

"Thank you."

We turned away from the enslaved men in the sand below us and left the colosseum for our opulent suite in the resort.

15

TORRANCE

"**Y**ou're not actually going to fuck him, are you?" The words flew out the moment Rori and I were alone in our suite, which was bigger and grander than her family home back in Four Corners. There were multiple huge bedrooms, a gourmet kitchen, a deck with a pool and hot tub with unobstructed views of the canyon, and tons of plush couches and armchairs centered around an ornate glass fire pit.

"I don't know." The dismissive answer hit me like a slap.

Dumbfounded, I watched Rori as she breezed from room to room, checking out the massive suite. She looked everywhere but at me. But I was fucking used to that, wasn't I? She never looked at me.

"Rori, he's a *slave*." The word burned my mouth like poison. "He can't consent to having sex with you. Jesus, I can't even believe I'm saying this. This whole place is way more fucked up than I imagined." I headed straight for the extensive liquor cabinet in the kitchen, then stopped myself right before opening the glass door. Fuck, I needed a drink, but all this top-shelf booze was likely bought with slave labor. I wanted to burn this whole place down and wash myself clean of its stink.

"I know." Rori leaned against an armchair, rubbing her forehead. "I'm using the time to talk to him, find out more about this place."

"So what's with the, 'I don't know' then?"

She spread her hands, palms up, as she shrugged. "I mean, what if he gets in trouble if I *don't* fuck him? What if they see it as, like, he didn't please me or whatever and he gets punished?"

"Listen to yourself. That's your anxiety playing the what-if game again."

"But it might not be, Torr. You saw how beaten and broken down those men were. Who knows what they do to them?"

"Well, we know they fight to the death and get whored out like rentable dildos." I rubbed my mouth, spinning around in search of a bathroom. Ah, there it was, between the kitchen and bedrooms, the size of a conference room with a walk-in shower taking up one entire wall and a bathtub the size of a small swimming pool. "God, this place makes me sick," I groaned.

"Me too."

I turned back around to face Rori. "Not so sick that sampling the goods is out of the question, huh?" I knew I was being an asshole, but in that moment, I just couldn't bring myself to care.

She narrowed her eyes at me. "Torr, I'm just trying to be realistic. Of course I don't want to take advantage of a guy in that situation, but if the alternative is him getting beaten to death? Sure, I'll have sex with him to save his life."

"Fuck." I turned away again, physically unable to look at her.

"We don't know what we're actually dealing with here," she continued. "So talking to him and getting more information is our number one priority."

"Yeah, and what if they've thought of that, huh? What if

he's so beaten down and brainwashed that he reports you to fucking Nella once you start probing?"

Rory scrubbed her hand down her face, smudging her makeup. "I'm not an idiot. I won't be obvious."

"Maybe not, but who knows if we're on her radar already?"

"We've passed through all of their security measures, thanks to Gwen. If they had a whiff of suspicion, we wouldn't be here." She smiled wryly. "Listen to me. Telling *you* not to be paranoid for a change."

"This place just makes my skin crawl. Nella looks like she wants to throw *me* in the gladiator pit."

Rori gave me an appraising look from head to toe, and it was really fucking annoying how my stomach flipped in response. Even now, with a slightly better idea of the deep shit we were in, I wished she wanted me.

"I could see it," she said with an approving tone.

"See what?"

"You, fighting half naked in the sand pit. The crowd'll pay good money for that."

"Enslaved and fighting for my life every day, you mean?" I snapped. "Maybe having my dick rented out to the highest bidder too, while I'm at it?"

Her face fell. "Sorry, Torr. I'm just trying to make light of the situation a little."

"Well, I don't find it funny. But then again, this place doesn't cater to *me*, does it?"

"You're right. I'm sorry, it's awful. If it was women in that situation, I wouldn't be making jokes."

A small amount of tension bled out of me. I knew she'd be able to see the double standard. But it was the mental image of her and a gladiator alone in a room that kept my teeth grinding.

"I don't want you to see that guy," I bit out. "Cancel that appointment. Please."

Rori pinned me with a hard stare. Fuck, she was really going to fight me on this. The smudged makeup on her face now looked like a mask of war paint. And it was way hotter than the glammed-up look she'd been wearing all day.

"Do you have any better ideas for finding intel?" she asked.

"Not right now, but let's take some time to get our bearings here. You talk to the ladies at the spa. I'll talk to other guys in the gym. You know, get a lay of the land first."

Her gaze hardened. "So how many gladiators are you willing to let die because you want to be slow and careful?"

"If we're *not* slow and careful, it could be *us* getting fucked over."

Rori threw her hands up in exasperation. "I'm not seeing the guy until three days from now. We can certainly do both methods."

She was right, and it was a good plan. What better way to find out what was really going on than private one-on-one time? But fucking hell, the thought of her in close proximity, alone, with one of them, made me want to send my fist through a wall.

Not because it was potentially unsafe or that our cover could be blown. No, it was all over the simple fact that she'd be alone with another man. And she wasn't completely writing off having sex with him.

After watching her head off with other guys so many times, I couldn't begin to understand why this time made me especially ragey. Maybe because it was just the two of us without a buffer of friends to keep me distracted. Maybe because finding my own piece of tail in this place wasn't an option. Or maybe, just maybe, I had secretly hoped this trip would bring us closer in a new way.

When she'd woken up in my arms that morning and didn't immediately pull away while I pretended to sleep, I stupidly thought we might be able to head in that direction. But that was just me when it came to Aurora Wilder. Stupid.

Now, being in completely unknown territory with only each other to look out for, evidently made me even stupider.

"I just don't want you to do it," I hissed through clenched teeth. "Seriously, Ror. I got a bad feeling about it, and I don't want you to meet up with the guy."

Rori stood from the chair, staring me down. She hadn't taken her heeled shoes off yet and was almost as tall as me. Her shoulders squared like she was ready to fight.

"You don't dictate what I do here, Torr. You came to back me up, remember? That doesn't mean you boss me around. If I have a chance to talk to someone with no interruptions, no eavesdropping, I'm going to take it."

I couldn't stop the next words that came out. "And a ride on a cock, too. To protect the guy and your cover. Awesome. Great plan, Rori."

She reeled back with a surprised huff of breath. "Are you jealous, Torrance Knight?"

The large, airy suite suddenly felt cramped and cluttered. I needed space. I needed to lift heavy shit until I collapsed. And I really needed Rori to stop fucking looking at me like that.

"Pick which bedroom you want," I told her, turning away and heading for the massive bathroom. "I'm hitting the gym."

16

RORI

Torr and I didn't talk much the rest of that day or the next. The tension between us was beyond awkward. He seemed pissed off at me, and every moment of being in the same room together felt like navigating a minefield.

I picked the smallest bedroom to sleep in, and he chose the one farthest away from mine. Every time I tried to make casual conversation while in the suite together, he'd ignore me or answer with a grunt.

After spending our first night in the suite, I let him know there would be a gladiator fight that evening and that it would be smart for us to attend. He mumbled out something like, "Okay," chugged the rest of his coffee, and left for the gym.

I decided to give him space and not push him. Whether he was angry at me specifically, or the fact that this glamorous resort openly profited off of enslaved people, he needed to get it out of his system so he could focus. It was jarring, seeing Torr so frazzled. I knew he had a lot of pent-up aggression, but he usually seemed in control of it. Working out was his outlet, but now he acted dependent on it, like a drug.

While he did that, I spent too much time sitting and thinking. Because I had to keep up the guise of being from Blakeworth, I spent a good chunk of my day in the makeup chair, both for my daytime and nighttime looks.

The maid assigned to help me with makeup and clothes was a young woman named Paige. She had bright red hair pulled back in a long French braid and lots of freckles dotting over her pale skin. Her vivid green eyes were shrewd as she skillfully contoured my face and applied a new set of fake lashes and colored contacts.

For my evening look to attend the fight, I chose a dark pink eye color, bordering on purple, and Paige picked out a dress and makeup colors to coordinate. Like most of the resort staff, with the exception of Nella, she was quiet and agreeable. I wondered how much of that was the persona she put on for her job and how much was actually her.

"How long have you been doing makeup?" I asked, eyes closed under the soft brush sweeping over my skin.

Paige hesitated before she answered. "Since I was five, maybe six." The brush fell away, and I felt a fingertip gently dab at my eyelids. "The daughter of the family my parents worked for always threw away old makeup pallets in favor of buying new ones. Some of the colors were never touched, and they were so pigmented. My sisters and I would pick them out of the trash and practice on each other." Her finger pulled away and I opened my eyes to find her looking at me with a worried expression. "I'm sorry, ma'am. I didn't mean any offense, I just ramble too much. I swear the makeup was thrown away, I never stole it."

"Hey, it's okay." I held up a hand and smiled. "I believe you, and I like hearing you talk. It's why I asked the question. And besides," I lowered my hand and returned to looking vacantly straight ahead, "listening to you keeps me out of my own head."

Paige wiped her hands on a small towelette and picked up

another makeup brush. "That's kind of you, ma'am. Most of the guests prefer us not to speak unless absolutely necessary."

"Sounds boring as fuck."

She laughed softly and returned to painting my face. "You don't speak like other guests either. Both in your accent and the words you use. It's refreshing, if I may say."

"You may say anything you want," I told her. "I mean that. Don't worry about offending me or talking too much. I'm used to people speaking their minds with crass words."

A pang of homesickness hit me. I missed my loud, rough-necked family. Everyone said foul words and didn't pull any punches when expressing their opinions, but they were always genuine. The love and loyalty back home was real.

Here? Everything was too fucking fake.

Once I settled into the suite yesterday, I dug out my phone and walked laps around the place, trying to get a signal. I got nothing, and that was probably by design. The resort probably couldn't be kept a secret if guests could freely send texts and photos. I didn't know when I'd be able to make a quick call simply to let everyone know I was alive, and that just made my homesickness worse. Now with Torr giving me the cold shoulder, I felt even more alone in this place. A single word of encouragement from my mom or any of my dads would have put a little pep in my step.

At least I had Paige to talk to.

"Do you come from a big family?" I asked.

"Not really," she said. "Just me, my sister, and my two parents."

"Did your mom and dad both work for a rich family?"

Paige hesitated and I popped an eye open, watching her hand hover nervously over a selection of lipsticks. "I don't... exactly have a father," she mumbled, avoiding my gaze.

"Two mothers?" I guessed.

Her nod was hesitant, and my heart broke as she searched for judgment in my eyes. "I have two aunts who've been married over twenty years," I said. "Well, neither one is blood-related to me, but they're still my family, and I love them. Oh, and I have three uncles who are with each other plus a woman, my other aunt." I grinned at Paige's open-mouthed shock. "So yeah, my family's pretty big. And there's all kinds of fun relationship combinations. It's pretty great. Just more people to love and support you."

"I...wow. Pardon me, ma'am. I've never heard of such dynamics."

"Like I said, you don't have to censor yourself around me. I've heard it all, due to the sheer amount of people in my life. I find silence to be pretty eerie, if I'm being honest." The only kind of silence I liked was the steady roar of my motorcycle and the wind in my face. Fuck, it had barely been a day and I already missed riding something fierce.

"Can I ask where you're from, ma'am?" Paige asked.

Shit. I bit the inside of my cheek, remembering what Torr said last night. The staff could report anything suspicious to Nella. I had to be more careful and probably already spilled too much.

"Blakeworth." I silently prayed she had worked somewhere else and wasn't familiar with the elite families. "A cousin helped us with our resort application as a wedding gift, and we were thrilled to be accepted."

"Congratulations!" Paige's tone betrayed nothing as she applied a final swipe of lipstick before she capped the tube and stepped away. "You're all finished, ma'am. Is everything to your liking?"

I leaned toward the mirror, inspecting the look. She put wispy green feathers in my lashes and stuck small green gemstones at the corners of my eyes to contrast with my pinkish-purple irises. My eyeshadow was a dark, smoky purple and my lips the color of a ripe plum.

"Thank you, Paige. I love it." I turned to smile at her. "You do great work. I look like a sorceress."

She dipped her head in respectful nod. "If I may say, ma'am, thank you for the opportunity to work with you and...to talk with you. I felt inspired while creating your look, and, well, I enjoyed doing it."

A warm glow filled my chest, and I smiled so hard I was sure I'd crack the lipstick. "Thank you for the conversation. I enjoyed talking to you too. Maybe I..." I stood from the chair, smoothing my hands down my dress. "Maybe I could keep you to myself while I stay here. Would that be alright with you?"

Paige's mouth gaped open and closed a few times before she bowed her head. "I would be honored, ma'am! I...I'd love nothing more than to assist only you. I, holy shit!"

Her muttered curse made me laugh. I liked this woman, and while I would remain cautious about what I told her, I felt like I could trust her. "How should I go about that?" I asked her. "Just tell Nella that I want you assigned to only me?"

"Yes, ma'am. Her extension is by the phone on the side table in the foyer. You can just leave a message for her, and she'll see to it."

"Perfect. Say, does that phone make outside calls?"

Paige shook her head. "No, ma'am. Only within the resort for whatever services you may need."

I thought so, but it was worth a shot. "Thanks, Paige. And you can call me Rori, by the way."

She blinked. "Ma'am?"

I shook my head. "Don't know who that is."

A smile pulled at her lips, and she looked from side to side like she was about to say something utterly scandalous. "Alright, um...Rori."

"It's fun to be rebellious, isn't it?" I grinned at her and did one last check in the mirror. "Thank you again."

"It's my pleasure." She did a little curtsy. "Will you be coming back here after the event? I can prepare your room for bed."

"That would be amazing, thank you." I didn't know exactly what all that entailed, but she seemed excited to do it.

A knock on my bedroom door had us both turning around. "Come in, Torr," I called, recognizing the signature pattern of his rapping.

A few seconds passed before he appeared. Despite picking the smallest bedroom, it still had its own mini foyer, sitting area, walk-in closet, and luxurious bathroom before the actual room with the bed in it, which was also stupidly big. Torr's heavy footsteps bypassed all of that to stand before us, and damn, what a sight.

He was in his workout pants and sneakers, topless except for the towel around his neck, which he used to wipe the sweat from his forehead and neck. His skin was flushed, breaths ragged like he literally just stepped off the treadmill. After barely talking to me for a full day, I couldn't imagine why my room was his first stop after the gym and not the shower closest to his own room.

"Hey," I said, keeping my gaze firmly above his collarbones.

"Hey, Ror."

Torr dropped the end of the towel he'd been using to wipe his face. He studied me from head to toe, mouth flattening with displeasure. I tried not to take it personally. I looked fucking hot, thanks to Paige. It was the whole rich-lady facade he hated, not how *I* looked in particular. Still, it stung that he looked at me with such disapproval.

"So, there's a dress code for this gladiator fight?" he grunted out.

"For us, yes. We're guests of the resort, so we're in the VIP boxes, remember?"

"Right."

Paige stepped forward. "I can call a male staff member to assist with your clothes and makeup for the event, sir. We have several who—"

"No, that's alright." Torr turned to leave, presenting his wide, muscular back to us. "I can manage on my own."

He left the room, and Paige and I both let out sighs at his departure, albeit for different reasons.

"Sorry about him," I said. "He's a fucking grump lately."

"It's no problem, ma—um, Rori." She gave me another salacious smile. "You're very lucky, if you don't mind me saying so. He is, well, very nice to look at."

"Don't I know it," I mumbled, my own mood now souring. I'd enjoyed looking at Torr so many times over the years I'd known him, even before he packed on all the muscle. Always looking, always yearning. Never having.

It felt especially cruel now that we were posing as married, and he couldn't even pretend to like me. We had this gigantic suite to avoid each other now. For a moment, I missed the little bed we were forced to share in the tavern. I missed how easy it was to distract myself with riding, drinking, and other guys back home.

I sure as shit didn't feel lucky.

17

RORI

Torr and I walked with our arms linked to a section of VIP boxes on the colosseum's floor level.

Just outside of our box was a lounge area with a bar, a few tables, and plush seating. We put on fake smiles as we mingled and made introductions with some of the other guests, lying through our teeth about who we were. It was easy, really. Everything was a subtle power move, a sly one-up to show you were better than the person you were talking to.

Torr held me against his side with his arm around my waist, spinning all kinds of bullshit about who we were, where we came from, and how he proposed to me with the exact, rare black diamond I'd wanted. He was a natural at charming people, and I just followed his lead. I leaned into him and extended my hand to show the ring off, letting everyone *ooh* and *ahh* over the rock. I hadn't taken it off once since he'd put it on my finger back at the tavern.

I'd been sitting and staring at the thing a lot more than I'd like to admit, especially since things had gotten awkward between us. I felt like an idiot for even entertaining the idea that his vows had an ounce of truth to them. We'd only been here a matter of hours before he stormed off. So much for guarding me at every turn.

We settled into our box after roughly a half hour of mingling. The drinks and appetizers we'd ordered waited for us on a low table in front of a pair of chairs that looked more like thrones. Beyond the massive window and a short barricade, we had a perfect view of the entire fighting arena.

Torr sighed with a groan as he sank into his seat, letting his body slide toward the polished tile floor.

"It's fucking exhausting dealing with these people," he said.

"You were a natural out there," I told him. "You're really good at that."

"Acting like a rich asshole?"

"No, just schmoozing, networking. Whatever you want to call it. You just know how to work a group of people."

There was a beat of silence. "Thanks, Ror."

I reached for my champagne glass, mainly to keep my hands occupied. "Are you gonna be okay watching this?"

"I'll get through it."

He grabbed his own glass and downed it in one gulp, then pulled the bottle from the ice bucket to top himself off. Then he threw back his second glass just as quickly as the first. If by '*get through it*' he meant becoming completely obliterated by the time the fights started, he was well on his way.

Part of me wanted to comfort him, to reach for his hand or shoulder. But he was still treating me coldly in private. It was like a light switch, how he flipped on the charm and affection when in front of others, then shut me out the moment we were alone. He'd even scooted his chair away from me, keeping a good few feet of distance between us.

As tempting as it was to try breaking down this barrier between us, I wasn't going to capitulate to his mood. I was his only ally here. If he wanted to shut me out and stew in his own head about this fucked up place, so be it.

I sipped daintily at my drink and watched the colosseum seats fill through the large window of our box. The sky darkened and huge floodlights cranked on with a hum of electricity. Torr and I had to shield our eyes and blink while the lights were adjusted, pointing directly at the sandpit to illuminate it like a spotlight.

There would be two main fights tonight, according to the schedule. The second one, featuring the Butcher, was the most highly anticipated. The program didn't give any details about who his opponent was or what the fights would entail. Surprises were the best part of the fights, as some of the other guests had just explained to us.

A group of four young men walked out onto the sand from one side of the colosseum. I recognized one as the sunburned fighter from the lineup yesterday. His shoulders had already darkened and began peeling.

The crowd's low murmur shifted into loud booing. All four men huddled with their backs together, weapons and shields pointing outward. One yelled back at the crowd. Another waved his middle finger in the air. Some audience members even started throwing things down into the pit. I saw food, drink cups, crumpled paper programs, and all kinds of random items landing on or near the four men. The fighters raised their arms and shields against the thrown objects, protecting themselves as well as each other.

"They're fighting as a team?" I wondered aloud.

"Doesn't seem very gladiator-like," Torr muttered, leaning forward.

Two figures emerged from the opposite side of the sand pit, and the crowd immediately shifted to cheering. The figures raised their arms, turning in circles as they looked back at the audience. These two were clearly seasoned fighters, covered in scars, muscle, and dark tans from long hours in the sun.

"Who are they?" Torr asked, leaning toward me to see the paper program.

"The Animal and the Hatchet," I answered.

"And the four musketeers?"

I blinked at the written name. "The Maggots."

"Huh, that's harsh."

There was no announcement, no referee to signal the start of the fight. The veteran gladiators simply rushed at the group of four, weapons raised while screaming war cries.

Two of the Maggots broke off from their tight formation to dodge assault, leaving their comrades exposed. One guy immediately got a sword through his gut, the sound of metal through flesh unmistakable.

I jumped in my seat, covering my mouth. The champagne I just swallowed threatened to come right back up. The sight before me almost didn't seem real.

"Better get used to it," Torr said grimly. "That was just the first strike."

The man who got stabbed didn't appear to believe it either. He just looked down at the bleeding wound on his stomach until his opponent withdrew the sword and stabbed him again, this time through the neck.

When he fell, bleeding from two mortal wounds, the gladiator who made the first kill of the night spread his hands to the side, waving them up and down as he spun in a circle, getting the crowd riled up. They started chanting *"Ani-mal! Ani-mal! Ani-mal!"*

The Animal's partner, the Hatchet, went after one of the Maggots who had broken away from the group and was now running the perimeter of the sand pit. The running man grabbed doors and gates, trying everything that looked remotely like an exit. He jumped over a short fence and started climbing up the front of the stage where Torr and I stood yesterday.

I blinked and then there was a small ax in the center of his back.

"Oh my God!" I cried.

He was still trying to climb out, and the Hatchet only laughed, juggling two of his namesake weapons for a moment before the blades sailed through the air at the other man. The Hatchet's victim fell, and he turned to one of the armed guards with tasers and batons at their belts.

"Aren't you going to get those back for me? That last one was my favorite!" He let out a deep belly laugh, and the crowd's chanting shifted to, *"Hat-chet! Hat-chet! Hat-chet!"*

Seconds later, the three hatchets sailed over the short fence and landed harmlessly at their owner's feet. He picked them up and raised them in the air, the crowd's noise reaching a new level of frenzy at the sight of those blades covered in blood.

In the middle of the pit, the Animal and one of the two remaining Maggots were trading blows. The Animal was big and slow but seemed to be biding his time, while the other man moved in quickly and took aggressive shots. The other guy's emotion was clear on his face, his jaw clenched and the rage potent in his eyes. Whether his anger was directed at his oppo-nent for killing his friend or at the two who broke away and ran off like cowards, it was hard to say. Probably both.

The newcomer was a skilled fighter but struggling on the shifting, sandy ground. I held my breath when he missed a forward jab with his sword, exposing his side to the Animal. The other gladiator didn't hesitate and brought a meaty fist encased in brass knuckles to the man's side. The crowd started chanting for the Animal again as the Maggot rolled and scram-bled to get away.

"Come on, throw some fucking sand in his eyes!" I hissed.

Torr let out a mirthless laugh. "Rooting for the underdog, huh?"

"I guess so." I chewed one of my nails and fully expected all ten fingers to be bitten down to stubs by the end of the night. "Those guys don't belong in here. That one that ran was scared shitless."

Finally, the man scrambling on the ground tossed a handful of sand up at the Animal, buying himself a few precious moments to roll to his feet. The two of them had neared our box, and I got my first clear look at their faces.

He's kind of cute. The thought was more sorrowful than admiring. If he survived tonight, I wouldn't be surprised if he were added to the sexual services menu.

The Animal swung a spiked club, narrowly missing the other man's head. The Maggot dodged low and drove his sword into the Animal's gut. Smartly, he pulled away, withdrawing his weapon in the blink of an eye. The Animal was enraged, roaring wordlessly as he pursued the other man. His stomach was badly bleeding, but the injury didn't seem to slow him down.

Their fight had gone down mere feet in front of our VIP box, blocking our view of the rest of the pit. When the Animal and the underdog moved their fight along, it seemed we'd missed some other action.

The Hatchet was now kneeling in the center of the pit, with one of his own axes held against his throat by the other Maggot. As the other two fighters came closer, the man holding the Hatchet hostage said something to the Animal. It looked like a threat, a *do-something-or-he-dies* kind of command.

The Animal just threw his head back and laughed. "We're all destined to die, you fucking worm! Kill him! Cut his throat with his own weapon! He won't hesitate to do the same to you."

That moment of distraction was enough for the Animal's opponent to finish the job. He thrust his sword through the back of the veteran gladiator's neck before he could say anything else. The Animal made a gurgling sound as blood poured from his neck, running down his chest to mix with the blood from the wound in his gut.

You could hear a pin drop in the colosseum as the Animal fell to his knees and then face-planted dead on the ground. Only after he fell did an uproar carry throughout the audience. They were an angry, yelling mass shouting and gesturing at the fighters below.

"Bet some folks just lost a lot of money," Torr said.

The Hatchet tried taking advantage of the upset by the Animal's death. He grabbed his captor's forearm, trying to wrestle the ax back into his own possession, but the other man caught on. The Maggot wrenched his arm free and this time did not hesitate.

He buried the ax blade under the Hatchet's chin, and pulled it across, releasing a river of blood. He must have gone deep, because the Hatchet died much quicker than the Animal.

The two men who had appeared to be on the same team now stared at each other across the sand.

"What happens now?" I asked. "Did they win?"

A new energy took over the crowd, starting as a low murmur but quickly taking over the whole colosseum. I even saw other resort guests in their VIP boxes standing up and pumping their fists. Within moments, a new chant emerged.

My blood ran cold as the horrific realization seeped in.

"There's no 'they'," Torr confirmed with a bitter shake of his head. "At the end of a fight, there can only be one man standing."

"Kill him! Kill him! Kill him!"

18

SANTOS

I could only give a sad shake of my head from the sidelines. The baby gladiators, Maggots, as they'd been called, looked horrified at the realization of what they had to do. They'd stuck together since being shipped to this hellhole. Now one would have to kill the other.

If they refused, more fighters would be released onto the sands. One man standing was the only rule.

"I tried to warn 'em," the Ghost, Devin, said with a regretful tone. "After training yesterday morning, I pulled Animal's killer aside and told him not to look too cozy with his boys."

"They never listen," I muttered. "They have to learn the hard way, like we all do."

It still wasn't easy to see. Part of, if not all, of your humanity was lost the moment you killed someone you once considered a friend. Even an acquaintance. Some of the kills that got to me the worst were the guys I had sparred with or just talked football with for a sense of normalcy. That was the main reason Devin and I acted like strangers in front of everyone's eyes. We likely wouldn't be able to bear standing across the sand from each other like these two were.

Both of the Maggots just looked at each other, not moving, until the crowd got bored and started throwing shit again.

"Glad I'm not going out there today." Devin started flipping one of the many hidden knives he kept on him. "At least the Animal's dead. Sick fucker."

I grunted out an agreement, though the bastard's death wasn't all good news. He'd been a favored fighter for the gamblers and had been something of a cult leader among the gladiators. Not that he had any leadership skills to speak of, he was just big, mean, and a fucking ruthless killer. People didn't want their skulls bashed in when he was in a foul mood, so they kissed his ass. His death created a power vacuum among his minions, and they'd be squabbling to take his place.

The seasoned gamblers would also be taking a huge loss. Even against four Maggots and the Hatchet, the odds had been highly skewed in the Animal's favor. Now that precarious balance had been upset by a scrawny dude with a sunburn.

The dude could fight though, and he had my respect for that. But it was his first time on the sands, and he'd have to prove himself time and time again.

"Ooh, they're arguing." Devin sounded like he was watching a TV drama.

I crossed my arms, scratching the stubble on my jaw as I watched. The two guys were circling closer to each other, both of them red-faced with anger as they shouted. The Animal's killer was repeating something like, "You ran! We were supposed to hold tight, but you ran and got them killed!" The sword was in a loose hold at his side, but his opponent clung tighter to the axes in each of his hands as he shouted arguments back.

The whole colosseum seemed to wait with bated breath, not daring to look away and miss who would strike first. In the end, it was the Hatchet's killer who raised his weapons against his friend.

The Animal's killer brought his sword up to block the attack. Metal sang as axes and sword clashed. Then there was a crunch and an "Oof!" as the Animal's killer drove his elbow into his friend's nose.

"Quit trying to be a good guy," I muttered. "There's no way for both of you to leave the pit alive. You want to be merciful, end it quickly for him."

With blood pouring down his face and a look of malice that wasn't there before, the ax wielder recovered and swung again. He was wild and uncoordinated now, sloppy. The swordsman dodged his friend's attacks easily, the hurt and anger in his eyes morphing into a grim determination. He waited until the axes finished another wide, lateral swing, then drove his sword through the other man's ribs.

The swordsman had clearly aimed for the heart in a valiant attempt to make his friend's death quick and painless. But he was off by several inches, and the man at the business end of his weapon would remain very much alive for a few minutes.

All the gladiators watched with grim silence as the two men crumpled to the sand together. One dying and being cradled in his killer's arms, the other with his head bent low and probably whispering all manners of regrets and apologies. We'd all seen it before. This was the consequence of getting attached to anyone.

The swordsman pulled his weapon free and, with a shaking hand, stabbed his friend again to end his suffering. My respect for him went up even higher as I watched the ax wielder finally go limp. Most wanted to hold on, to prolong their final moments with loved ones for as long as possible. He gave his friend one final kindness and sent him to a quick death.

A rough pat on my shoulder came from the Ghost. "You're up next, Butcher boy. Carve us up some steaks."

"Yeah." I shrugged his hand off and rolled my shoulders, then my neck.

While waiting for pitmasters to carry off the body and escort the last fighter from the sands, I pulled my machetes from their sheaths and rotated my wrists around to warm them up. Tezca rubbed the length of his body against my legs, circling me tightly. He usually came out to fight with me, mostly because no one wanted to deal with trying to corral the jaguar who'd killed a dozen of us. Every pitmaster that attempted to got a nasty bite or a scratch. One even got a bad infection in his hand and had to stop working.

The jaguar got free rein of the colosseum, a privilege even most of the employees didn't have.

Outside under the floodlights, the crowd had quieted down to a murmur. They were probably still reeling over the shock of the Animal's death. By the next fight though, they'll have moved on and picked a new favorite. We were expendable like that, going up and down in value like my grandfather's baseball cards.

Once the fighters were gone and the bloody sand had been quickly raked over, the gates in front of me swung open, and the audience exploded with new life.

The noise was deafening, even down where I was. I raised one machete in the air, turning around so everyone got a chance to see my face. Maybe I smiled, I didn't know. Putting on the act of a crowd-pleasing entertainer had worn thin for me. I was on autopilot for this shit. My singular focus was getting through this fight to live another day.

For what, I didn't know exactly. Tezca said change was coming, and I had to believe him. The talking jaguar god had been at my side for months. Despite more of the same since his arrival, I had to believe him. If I didn't, what else did I have to live for?

As I hit the center of the sand pit, I lowered my eyes from the stadium seats to the VIP boxes on the ground level. These were the resort guests who dropped a year's salary at my old job to get the best views.

The VIP boxes were protected by a half-wall barrier, armed pitmasters, and tempered glass windows. Gladiators weren't allowed guns, but it wouldn't surprise me if that glass was also bulletproof.

My eyes stopped on a woman behind the glass. Short, blonde hair in soft waves hit the edge of her jaw, showing off a graceful neck and slender shoulders. It was the same woman from the elevator, the one who had a personal appointment with me in a couple of days.

She sat a few feet away from her male companion, who I still wasn't convinced was her husband. They weren't talking or looking at each other, just staring blankly out at the sand. That honestly wasn't unusual with many of the resort guests. Many of the couples seemed to only tolerate each other, at best.

The woman's eyes caught mine, and our stares locked for a single, electrifying moment. She moved first, raising her glass a few inches as she mouthed, *Good luck.*

I jerked my chin down in a quick nod before turning to face the gates my opponents would come out of. By now, she must have heard other guests talking about me, or more specifically, my skills that had nothing to do with fighting. If she were anything like the others, she probably hoped I'd live through this fight just so our session wouldn't be canceled. These elite types all thought they were gods, after all. Everything on earth existed to serve them.

But damn. I'd be lying if I said I didn't want to miss that appointment either. Just like when I first saw her come down the elevator, I got a different feel than the other guests. Some buried part of me dared to wonder if our time together would be different too, if even fun.

God knew I was fucking tired of the same old shit. Both on the sands and in bed with the guests.

The far gate lifted slowly, and I gave another quick swing of my wrists to make my machetes dance. I never knew ahead of time what would come out of that dungeon. No one did, except the pitmasters scheduling the fight.

My heart sank at the sound of low growls and then a series of barks. I fucking hated killing animals in here. At least gladiators understood what they were getting into. These were likely stray dogs that had been rounded up, starving and aggressive out of pure necessity.

The pack shot out in a streamlined formation, running until they formed a circle around me and Tezca. These pups were hungry alright—their ribs on display and bodies scarred from previous fights.

Tezca and I faced opposite ends of the circle. I knew his back was arched and heard his feline warning growl over the dogs. He'd take care of a few while I carved up the rest.

What a fucking waste.

The first dog lunged for my leg, and I swung low. As the two halves of its body separated and the top half went rolling across the sand, another dog jumped, its teeth aiming for my neck. I swung the machete in my opposite hand, sending the dog's head flying like a soccer ball across a field.

It was a brutal dance of carnage, one that I hated with every fiber of my being. But the crowd loved it, and it was partly because of their passion that I continued to live. They stood from their seats, chanting, *"But-cher! But-cher! But-cher!"*

When I was finished, dogs lay slaughtered in pieces all around me and *on* me. I would have done anything for a private moment to throw up and take a shower, but I had more fighting to do.

I had barely caught my breath when the gate opened again, and a huge beast of a man came running straight for me. He wore a helmet that looked like something those medieval knights wore and spiked armor from his wrists to his shoulder. To complete the medieval getup, his weapons were two spiked maces. The man was pale, filthy, and I didn't have to speak to him to know he was half-crazed.

If I could see his face, I might have recognized him. Or maybe not, since he clearly hadn't been part of the regular gladiator population for a long time.

Sometimes, if we needed disciplinary action, we weren't thrown out in the middle of the pit right away. No, depending on the pitmasters' mood, gladiators would be tossed into a windowless dungeon with no light or human interaction for months. On top of the isolation, they would be creatively tortured. I'd heard stories of electrocution, sleep deprivation, forced injections of drugs, and all manners of things that weren't necessarily painful but fucked up a person's mind beyond saving.

It made me think of Hudson, Devin and my friend who'd been left behind when we were shipped off to this place. He'd been separated from us weeks before to fulfill an esteemed, special purpose, as they had said. We never saw him again but had heard his anguished screams every day until they loaded Ghost and I onto the truck that brought us here.

The crazed knight stumbled out toward me, swinging his maces blindly. I couldn't imagine he had a good field of vision in that helmet. He missed me by a mile, and the momentum sent him careening into the sand.

Uproarious laughter came from the crowd, making my skin

prickle with discomfort. This man had undergone torture that they couldn't even fathom, and they were laughing at him.

This type of fight was familiar to me, sadly enough. I was supposed to let the man bumble around like a court jester. He was little more than a rodeo clown, just some grim comic relief before I sliced him down.

He fell down more often than he was able to stand, run, and take swings at me. I couldn't bring myself to laugh with the audience, not even to pretend. While dodging his wild swings, I tried meeting his eyes through the slit in his helmet. Did he recognize me? Would I ever recognize who he was?

He never said a word though, only mumbling and grunting as he came at me again and again.

At some point, he went sprawling onto the sand by tripping over his own feet. The crowd's laughter was more subdued this time, which meant they were getting bored. Time to end this soon.

The man wasn't getting up though, and the crowd started shouting and jeering at him to get up and fight.

"Come on, man," I muttered under my breath. "Let me give you the respect of killing you standing up, alright?"

My gaze lifted, and I found myself looking at the blonde woman in the VIP box. Neither she nor her companion were laughing. She leaned forward, her shoulders tense. Her fingers were clasped so hard in front of her, the knuckles were white. Her eyes were glued to the armored man on the ground, eyebrows knitted together and her mouth a thin line.

Some motion caught my eye, and I lifted my gaze higher to see a white dove fly down to perch on the slanted roof of her private box.

In the sand at my feet, Tezca cautiously stalked over to the man on the ground and sniffed around his head. The jaguar then pressed his forehead against the man's helmet, leaning in to run his cheek and neck against the man, nuzzling him as he so often did with me.

"Kill him! Bite his throat!" someone yelled from the crowd.

The taunts and shouts faded as I felt a sense of calm coming over me. A reassurance and settling I so rarely felt in this place. The only other time I had was the day I met my jaguar. The man's body, which had been tense and twitchy since the moment he ran out, had calmed into stillness.

After a few moments, Tezca walked away, and the man pushed himself up to standing. He turned slowly to face me, his mannerisms completely different from the wild, uncoordinated lashing out from before. The eyes behind the slit in the helmet met mine, focused and lucid for the first time.

"Are you ready?" I asked, my voice tight.

He nodded once and I brought up my machetes, crossing them in front of my chest as I stepped forward.

"I'm sorry." I wasn't sure what I was apologizing for, but it felt like something that needed to be said.

"Me too, kid," he answered.

I slashed my blades down in two perfect arcs. A red X formed across the man's torso. I made sure to hit the arteries in his neck too. Blood pumped out in steady bursts from the cuts, and after a few seconds, he fell once again.

This time, with dignity.

RORI

I couldn't take my eyes off of him.

The Butcher was swift and brutal as he fought, but there was a beauty to his movements, almost like a dancer. He moved with precision and confidence but nothing overly flashy. Aside from the entrance he'd made, he acted as though the audience wasn't even there.

And when the pale man came out, dressed like a laughing-stock of a knight and falling down everywhere, the Butcher made no attempt to humiliate him further. He ignored the crowd's taunts to kick the other man while he was down, to shove a machete up his ass, and every other cruel, vile thing they yelled out. No, the Butcher waited until the man could stand up, and they even appeared to exchange a few words before he cut the man down.

I'd been so entranced with watching him, I didn't even notice Torr's eyes burning a hole in the side of my head until the staff dragged the knight's body off the sand.

"What?" I demanded.

"Enjoying the preview of what's to come later?" Torr asked, his voice heavy with derision.

"Being cut up with machetes is actually *not* one of my kinks," I shot back. "And like I said before, my plan is to talk to him, not fuck him."

"But you haven't ruled it out." Torr pulled the champagne bottle from the ice bucket and drank directly from it. I held my hand out, but he didn't offer me any. "And you've been eye-fucking him since he walked out there."

I dropped my arm, letting it flop against the side of my chair. "What is your fucking problem?"

"I could ask you the same thing."

"Torr, we're supposed to be working together." I put my hands in my lap and turned to face him. "When you're not ignoring me, you're picking fights with me. I know this shit is difficult to see. I know it's hard to pretend to be like the other guests. But we have the same goal, right?"

"I don't know." He took another swig from the bottle. "You tell me. What is that goal, Rori?"

I put my elbow on my knee, bringing my hand up to cover my mouth. The VIP box seemed private, but I still wanted to be careful. "We have to shut this place down. I don't think it's just the gladiators they exploit. I was talking to my maid earlier and...she didn't outright say she was enslaved, but I could read between the lines."

"Fuck." Torr rubbed his eyes and took another pull of champagne. "And how are the two of us supposed to do that?"

"You see the Butcher's jaguar?" I nodded toward the sand pit, where the fighter and his animal companion paced in the center. Shit, was there even more fighting to come?

"Yeah, so?"

"What if it's a god like Astarte? Did you see how it protected his back? When it rubbed against the other man and then he stood up?" Torr remained silent, his brow furrowed as his mind put the pieces together. "That's why I need to talk to him. I'll bet you he's the one we needed to meet. Maybe he can...I dunno, get the gladiators to revolt. Tell us what we need to know."

Torr's eyes shifted toward me. "You didn't see the jaguar around when they lined up during training."

I stared at him, confused. "Okay, so? Astarte isn't exactly glued to me at all times, either."

"I'm pointing out the fact that you were up for fucking—I'm sorry—*talking* to him before ever knowing he had a jaguar."

"Torr!" I barked so loudly, my voice echoed off the glass window. "Why the fuck is that such a stick up your ass? It's a perfect opportunity to find more intel, and you're acting like it's some big fucking betrayal."

"You know why."

He continued hogging the champagne bottle, so I snatched it out of his grip because I sure as hell wasn't going to have this argument sober.

"Is it *really* because he's a gladiator and can't consent? Or is it something else? What do you want me to do, pinky-swear that I won't fuck him? Why is it such a big fucking deal to you?"

Torr stood abruptly from his chair, towering over me for one intense second that felt like minutes. His shoulders and jaw were so rigid from held-back energy, I thought for a moment he might hit me.

Or throw me against a wall and fuck me, if he was that bent out of shape about me *potentially* fucking someone else.

The familiar fantasy hit my frontal lobe, playing out like it had so many times before. Torr lifting me by the waist so I could wrap my legs around his hips. Kissing me like he needed my air to breathe. Walking forward until my back hit a wall and pinning there while we fumbled with passion and desperation to get clothing out of the way of our goal.

I'm right here, I thought, meeting his heated gaze. *I'm right fucking here. You don't want me alone with another man? Prove it. Show me the real reason why.*

Torr broke his gaze away, his shoulders cutting stiffly through the air as he crossed the space to the door in a few strides. "I'm gonna finish drinking out there." He angled his head toward the guest lounge on the other side of the door. "Probably won't head back to the suite until later. Gonna need some space."

He didn't slam the door behind him, but he might as well have from the way I flinched at the sound.

Alone in the VIP box, I turned slowly to face the sand pit again. The Butcher was in the middle of another battle, another free-for-all with other gladiators like the first fight had been.

"Fuck Torr," I said to the small, empty room I now had to myself. "Fuck me."

I settled back into my chair and grabbed the half-empty champagne bottle. Bringing it to my lips, I leaned back, kicked off my shoes, and placed my feet on the table in front of me. My skirt slid up my legs, exposing me from my feet to just about my knees.

I drank my fill, both of the expensive booze and the beautiful display of strength and grace from the Butcher. Torr thought I was eye-fucking him before? That was nothing compared to this.

I watched the sweat roll down his neck to disappear under his thin shirt. The shape and tension of the muscles in his arms and shoulders as he swung the machetes at his opponents. I watched his tongue dart out to lick his lips and the intense focus in his dark eyes. His eyelashes were so thick and full, beads of sweat clung to them like tears. When his shoulders and chest rose and fell with great gulps of breath, I wished I could see that motion on a repeating loop.

When all motion stopped, I realized it was over.

Roughly a dozen gladiators had been released to the pit for this final fight, and now only the Butcher stood, with his jaguar at his side.

He stood in the center of a massacre, all manner of blood and gore surrounding him. He was exhausted but appeared uninjured. Everyone in the audience was on their feet, chanting his name, pumping fists, and clapping.

The Butcher didn't acknowledge them, though. He looked straight at me.

I watched his gaze start at my ankle, then travel up the length of my bare calf. When our eyes met, I raised my champagne bottle in his direction and shot him a smile.

"Well done," I said, even though he couldn't hear me.

He gave a small nod in return, the corner of his mouth ticking up for one mere second. It was barely a smile, but it sent my chest pounding all the same.

* * *

I RETURNED to the suite alone, not bothering to check in with Torr when I left the VIP box. He'd been sitting at the lounge bar, engrossed in conversation with the beautiful bartender. She'd laughed uproariously at something he'd said, tossed her dark, braided hair over her shoulder, then leaned across the bar to stick her cleavage in his face and whisper something in his ear.

Whatever. If he hooked up with her, he'd be an even bigger asshole for trying to dictate what *I* did. And a hypocrite at that.

I glanced over my shoulder after passing him and wished I hadn't. It still hurt that he didn't pull away from her but smiled all lazily and flirtatiously instead. It still hurt that his gaze flicked down to all the business happening in her bra.

I hated that we'd been thrown into this crazy mission full of secrecy and corruption and things were still exactly as they'd been back home. Torr flirting with, and almost definitely fucking, the prettiest woman in the room. Me shoving down my feelings and trying in vain to distract myself with other men. Same old fucking bullshit.

His weird possessiveness was new, though. For a minute, I thought it might be due to him wanting me after all. What else was I supposed to think when he got all squirrelly and ran off to the gym when I'd semi-jokingly asked if he was jealous?

But it was crystal clear to me now. He'd rather flirt with a boobilicious bartender than be near me. For fuck's sake, why did he even want to come with me if he couldn't stand to be around me? We barely looked like a honeymooning couple and had spent most of our time apart since we'd arrived.

My thoughts stewed, roiling around my head like a stormy sea as I walked back to the suite. Once there, I headed straight for the bar next to the kitchen. It would probably cost Gwen's employer extra to keep this place fully stocked, but I couldn't bring myself to care. That champagne bottle had barely touched my tolerance, and I was intent on getting obliterated. I grabbed a whiskey bottle and headed for my bedroom.

Paige, the sweetheart, had made my bed, folded down my sheets, and laid out a soft, neatly folded robe on the bed. She placed a note on the garment, handwritten in a pretty, feminine script: *Rori, dial *6 for maid service and ask for me if you need a bath, food, or anything else for your evening. I'm happy to be of service! -Paige*

"Too damn sweet," I muttered, setting aside the note and robe so I could flop onto the bed without ruining them. It would be nice if I could smuggle Paige out and take her with me whenever we left this place. She and her family would be happy and free in Four Corners.

I swallowed a big pull of whiskey, sinking down into the

mattress as the liquor made a warm path down my throat to my belly. I could almost pretend it was someone's hand, or a mouth, moving down my body like that.

A frustrated sigh left my chest. We had a whole month to spend here and were off to shit-tastic start. I knew in my gut I was right about the Butcher's jaguar. That gladiator was the one I needed to talk to, and on some instinctivel level, I knew it before I ever saw the black cat prowling at his side. But even if the Butcher and I got a plan together, how much could I really do if I didn't have Torr to back me up?

How far would he really go in *not* supporting me?

Round and round went my mind with questions. The only reason I wasn't speaking them aloud was because I didn't have anyone to listen. If Torr were here, he would tell me it was just my anxiety.

I took another pull of whiskey with an annoyed groan. Closing my eyes as I swallowed, I imagined the Butcher's fingers trailing from my jaw, down my throat, between my breasts, and settling on my belly.

Only...I imagined his touch continuing further down, a hunger in his dark eyes as he watched me with rapt attention. With my own hand, I followed the path I imagined him taking, sliding a palm down my thigh to bring the dress up higher, until it bunched around my hips.

I was just on the edge of tipsy, pleasantly warm and languid with just the slightest buzz in my brain. But it was enough to quiet my racing thoughts and replace my fantasies about Torr with those of someone completely new.

I couldn't believe how easily I pushed Torr from my mind and slotted the Butcher seamlessly into the same place. Whenever I had tried to fantasize about other men before, it never worked. Thinking of them just didn't stimulate my body and brain the way Torr always had. But for some reason, my brain chemicals decided that the Butcher was just what I needed.

In my mind, his hand gripped my thigh, kneading it before traveling to the space between my legs. Maybe he'd cut my underwear off with a machete, that'd be hot.

Imagining it was his hand doing the work, I rubbed myself. My head went back, eyes firmly shut to stay in the fantasy. Instead of my own two fingers sliding across the thin material of my panties, they were his. Hands much bigger than mine, with callused fingertips for added friction, stroked my lips with a firm pressure that continued up to my clit.

My skin, my breathing, and heartbeat, everything reacted to his touch. I arched on the bed, splaying my legs wider as I sighed under my—no, *his*—ministrations. If I peeked, I'd definitely see dark, hungry eyes framed by thick lashes drinking me in. Those eyes would drop, traveling the length of my body before zeroing in to watch where his hand played with me.

What did the Butcher's voice sound like? Was he a dirty talker? Would he tell me how I looked to him stretched out on the bed like this? Would he describe all the ways he wanted to fuck me in filthy, clear details? Or would he just watch silently during the foreplay, observing me closely for what I liked and responded to the most?

His mouth would definitely be occupied if I had anything to do with it. He had nice lips, and I wondered if he allowed kissing when he met with guests.

He's enslaved. He can't set boundaries or say no to anything.

That was Torr's voice in my head, and it was as sobering as a bucket of ice water to the face. My eyes snapped open, and I pulled my hand away from between my legs, panting hard. A flash of anger hit me, and I reached for the whiskey bottle on the nightstand, pulling another long, burning swig.

Chances were high that I wouldn't actually fuck the Butcher, despite Torr's utter lack of faith in me. But he sure as hell was not going to come barging into my brain and ruining a harmless fantasy, especially after being such an ass tonight.

Determined, I brought my legs together and slid my panties off, then slingshotted them to a dark corner of the room. After settling back and spreading my legs again, I closed my eyes and allowed the Butcher to explore me bare this time.

I was wet, my flesh swollen and sensitive. The Butcher traced my lips with his fingers before pushing them inside my mouth. I sucked and licked at the digits, imagining his groan as he thought of me sucking him in other places. Those wet fingers skimmed down my body, leaving trails of heat before they teasingly circled my clit hood.

A whimper escaped my mouth as I arched higher for more, then those fingers trailed down and stroked inside me. My teeth sank into my lower lip, hips lifting off the bed to match the thrust of the Butcher's hand. I imagined his breath ghosting over my skin, maybe even kissing my hip and lower belly as that mouth moved closer to where his fingers played.

It wasn't the same as a tongue but flattening my palm over my clit was close enough to let my imagination take over. The Butcher licked over the sensitive nub while his fingers curled and spread inside me, demanding a response from my nerve endings with every stroke.

I had no restraint, no self-control, and no desire to draw this out with teasing. Once the orgasm started building, I headed straight there, accelerating like I just hit the gas on a straight stretch of road.

The release locked up my muscles, sent my hips spiking up to grind against the Butcher's face. I could feel him riding out my pleasure, keeping steady on all the right spots to carry me through the peak and descent.

When I finally fell back to the mattress, limp, panting, and sweating, I didn't dare open my eyes. Reality could wait because I wasn't ready to face it yet.

I'd much rather stay in the fantasy of someone, the Butcher, crawling up the bed to lie next to me and hold me in my sleep.

20

SANTOS

My appointments with guests were the only times I was allowed a long shower, complete with hot, running water. So I made it count.

I shaved my face and manscaped, lathering myself up every-where. Then, when I dried off, I made sure I kept smelling decent with a few spritzes of cologne. Less was more, as I'd learned from experience.

I dressed in loose, linen pants and a matching shirt. My feet were bare, and my trusted machetes were back in my room in the bowels of the colosseum. I always felt the most naked without my weapons, but they wouldn't serve me here. No matter how much I occasionally wanted to murder the guests.

I gave myself a final once-over in the bathroom mirror, then nodded at the pitmaster to let him know I was ready. It was always the male staff keeping watch over those of us who met privately with guests, just as a precaution.

My guard's face was blank as he patted me down for hidden weapons, his expression never changing as he unlocked the door and held it open for me. I went through the short corridor and stopped before the door at the other end. He unlocked that one for me while I waited, then held it open as I crossed the threshold.

The guard didn't enter the lavish room with me. He would stay on the other side to give us privacy, keeping the door unlocked just in case I, or the guest, hit a panic button during our time together. Then he'd be able to rush in at a moment's notice.

In my four years of being at Mystic Canyon, I'd only heard of a panic button being used once. A gladiator had taken a guest hostage in hopes of negotiating for his freedom. The staff had been able to diffuse the situation and the guest was unharmed, but that guy was immediately thrown into the next fight—a brutal five-on-one. Devin was the one who put him out of his misery with a knife thrown to his frontal lobe.

After that, they almost stopped whoring us out, but Nella wouldn't have it. She claimed the demand for fucking gladiators was still high among the guests, despite the risks. So the service remained, just with extra security measures. Apparently, the guests also had to sign a liability waiver too, saying they knew and assumed the risks for spending time alone with dangerous criminals.

As I'd come to find out, it was because of those risks that we were in such high demand, not in spite of them. Some people rode motorcycles, lit things on fire, or took drugs for a thrill. And some liked to fuck unhinged killers.

My current guest, who had been sitting on a loveseat, stood abruptly as I walked in. My heart did a little extra kicking motion in my chest. I'd been antsy for days about this session, the pretty blonde who'd requested me personally and watched my last fight from her VIP box. There was no tangible reason for this private spark of excitement behind my sternum rather than the resigned dread I usually felt. And yet it was there all the same.

With a few exceptions, I was not attracted to most of the guests and loathed the type of the sex the majority of them wanted from me. It was usually a grin-and-bear-it type of thing, but maybe this time, I could actually enjoy it a little.

"Good afternoon," I said with my politest tone and smile. "No need to stand for me. Make yourself comfortable."

"Hello," she returned in a soft, husky voice. "Thank you for, um, seeing me."

Her smile was nervous, and she clasped her hands in front of her like she didn't know what to do with them. Ah, a newcomer then. Every once in a while I got one of those. The first order of business was making her comfortable.

"It's my pleasure. Would you like something to drink?" I made my way to the minibar while she settled back on the loveseat and smoothed out invisible wrinkles in her dress.

She seemed to perk up at the prospect of a drink. "Do you have whiskey?"

I paused, hands frozen in midair for a second. We had every spirit and fermented alcohol the guests could desire, but whiskey was an unusual choice for a woman. It threw me a little, but I recovered quickly and grabbed two short tumblers.

"Will a pre-Collapse single-malt do?" I asked, showing her the bottle.

Her eyes, an unnaturally bright turquoise from the colored contacts she wore, widened. "I don't think I've ever drank anything pre-Collapse before."

I kept the surprise off my face. The Blakeworth elite loved their relics from before the Collapse. They hoarded aged wine and spirits from that time like it was gold. "It's extremely diffi-cult to find these days, but we have more whiskeys if this one isn't to your liking."

I poured a small taste into one of the glasses, but the woman waved her hand at me to continue. "I'll take a full pour, I'm sure it's excellent."

I obeyed silently, pouring myself slightly less alcohol than her. If she was nervous, she'd want the edge taken off. And I couldn't allow myself to drink much and risk running into performance issues. Curiosity or not, I was here to get a job done.

Instead of swiping the drink out of my hand like I was a waiter, the guest held my gaze and kept her drink level with mine. "Cheers," she said softly, toasting me as she had during the fight.

It was getting harder and harder to keep the surprise out of my expression. Already, this woman was treating me closer to an equal than a body hired to do a service.

"Cheers," I returned, touching my glass to hers.

She held my gaze as we took our first sip, but I broke eye contact to sit on the loveseat next to her. We were close, but still far enough for me to not crowd her if she was nervous.

"Are you enjoying your stay here?" I set my drink on the side table and turned to give her my full attention. The guests loved talking about themselves like they were on a date with someone who actually gave a shit, actually wanted to fuck them. I knew how to fake it well enough, but with this woman, I was genuinely curious to hear what would come out of her mouth.

"Yes. I am, thank you."

Bad liar, I thought, my curiosity piqued to a new level. The words were stilted, forced out after a moment of hesitation and a tight smile. She took another drink, and I wondered how many whiskeys she'd need before those pretty lips started spilling truths.

"What has been your favorite part of the resort so far?" I leaned back against the arm of the loveseat, putting on an air of being open and relaxed.

Her eyes sharpened, and I wondered what their natural color was. "Watching you fight."

I smiled wider. It wasn't an especially unique answer, but she was telling the truth. And when she said it, I wanted to gloat and beat my chest. "Thank you, that's very kind."

"You're very precise with those machetes, and your technique is incredible. I know they call you the Butcher, but the way you fight is so much more than a messy hack-and-slash job." She took another sip of her drink. "Did you fight before becoming a gladiator?"

"Um..." I rubbed my chin, stalling with an awkward laugh to cover up my surprise. Blakeworth elites didn't know shit about fighting, aside from its entertainment value. They loved the blood I spilled and how brutally I cut up my opponents, not my technique. Who the fuck was this woman? "I was a mercenary in a past life," I admitted, figuring the truth was the easiest.

"Really?" Her head tilted, a golden, wavy strand falling across her forehead. "Who hires mercenaries these days?"

"Crime syndicates, usually the ones wanting to take over territories. But I haven't been in that game for about six years, so who knows if any of them are in business anymore."

"You ever work for any motorcycle clubs?"

"Nah. Bikers tend to run pretty tight ships. They're big on loyalty among members and don't usually hire outside help." I picked up my drink again, if only to keep my hands occupied. "You ask a lot of interesting questions."

It probably wasn't the smartest thing to say. We were supposed to be agreeable with the guests, to stroke their fragile egos and make them feel even more important than they already believed they were. It was frowned upon to give direct statements that may put them on the spot or make them uncomfortable. If someone got offended and complained to staff, I'd have one hell of a beating to look forward to.

But this woman was unlike anyone who had requested my services before. And to my relief, she didn't seem offended.

"I'm just curious, I guess." She smiled again, taking another sip of whiskey like she drank it all the time. She never even coughed or made a face at the taste. "I haven't left home much, so it all sounds very adventurous."

"Where are you from?" I scooted closer to her, sensing that she was becoming more comfortable, and felt pleased that she didn't pull away.

Her lips pursed, and she made a soft exhalation like she was about to say an F sound, but then she quickly changed her mind. "F—Blakeworth."

I didn't hide my smile or my skeptical look as I allowed myself another small sip from my drink. "You have secrets. I understand and respect that." I stood firmly in forbidden conversation territory now but was enjoying myself too much to care about the consequences. This wasn't the usual tired, rehearsed small talk before getting down to business. This was a real conversation, something I experienced so rarely.

"Just know that anything you tell me is confidential," I said. "The privacy of our guests is of utmost importance." Okay, that was a rehearsed line, but with her, I actually wanted to know. Of all the drunken and drugged-out confessions I'd heard before, the basic details of this woman's life were the ones that I wanted to collect and hoard. What was her name and the real color of her eyes? Where was she really from? Was that man actually her husband?

"Really?" Her eyebrows went up in surprise. "You're not mandated to report anything to the staff?"

Another interesting question that I filed away. "Intimate details about our guests, no."

"But other things?" I paused to consider my answer. "If it

would endanger other guests or interfere with how the resort is run, yes, I am supposed to report things of that nature."

Her wry smile returned. "But do you?"

"Why?" I grinned back at her. "Do you have nefarious plans for this place?"

"If I did, would I risk telling you?"

I swallowed the remainder of my drink, put it down, and moved in much closer, until my thigh pressed against hers, and I could take her delicate chin in my hand.

"That might depend on how well I do today, won't it?" Flirting and banter were great, but she'd come to me for a purpose, and we only had an hour. Now that her nerves were gone, it was time for me to do my job.

The woman's pupils dilated, and her lips parted on a soft gasp. Damn, I might even enjoy kissing her. That usually wasn't on the table for these kinds of sessions, but if she was on board, I sure as hell was.

I leaned into her, allowing my eyelids to fall closed, only to find fingers pressed to my lips at the last moment. My eyes popped open, and I saw her eyebrows knitted together in some conflicted emotion as she leaned away.

Panic fired through me like a gun going off. Oh shit, I read this completely wrong. Where did I fuck up? If she was stopping me, she was definitely going to complain to the staff. Fuck! I was usually good at this shit.

I slid back until a good two feet of space separated us on the love seat and cast my eyes downward. "I'm sorry." My mind raced, grasping at things to say to hopefully avoid the beating from the pitmasters that would surely come out of this. "I'm very sorry. I...completely misinterpreted and did not intend to make you uncomfortable. I can have them send in another gladiator, if you wish."

"No, don't apologize." The woman reached across the

distance to place her hand on my forearm. "You did nothing wrong. *I'm* sorry."

I could only stare at her, even more thoroughly confused. Guests were never wrong. They never had anything to apologize for, no matter what they wanted. If something wasn't to their satisfaction, it was *our* fault. Always.

"I'm sorry," she said again. "I'm...new to this and probably still not ready to...you know, sleep with you."

I swallowed. "Would you like someone else instead?"

"No! I meant in general. I don't think I can sleep with anyone being, you know, offered here. It just doesn't feel right."

"Oh. Okay." My throat remained a tight knot, but my heart rate started to calm. It had been so long since I'd been around anyone who had ethical issues with prostitution. I had forgotten there were people like that at all. "So you're not going to tell anyone I didn't...satisfy you?"

Her expression turned horrified. "No, of course not! In fact, I'll tell them the opposite."

"You really will?"

"Yes! You did nothing wrong. I would never throw you under the bus."

A sigh of relief left my chest. "Thank you."

She shook her head, looking around the ornate room furnished and decorated for the sole purpose of satisfying guests. "It's terrible that you even have to thank me for that."

"That's just how it is." I couldn't stop looking at her, couldn't stop wondering how this woman ended up among the elite clientèle of this place. She seemed almost...normal. And yet lovely and fascinating. If I wasn't so relieved about not getting reported, I'd be bummed about not sleeping with her. She seemed like a girl I would pursue if I was, well, not enslaved.

"Well, I like talking to you." She tilted her head again in that way that made her hair shimmer. "Would it be so bad if we spent the rest of our time doing that?"

"Not at all." A weight felt lifted off my chest now that I didn't have the pressure of satisfying her sexual needs or her ego. I propped my arm on the back of the loveseat. "And the feeling is mutual."

Her smile was warm and sultry. "Do you say that to all the girls?"

"Yes, but with you, it's the truth." Damn, she made it so easy to flirt and just pretend to be two people getting to know each other.

She played with some loose fabric on the couch, reserved but no longer nervous. "My name's Aurora. I go by Rori."

"Aurora." I rolled the R's in her name, enjoying the vibration of it in my mouth. "That's beautiful."

"You're a show-off with that tongue, huh?"

I laughed. "If I really wanted to show it off, we wouldn't be having a conversation right now."

"Hm, maybe next time," she mused.

My eyebrows lifted. "Are you saying you'd want to see me again after this?"

"I mean, we got off to such a great start." She chuckled.

"We sure did. I'll never forget it, Aurora."

Her next smile seemed a bit sad, and I felt it too. She'd be here for a few weeks, at most, and then leave. Maybe we'd have sex, maybe we wouldn't. But sitting and talking as two people, just because we could, was such a rarity for me. I wasn't bullshitting to flatter her. I'd remember this for however much longer I lived.

"What's your name?" she asked.

"I'm the Butcher." My response was automatic. Real names were forbidden, especially to the guests. Our names humanized us, gave us an identity outside of our roles. But fuck, I *wanted* to tell her.

"You know what I mean." Aurora's look was playful but stern. "I gave you mine."

I sighed, disappointed that I could no longer live in the fantasy of being on a date with her. Reality had to whisper in my ear and remind me of the consequences. "I'm really not supposed to tell you that."

Her face fell, the realization dawning on her. "Oh, I'm sorry."

"It's not your fault."

"It's pretty unfair, huh?" She leaned closer to me. "What you go through here."

I thought of the last beating I got. It was a few months ago, shortly after Tezca had arrived. The guest wasn't satisfied because I didn't choke her hard enough.

I thought of the Tank, a ruthless fighter and a decent enough guy, for a gladiator. He was made bait at last month's animal-mauling fight because he developed feelings for a guest, to the point of being convinced she would free him and they would run away together. The guy ran his mouth too much and died in an excruciatingly painful way—ripped to shreds by a pack of starving dogs. And the guest he fell in love with? She added me and a few others to her rotation to replace him.

Unfair? That was the fucking understatement of the year.

"You could say that," I answered through the tightness in my chest.

Reality kept me alive, so I had to stay firmly anchored to it. No matter how much good conversation, laughter, or flirtations I shared with Aurora, she didn't feel a thing for me. She wasn't here to save me.

Aurora looked like she was about to say something, then

jumped in her seat, pulling her feet up to the cushions. "Oh my God, is that...?"

My head snapped around to where she was looking, where Tezcatlipoca sat like a cat-shaped shadow with yellow eyes. Fuck! My blood pressure spiked for the second time that day. He was absolutely *not* allowed anywhere near the guests.

"Tezca!" I hissed. "What the fuck are you doing here? Go!"

He ignored me, naturally, and walked forward. The black jaguar went around the coffee table and approached Aurora. I thought I was going to have a stroke when he placed his fucking chin on her knee and looked up at her with wide *please-pet-me* eyes.

"Well, hello." Her voice was calm, even amused as she reached a tentative hand out toward his head. She glanced at me, fingers pausing in midair as she asked, "May I?"

Not that she needed my permission to touch a god, but I nodded. "If you promise not to tell anyone about this either."

"I promise. My lips are sealed." Her palm came down on the big cat's head, and his eyes closed, lifting his head to press against her hand. "Oh, you are just beautiful," she cooed, scratching his ears. "Aren't you? Such a handsome boy, yes. Oh!"

Aurora yelped with surprise when Tezca jumped on the loveseat, effectively shoving me out of the way while he lie across her lap. She laughed as he flipped over to his back, silently demanded more scratches under his chin and on his belly. "You remind me of a cat I had growing up."

Her nails raked gently over his neck and ribcage, fingers smoothing out to rub in circles over his belly. Tezca opened one eye to stare at me, taunting me as if to say, *she could be running her hands all over you, but too bad.*

"Is he usually like this?" Aurora massaged Tezca's front paw pads, gently pressing on the muscle that exposed his claws, the sharp curve as long as my pinky fingers.

"He's never like this," I admitted. "Not even with me."

"I guess he likes me." Tezca flipped over so his chest and chin rested on her legs, and she stroked down his long back to his tail. "Well, I feel the same way, Tezca. You are just absolutely gorgeous."

The tip of Tezca's tail tapped against my thigh. *Yeah, I'm jealous, you jerk. Is that what you wanted to hear?* I thought.

He answered, not with words but with a feeling pushed into my mind. It took me a moment to recognize it as trust. It was the same way I felt around him and Devin, and it made me pull in a surprised breath. He was telling me we could trust Aurora, if even challenging me to try.

Well, if this wasn't a day full of surprises.

Aurora glanced up at my sharp inhale, her hand pausing on Tezca's back. "You okay?"

I nodded, swallowed, then took another breath. "My name is Santos."

21

───────

TORRANCE

"**I**'ll take another, Andie."

The bartender paused, narrowing her eyes at my empty drink. "You're getting started awfully early today. You sure you don't want to slow down?"

I shot her a stony look right back, not having any of her fake concern. "You can give me a water to chug too, if that'll make you feel better."

She shrugged and took my empty glass, then placed a cup of water in front of me. I nursed it while she poured me a fresh whiskey and was grateful when she disappeared to the other end of the bar.

Andie and I had gotten to know each other pretty well over the last few days. When I wasn't working out to the point of collapse in the gym, I spent nearly every waking moment at this bar.

Rori and I had barely seen each other, let alone spoken to each other, since the gladiator fight. She had been right to confront me in that VIP box. I was being a total ass and knew it would only get worse the closer she got to her private appointment with that fighter.

186

I avoided her because she deserved better than seeing me go apeshit. I didn't trust myself around her, and even if she had sworn up and down she wouldn't fuck the guy, it probably wouldn't have reassured me at all.

Instead of manning up and being honest, I, of course, went to drink and chase tail. Because that was how I dealt with not having the woman I wanted. That was how I dealt with getting passed over for someone else. Again.

I had every intention of hooking up with Andie after the gladiator fight. She had even invited me to a vacant guest suite, which she had access to because her friend was a maid. But no matter how sloshed I was, no matter how badly it hurt to watch Rori eye-fuck that gladiator, I couldn't bring myself to say yes.

So I made a lame excuse about having drank too much, and said I'd be back the next night. I got back to Rori and my suite late. Her bedroom door was closed, and the whole place was dark. When I got up the next morning, she was already gone.

I worked out, showered, ate. Checked out the gentleman's club and golf course in the resort, got bored, then came to the bar. Andie invited me back again. And again, I couldn't say yes.

She gave up trying after that, and I couldn't blame her. I almost suggested it myself the day Rori went to see the gladiator, but I had *really* obliterated myself, to the point of passing out at the bar. I woke up to a maid gently shaking me and informing me meekly that she needed to clean.

I went to my suite and crashed for a few hours. At some point, I was awake enough to hear Rori's bedroom door open and close, then the soft voices of her and her maid.

So it was done then. Great.

Part of me wanted to storm over there, rip the door off its hinges, and demand to know what happened. Part of me wanted to know everything she'd done in explicit detail. Was he actually good in bed? How many times did he make her come and in what ways?

The other part of me wanted to throw the covers over my head and pretend none of this was real, and that was the side that won out.

That day had come and gone, and it still wasn't sitting with me any easier. Not knowing what happened was the worst part, but the thought of swallowing my pride and asking Rori made me want to drink myself into oblivion again.

I had to just...figure out how to be okay with the possibility that she'd done him.

Might as well tell a fish to learn how to breathe air.

On top of all that, we were supposedly meant to be doing something important here, important enough to get gods involved. Rori may have found things out from the Butcher, or, considering she hadn't yet told me anything, maybe not.

Sure, I wasn't exactly making myself available to her, but there were only so many places I could go here. If she needed me, she was smart enough to find me.

"You're a fucking bastard, Torr," I mumbled into my drink before swallowing it down.

It was easy to ignore the shouts and the scuffling sounds. This bar was just outside the underbelly of the colosseum, and gladiators were training in the sand pit. But when someone shouted, "You lost me five thousand TCs, you piece of shit!", that got my attention.

The bar staff, on the other hand, put their heads down and became particularly engrossed in their work. Andie turned her back to the corridor heading to the pit and began slicing lemons to add to her already-full stash in the refrigerator.

I heard more yelling, thuds that sounded like kicks and punches, and began sliding from my barstool. "The hell is going on?"

Andie's head snapped around. "Don't get involved."

I heard an electric crackling sound, like a taser or cattle prod, then a yelp of pain.

My feet carried me toward the dark corridor, not wanting to believe what I was hearing but too horrified to stop. "Are they beating up a gladiator in there?"

"Sir, please!" A maid jumped in front of me, then lowered her eyes meekly. "You are an esteemed guest here, please do not bother yourself with the staff's disciplinary actions—"

"Excuse me." I went around her in a wide circle, fearing I'd be too rough if I'd touched her, because I was already seeing red.

It wasn't her or Andie's voice I heard anymore, yelling at me to stop and not get involved. It was teachers at school and other sixteen-year-olds like me, trying to pull me back from a defenseless kid getting ganged up on by bullies.

This situation wasn't any different. I'd gotten too many black eyes, broken noses, and bruised ribs of my own to let that kind of humiliation happen to someone else, no matter who they were. From the moment Shadow put a dumbbell in my hand and told me to pick it up and put it down over and over again, I knew I'd use the strength I'd gained for those who couldn't defend themselves.

The lighting was dim in the colosseum's underbelly, so I followed the sounds to a dark corner. Sure enough, four of the male colosseum staff stood in a circle, surrounding someone crumpled on the floor. One had his taser out in his hand.

"Can't believe this little bitch killed the Animal," one of them sneered, then spit on the man on the ground. "You call yourself a fucking gladiator?"

Another one kicked the guy who, to his credit, didn't scream or beg. Come to think of it, he hadn't said a peep except for when he got tased.

All four shitbags were so preoccupied with the guy on the

ground, they didn't even notice me walk up to them. Most bullies were like that, as I'd found out over the years. Pea-brained and single-minded.

I snatched the one asshole's taser first. He barely had a moment to look up in surprise before my fist crashed into his jaw. He whirled away like a spinning top, and only then did his friends get the memo.

The next guy that came for me got his buddy's taser right to his fucking gut. I kicked his knee so it bent in the wrong direction with a satisfying crunch. His scream gave me wicked tinnitus, but I still had two of the gang to deal with.

They tried to arrange themselves in front and behind me, typical dumbass bully behavior that I'd seen a thousand times. I backed up to a wall and lifted my hands, feigning surrender. As I expected, the dumbfucks thought they had me cornered and lowered their fists.

"You're a guest?" one of them said, gawking at my clothes. "Why are you getting involved? This doesn't concern—"

My left hand snapped out with the taser while my right fist connected with the other guy's nose. Both guys went down, one convulsing from electricity, the other groaning as blood spurted from his face.

None of the four dickbags were mortally injured, though they were in a world of pain. I stood in front of the gladiator they'd been beating up, blocking their path to him while they watched me with wary, confused eyes.

"What the fuck is wrong with you?" asked the first guy I'd hit, rubbing his swollen jaw.

"Could ask you fuckers the same thing." I dropped the taser and shook out my fists, resuming a fighting stance. "You want more? I got all fucking night."

"You're gonna get kicked out of the resort," hissed the one whose knee I fucked up, listing heavily to one side. Okay that might be semi-permanent damage, but I wasn't sorry. "And you'll be blacklisted from ever coming here again," he went on.

"Aw, damn. Can't wait to go up to my room and cry about it."

"You really have no idea what you've done." The four of them started edging toward the doorway, keeping their eyes on me like I'd pummel them again if they turned their backs.

"You're gonna regret this," another one of them echoed.

"Oh no, I'm fucking shaking."

They weren't amused by my deadpanning and slunk out the door like the slimy pieces of shit they were. Only after I no longer heard their footsteps scurrying away did I turn to see how their victim was faring.

"Hey. You alright?" I held my hand out to the guy, but he ignored it.

Rather than accept my help, he scooted back to use the wall as a support. One hand pressed to his ribs while he slowly stood to full height, his face grimacing, although he still didn't make any sounds of pain.

"They were right, you know," he growled at me in a low voice. "You made a big fucking mistake jumping on them."

"Well, you're fucking welcome, I guess. Didn't know you liked having your ribcage used as a soccer ball, but I'll remember that next time." I turned to leave, not offended or entirely surprised by his reaction. The sad thing was, some victims of bullies didn't always believe they deserved help.

"Hey," he called when I'd almost made it to the exit.

I stopped and looked back at him. "Yeah?"

"Why'd you get involved, anyway?"

"Because what they did is fucked up. And to be honest, I was in the mood for spilling some blood."

He let out a derisive snort. "Welcome to my world."

He was tough, this guy. And not just physically strong. I

could only imagine the headfuck of not only being thrown into a fighting pit and beaten up by guards, but being forced to kill a friend. And here he was, standing tall and rolling his shoulders like it was all water down his back.

"Yeah, I guess." I paused, then turned all the way around to face him. Come to think of it, it had been a while since I'd talked to another guy, just man to man. Shit, if Daren was here, he'd be right at my side, taking those assholes down. My best buddy would probably be piggybacking this guy to the hospital, he was such a saint. Unlike me. "I don't know how you can stand it," I blurted out.

"Stand what?"

"All of it. Everything you have to do out there." I jerked my head toward the sand pit. "Being whored out to female guests. Dealing with those pricks ganging up on you when you can't even fight back."

The gladiator shrugged one shoulder with a scoff. "When the alternative is bleeding to death for the mass' entertainment, what else can you do?"

"Yeah, you're right. Sorry. I can't even imagine what that's like."

He cautiously dropped one hand from his ribs and tried to take a deeper breath, wincing a little. "Sometimes that's just the hand you're dealt."

I still wasn't ready to head back to the bar, to face Andie and whoever else saw those assholes run with their tails between their legs. The consequences would come, and I'd shoulder them like a man. But not quite yet. I especially wasn't ready to tell Rori that I'd fucked everything up.

"You got a name?" I asked the gladiator.

He shook his head. "We don't do real names. That shit's burned and buried." He straightened a little taller anyway.

"Since I defeated the Animal, they've been calling me the Hunter."

"Right on. It's fitting, with the way you fight. Really strategic. Congratulations, by the way. On surviving that, I guess."

"Thanks." He gave a lopsided smile, one that showed he was enjoying this bro-talk as much as I was. "That was my first fight here. I was shitting bricks, you know? I *knew* I was gonna die, I was so fucking scared."

"I don't blame you. Where'd you come from?"

The smile instantly disappeared from his face. "Somewhere really fuckin' bad. Honestly, I don't know if this place is any worse. At least I can make a name for myself here."

My eyes narrowed. "Seriously? What's worse than here?"

The Hunter met my stare, squaring his shoulders. "What's it to you? If you're trying to take me on as your new charity project, I'm not interested."

"What? No, it's not that." I looked down, realizing that he was still seeing me as a resort guest and from the perspective of miles stretching between our social classes.

Well, fuck that.

"Look, can I trust you to keep your mouth shut?" I asked. "At least for a little bit?"

He cocked his head but humored me. "Sure. We gladiators aren't exactly all buddy-buddy with each other. And I'm obviously not getting along with the staff."

"Right, makes sense. Well, my name's Torrance. You can call me Torr. And this shit?" I pinched at the fabric of my shirt, looking around as I lowered my voice. "It's all bullshit. I'm not one of these people."

The Hunter's expression didn't change, though I saw his gaze sharpen. He was observing me for any twitchy, lying behavior. "How are you here then?"

"I'm still not sure exactly. Connections, I guess. But we're undercover, sort of. Trying to sniff out this place, and yeah, it's fucking rotten."

"We?" he repeated. "You mean, you and your wife?"

I wish.

"She's not actually my wife, but yeah, the two of us are just regular folks from Four Corners."

"Shit," he breathed, eyes widening. "So, what, you're here to like...free us?" He whispered the word so cautiously, like he didn't dare believe it.

"That's just the beginning. We want to find out who's on top, funding all of this. This whole fucking business model is just sick, and we want to root it out for good."

The Hunter's jaw hardened. "Get us out. Burn this place until it's nothing but a scar in the ground. Do what you came here for, and I'll tell you about where I came from. I have a feeling I know who's at least supplying fighters to this place."

"That'll help us a ton," I said. "We want to stop it. This whole place has made my skin crawl since I set foot in here. It's just...fucking inhumane."

He continued to observe me coolly. "I haven't been a gladiator long, but I'm pretty sure this is a big, complex machine that I've been a cog in for years. You won't be the first to try putting an end to it. But I sure as fuck hope you're the last."

RORI

"No jaguar hanging out with us today?"

The Butcher chuckled, sending me a warm smile over his shoulder as he poured drinks for us at the minibar. "No, I think he'll leave us alone today."

"Aw, too bad." I propped my elbow on the back of the couch. "He's the whole reason I was excited to see you again so soon," I joked.

By some fluke in the schedule, I'd been able to see the Butcher, er, Santos, again only two days after our first appointment. I was a lot less nervous this time, less conflicted about my feelings for Torr, who seemed hellbent on avoiding me for the past several days.

That was fine. I could at least spend time with someone who pretended to be interested in me.

Although Santos didn't give me a lot of fake vibes. He, too, seemed warm and relaxed today. A nice change after he'd been so worried about being reported the first time we met. After his jaguar had showed up, we'd small-talked about mundane things until our time was up. There had been a little tension and awkwardness hanging between us then, but I didn't feel any of it now. The nerves in my belly were solidly about spending time with a guy I was attracted to, and if things went in a physical direction, I just might let it happen.

"I can do my best jaguar impression if you want," Santos said, coming around the couch with our drinks. "Crawl around on all fours, lick myself in unseemly places, stretch across your lap in hopes of head scratches."

"Hmm, tempting. Your head does look very scratchable." I accepted the whiskey from him. "Thank you."

"If you ever need a scratching post, it's there for you." He settled on the couch next to me.

A laugh burst out of me. "Wait, am *I* pretending to be a jaguar now?"

"Hey, fair's fair." His smile and warm, dark gaze made me bashful to the point that I had to take a drink just to have a break from the intensity of his eye contact. "So, what have you been up to since we last hung out?"

Oh, nothing. Just being completely shut-out by the guy I'm in love with and thinking of you while I masturbate so I'm not focused on him.

"Not much," I said, keeping my tone casual. "Going to the spa, breakfast at the cafe, dinner and drinks. The usual. You?"

The pause before he spoke stretched on long, giving me the sense he didn't believe me, but he humored me enough not to address it. "The life of a gladiator is much more boring than that," he said with a smirk. "It's just eating, training, sleeping. Watching your back and preparing for your next fight."

He didn't mention his private time with other guests, which I was morbidly curious about. Nella hinted that he was popular, so how often was he in this room with other people, having sex with them? Did he have regulars that kept coming back?

I wanted to know everything, but couldn't bring myself to ask. I asked Torr about his sex life all the time, at first thinking it would help me get over him. But my feelings never went away and hearing about what he did with others only hurt me more. Santos felt like the beginning of a crush, and I knew the end result would only be the same. Hurt and rejection that I'd only brought upon myself.

"How often do you fight?" I asked instead.

"It's different for everyone, but since I'm a headliner that draws crowds, I'm out there once a month. Guys that are lesser-known, they're tossed out there once a week sometimes."

"Wow, doesn't seem like a lot of recovery time."

"It's not, which is actually by design to weed out the weaker fighters. If you keep proving yourself, keep winning, you earn longer recovery times and little perks here and there."

"A jaguar bodyguard seems like a hell of a perk," I mused.

Santos laughed softly. "Yeah, they don't exactly hand out kittens for us to bond with."

"How *did* you end up with Tezca, if you don't mind me asking?"

He paused again for a while, this time seeming as if he was wrestling with how much to tell me. "Tezca was released into the pit during a fight, a pretty routine thing. But he just...kept killing everyone."

My eyebrows shot up. "Holy shit."

"He couldn't be captured, couldn't be beaten. Gladiators were dropping like flies. And then they sent me out."

I cocked my head, waiting for him to continue. "Well, I'm glad to see you're still here."

"Yeah, me too." Santos laughed dryly. "I went out there, and he...spoke to me."

Dark eyes flicked up to mine, gauging my reaction. "Did he tell you his name?" I asked.

Santos blinked. "Yes. How did you know?"

"If you've noticed a white dove hanging around me, it's the same situation. Her name is Astarte. She chose me."

"Yes!" Santos shifted on the couch, sitting straight up as he faced me. "Tezca chose me. He said that...something was in motion and that he would be my protection."

"Astarte led me out here," I said, relieved to get it off my chest. "So it's probably no coincidence we've met."

Now Santos cocked his head, a grin pulling at his delicious mouth. "So you're not really from Blakeworth, are you?"

"No, Four Corners," I said. "And the guy I'm here with, he knows everything."

"Is he really your husband?"

"No."

Santos nodded as if that confirmed what he'd already guessed. "Boyfriend?"

"Definitely not."

He grimaced. "He's not your brother, is he?"

"No!" I laughed.

"So, it's...platonic?"

I hesitated before answering and knew he took note of the silence. Those eyes missed nothing. "We've been friends a long time. But, on my end at least, my feelings are... complicated."

It felt good to be honest. I'd never breathed a word of my feelings for Torr to anyone. But I felt like I could trust Santos and that he wouldn't be judgmental about the situation.

Santos nodded again, nothing changing in his expression. "And on his end?"

I shrugged and took a long sip of my drink. "You'd have to ask him."

The handsome gladiator made a dismissive noise, leaning back as he spread his powerful body across the loveseat. "He's a fool if he's not crazy about you."

My stomach flipped. "That's sweet of you to say."

"I'm not blowing smoke up your ass. I mean it."

I couldn't help the smile as I looked away from him bashfully. "You don't even know me."

"I know enough."

I shook my head, but my smile only grew wider from the attention he poured on me. "Callate," I told him with a soft laugh.

His eyebrows lifted, and a pleased grin spread over his face. "A white girl that speaks Spanish? I'm half in love with you already."

Heat burned my face like I'd just stuck my head in an oven. No man that I wasn't related to had ever told me they loved me, even as a joke.

"My mom's Latina," I told him, awkwardly ignoring that last thing he said. "So's one of my dads. I grew up speaking both languages."

Santos' eyebrows went higher. "*One* of your dads?"

"Yeah. I have four." I covered my eyes with a soft laugh, only somewhat pretending to be embarrassed. People had all kinds of reactions to my family's dynamic, and while I usually didn't care, I found myself anxiously wondering what Santos thought.

"Like, all at the same time? I don't mean any disrespect, I'm just curious."

"Yeah. They've all been together almost thirty years. Well, none of my dads are together-together. They're just with my mom."

"They don't get jealous?"

"Not that I've seen. They're all best friends with each other." I straightened my spine, feeling a little defensive of my family. "It's worked out great for us. Me and my siblings are all so close, and we're supported and loved by all our parents. I wouldn't change my family for anything."

"That sounds amazing." I was relieved that Santos' tone sounded genuine. "I'm a little envious, honestly. I had it pretty rough growing up."

"I'm sorry to hear that. We don't have to talk about family if it's a sore spot."

He shrugged, his expression and body completely at ease. With his arms draped over the couch like that, he really did look like a jaguar—all powerful, dark muscle forming sweeping, graceful lines that I couldn't stop looking at. A predator at rest.

"There's just not much to tell. I was an orphan. Been a little street punk for as long as I could remember. I was a small kid, so getting by was tough when I had to fight for food and shelter. I was a crafty little shit though. I learned how to get by and just took it day by day." Santos rubbed his chin, his eyes lighting up with amusement. "Kinda like how it is now."

"You're a survivor," I said. "That's how you got through it all. The fights, everything."

"Yeah. It surprises me sometimes that I'm still here when I've known a lot of people, either smarter or stronger than me, that didn't make it."

"You need some of both, I think. Sounds like you have a good balance of smarts and muscle." His story reminded me of Torr's, and the thought of the two of them trading war stories, maybe even becoming friends, was oddly pleasing to my brain.

"I dunno, maybe." Santos drank me in with those warm, beautiful eyes again. The look he passed over me made me want to burrow into his chest to find out if that big, powerful body of his was as huggable as he looked. "I think luck plays into it too."

"Luck or gods, you think?"

"That's the question, isn't it?" His smile was slow and just as warm as the gaze he fixed on me. "Maybe that's what luck is, an extra little nudge from the gods."

"You think they're up there, content to just watch us most of the time?" I went to take a sip from my glass but found it empty. "But when they feel like it, they'll give us a little poke in one direction or another?"

"I mean, if they can inhabit animals and speak directly to our minds, what's off the table?" Santos ran a palm over his buzzed hair, and I remembered his offer to lie in my lap for head scratches. "But what I want to know is," his hand fell to his lap, "why did the gods bring together a beautiful girl from a good family and a street punk turned gladiator?"

There he went, making my face hot again and probably as red as a tomato. I didn't know how to respond to compliments and flattery. The guys I had dated back home were punks too, wannabe bikers usually, but none of them had talked to me like this. So my only natural reaction was to ignore and deflect.

"Do you want more to drink?" I got up from the couch abruptly, circling around the back of it on my way to the minibar.

Santos was up in a flash, prowling around the other side of the couch to cut me off. My breath stuttered as he towered over me, not as tall as Torr but enough for my head to tilt back. Still a good kissing height though. *Now where did that thought come from?*

Not to mention he was also a broad, muscular wall, his hands and feet widened out slightly as if anticipating my going around him.

"What are you doing?" The question almost sounded playful, his eyes alert and a wry smile pulling at his lips. A jaguar ready to pounce.

"Getting another drink?" I hated that my answer came out like question. Why the fuck did my spine turn all noodley when it came to him? "I'll get you one too." I held my palm out, thankfully sounding much more sure of myself.

"No." The single word rumbled from a low place in his

throat, a growl. "You don't do that. I'll get us drinks." He held his palm out, mimicking my gesture. "Give me your glass."

Part of me wanted to cave, to melt under the firm weight of his words, but another side was dying to see how far I could push this.

"I'm perfectly capable of pouring drinks for us," I said, standing my ground.

"It's not that you're incapable." His voice went lower, and I found myself leaning closer to hear him. "It's just not your role here. I serve you. Not the other way around."

"You do more than enough for others already," I shot back. "Let me do this one small thing for you, please."

Santos took a sharp inhale, looking away for a moment. He licked his lips and...fuck, I swore I even saw him biting his lower one. Could he possibly be enjoying this as much as me? Why was this back-and-forth arguing such a turn-on? My core was pulsing, and every inch of my skin was alight and eager for his touch.

"What if I told you..." He paused, drawing out the moment. Teasing me like this really was foreplay. "That I genuinely enjoy serving you? Not because that is my duty at this resort, but because it pleases me, as a man, to do something for *you*, Aurora."

It took all my focus to not let my eyelids flutter half-closed when he said my name like that, all seductive with his rolling Rs.

"Then you are welcome to serve me when you're no longer a gladiator," I said. "But when you're in a position where you can't say no...I can't let you do that. It feels wrong."

That slow feline smile returned, and God damn it all, it almost made me whimper with need. It became achingly clear in that moment how long ago I'd been touched by a man. Months, coming up on a year almost. I desperately wanted

Santos to touch me, but only if this fucking enslavement situation wasn't a factor. Fuck, it was hard to remember that annoying little detail right then.

"That's a tall promise, to even speculate about a future in which I'm not a gladiator." His gaze flicked once to my lips. "That kind of hope sends men to early graves. I've seen it happen many times."

"I'm not trying to make promises I can't keep." My skin became prickly, uncomfortable. "I just...don't want to exploit you."

A long pause stretched on after that, and I couldn't shake the fear that it widened the distance between us, like the mouth of a canyon.

"You're not exploiting me, Rori." He went for the glass in my hand, but I swung it out of his reach.

Our eyes met again, and the playfulness there drained all the tension from the room. The two of us stood frozen like statues for a second, then I jumped into action. "You'll have to catch me if you want this!" I yelled, running away.

Santos' laugh was gorgeous, deep and musical. I felt it in my ear moments later, because he caught me easily with an arm around my waist, lifting me off the floor. His hold on me was loose though, probably in an effort to not hurt me. I was able to wriggle free to his frustrated cursing and started another lap around the furniture.

I made it to the back of the couch, and he faced me off from the front. We must have looked ridiculous, feet wide, giggling as we stared at each other, feinting to the left and right to throw each other off.

After a stand-off for nearly a minute, the victory went to the gladiator. Santos made a convincing dive to the right, then bounced back the other way before I could change my direction.

"Damnit!" I laughed when he caught me by the waist again,

lifting me up like I was a dainty little thing that was closer to five feet tall than six.

"And now my prize." Santos held me pinned against him with one arm, holding his palm out expectantly with the other.

I hesitated a long time before placing the glass in his waiting hand. Both because I was a sore loser who hated admitting defeat, and because of the fact that I enjoyed the firm heat of his chest against my back. Maybe too much.

Likewise, Santos seemed hesitant to let me go. His arm unwrapped slowly from around my waist, fingers trailing along much like how I imagined they would when I touched myself.

"All that just to pour a girl a drink, huh?" I said, panting slightly.

"Not just a girl," he corrected, unscrewing the whiskey bottle. He poured two fingers in the glass and then held it out to me. "For you. The dove to my jaguar."

"There you go, being sweet again." I accepted the drink. "Thank you."

"It's my pleasure." He turned to me, all smoldering and sexy. "And I truly mean that."

"Santos..."

There was so much I wanted to say, much of which didn't seem appropriate, considering this was only our second time meeting. I wanted to promise him that he wouldn't die a gladiator, that I would do everything in my power to give him and the others normal lives again. Not just the fighters, but those like my maid, Paige. Talk about giving a dangerous amount of hope. What could I do? I only had Torr to help, and barely, at that.

If only I were my father, Reaper. With a single command, he had not only an entire motorcycle club, but an army behind him. Back in his day, I figure he had the firepower to torch this whole resort until there was nothing left but rubble and ash.

"Yes, Rori?" Santos answered his own name with my own,

an eagerness to his voice that was delicious and tempting. But our time was limited, and he needed to be a free man yesterday.

"Can you tell me what Tezcatlipoca has told you?" I asked. "About what's coming? What steps you should take?"

His chin lifted with surprise. "Back to serious business, huh?"

"Yeah." I returned to the couch and sat down. "We need to figure out what the gods want us to do. How we're supposed to..." I paused for a breath, feeling the weight of my words before I spoke them. "Free everyone and shut this whole fucking place down."

Santos sat down so heavily next to me, he practically fell. "Damn, so you're serious-serious."

"I really am." I grabbed one of his hands, wrapping my fingers around the warm, callused skin of his palm. "I have no idea what I'm doing, but yeah, I *want* you to have a future where you're not a gladiator. I want that for you really fucking badly."

Santos blinked several times but said nothing. Then I felt his rough hand squeeze around mine just as his gaze fell to my lips.

A harsh banging sound tore through the moment, making me startle.

"Time's up, your session is over," the guard called through the door. "We'll give you three minutes to get dressed."

23

TORRANCE

"Hey, we need to talk."

I finally found Rori at the cafe the next morning, seated next to the aviary with a cup of coffee, an everything bagel with all the seeds and seasoning scraped off, and her nose in a paperback novel.

She lifted her eyes, an icy blue color today, slowly over the top of her book, then licked her fingertip before she turned the page and dropped her eyes back down. "Do we?"

"Yeah, Ror. We do." I looked around. She was relatively secluded over here by the giant cage filled with exotic birds, but there were still guests and staff milling about the cafe. I'd much rather talk to her in the privacy of our suite. "Like, right now. It's important."

"Huh. That's interesting, considering we haven't talked at all in the last four, oh no, five days." She picked up her coffee, eyes never lifting once from her book. "Surely it can wait until I finish this chapter."

Shit. I should have known that would have come back to bite me in the ass. "Look, I'm sorry. I've been a dick and a hardass about the whole gladiator thing."

I'd been more than that. I'd been a fucking mess. In the moments where I'd seen her briefly, from a distance or passing by each other in the suite, she'd looked...radiant. And not just from the clothes and makeup. She was glowing like she was on top of the world, with confidence in her steps and a secret smile.

I knew it was because of that gladiator, and that fucking killed me. I couldn't even pretend I was upset about the whole sexual slavery thing anymore. She was enjoying every moment of her time with that guy, and it clearly wasn't all sexual. Rori didn't just look well-fucked. She looked smitten, like she was in a new and highly satisfying relationship.

Fuck. Me.

"Hm," was all she responded.

"Rori," I hissed, eyes darting around again. "This is fucking dire. Like, we might have very limited time here. Hours, if that."

"I'll be done with this chapter in a few minutes. This is a great scene." Her teeth peeked out with a small smile, biting her lower lip. "They're about to have an orgy."

Oh, great. We were on the verge of getting kicked out or killed, and she was reading smut.

"Rori!" I ground my teeth to keep myself from yelling. "I fucked up bad, okay? I got in a fight with some staff. So they're most likely fucking onto us."

That got her attention. She lifted her head, the book falling away from her chest as she stared at me. "What did you say?"

"If you would really like to hear me out, I suggest we go somewhere more private."

She set the book down on the metal bistro table, moving slowly as if she were unsure. Then to my utter relief, she said, "Okay. Let's go to the suite."

"Thank you," I sighed.

As she stood, she carefully picked up her napkin covered in the scraped off seeds that were on her bagel. She went to the giant bird cage, stuck her arm through one of the bars, and shook the napkin so its contents fell on the floor. A flurry of wings and bird calls descended on the discarded seeds like it was the first time they'd seen food in a week.

"I can't save all of them," Rori said, returning to my side. "But I can make life a little better for them."

We walked to the suite in silence. I tried to keep my pace relaxed and not look like I was rushing anywhere. After an eternity, I opened our door for Rori and stepped in after her, locking it behind me.

"So, what happened?" she asked, leaning against the kitchen counter with her arms crossed. She was still closed off and angry at me. But I could handle that as long as she heard me.

"You know those armed guards that work the colosseum? I saw a group of them beating the shit out of a gladiator."

"Which one?" she demanded, eyes widening.

Not your boyfriend, don't worry. "The guy that won the first fight we watched. He killed the Animal and his buddy that he came in with. They're calling him the Hunter."

Rori's shoulders visibly lowered with a sigh of relief. "So what'd you do?"

"Jumped in and stopped it. Pretty sure I broke a guy's leg. Got a good few hits in on all four."

"*Four?!*"

"Yeah, they were totally ganging up on the poor bastard. He's okay, though."

Rori nodded. "That's good, I'm glad."

In all the years we'd known each other, she'd never condemned me for getting into fights. She knew I was defending those who were weaker, after all. She even used to try joining in, but Daren and I forced her to stay out of the way of flying fists.

As we got older, Rori and Lily would distract teachers and staff so I could make sure to end the fights before they were broken up too soon. I was usually done when Daren pulled me back, slapped the shit out of me, and told me it was enough. If it weren't for him, I very well could've been locked away for murder at sixteen.

"But now we've got a target on our backs," I said. "By now, I'm certain Nella is aware, and she's just figuring out what to do with us."

"If they think we're still regular guests, they'll probably kick us out." Rori chewed her thumbnail. "If they suspect something else...who knows?"

"Exactly my thoughts," I said. "Which is why I think we should beat them to the punch and get the hell out of here ASAP."

She blinked. "You mean, just up and leave? Now?"

"Yeah. Get some good walking shoes on. Let's take the elevator up and just go until we find a signal so we can make phone calls. Then we'll regroup and come back with some firepower."

"Torr." She shook her head. "We can't."

"Sure we can. Look, I told that gladiator about us, why we're really here. He might be able to help us out. It's a long shot, but it's something. But we have to get out of here first, together."

"I can't, Torr."

"Why the hell not?"

"I'm seeing Santos tonight."

"Who the fuck is Santos?" It dawned on me right after I said it, cutting through me like a machete's blade. "Oh, wow." I rubbed my jaw. "Gladiators are forbidden from giving their real names, and y'all are on a first name basis, huh?" It was worse than I thought.

Naturally, Rori ignored me. "I can let him know what's happening too. The more gladiators who know, the better.

Maybe they can organize a revolt while we're away. And by the time we're back, they'll be ready."

"How many times have you seen him?" Nothing else was on my mind. Not our exit plan, nothing. I could only think of Rori being intimate with this man, getting closer to him in a matter of days than we had in thirteen years.

"Twice." She bristled, her expression going as frosty as those fake contacts she wore. "What does it matter to you, anyway?"

"Have you fucked him?" For days that felt like centuries, I'd wrestled with the unknown, and it was fucking torture. The answer might hurt like a bitch, but I *had* to know.

"Oh God, fuck off, Torr. I'm not having this fight with you again."

"We're not fighting. It's just a question."

"It's never just a question with you, and I'm fucking sick of it! I'm done. I don't want to do this with you." She turned, heading for the liquor bottles on the minibar. It was late morning, early for drinking, but who the fuck was I to judge?

"What are you saying?" I followed after her, my panic riding high now. "What do you mean, you're done?"

"I'm done with you being an asshole and getting all up in my business about who I'm seeing." She aggressively opened a whiskey bottle and started pouring. "You've never cared about who I fucked before, and I don't believe for a second that it has to do with him being a gladiator. I don't even want to know why anymore. I just want it to stop, Torr."

My heart started to sink like a lead balloon, and it may have even been in pieces. "So you *have* slept with him?"

"Oh my God, did you hear *anything* I just said?"

"It's a yes or no question, Rori."

"I don't have to tell you jack-*fucking*-shit."

"I know you don't, but fucking tell me anyway!" The last word was accompanied by my fist slamming a side table so hard,

I left a dent in the polished wood surface. "Please," I added, my tone betraying how fucking weak I was for this woman.

Rori only stared at me with an expression of complete bewilderment, her drink hovering on its way to her mouth. A timid knock came from the other side of our door, echoing through our uncomfortable silence.

"Rori, ma'am? Is everything alright?" came the hesitant voice of her maid.

"Now's not a good time," I answered. "Come back later."

Rori's drink came down hard on the counter, spilling whiskey with the force of its impact. "You don't talk to her like that," she snapped. Paige is a friend, not a servant."

God, I was royally fucking everything up.

"Sorry," I said under my breath. Then louder, "I'm really so fucking sorry, Rori." The list of things to apologize for seemed too big to rattle off, so an all-encompassing apology seemed the most appropriate.

"You'd know I was getting close to her too if you'd actually, you know, talk to me." She looked past me to yell at the door. "I'm okay, Paige. I'll be out in a few minutes."

"Okay!" came the timid reply through the door.

"You're right." My hands clenched at my sides with the need to wrap around her, to pull her into my chest for real this time, not as an act. "You're right about everything, Ror. I shouldn't have shut you out."

Rori held up her left hand, examining the black diamond I'd placed on her finger back at the tavern, which felt like an eternity ago. "So much for guarding me at every turn, huh? Good thing I didn't need you anyway."

And yet I don't see you taking that ring off. I swallowed back that retort, despite it burning hot in my throat. If I wanted a fighting chance of us getting out of here alive, I had to keep my defensiveness in check. I had to leave behind all my jealousy, all the bitterness of the chances I'd lost. Chances I never took because I was too afraid of losing her.

Sure, she'd only met with this gladiator twice, and it might not go anywhere. But he wasn't some small-town guy like all the ones she'd had before. I'd known all of them, known they weren't good enough for her. But the Butcher wasn't just a man, he was a force. He might actually see her worth. Might actually take her from me.

And acting like a jealous, sad sack wasn't going to keep her. Shit, it might be too late at this point. I could already feel her slipping away.

"I meant those vows when I said them," I told her. "And I'm sorry that I let my pride rule me and didn't guard you like I should have. I really fucking regret that, Rori." She narrowed her eyes, but I went on before she could respond. "I also said we would come out of this together or not at all. And I still have every intention of doing that. But Rori, I cannot stress how much we need to leave *now*."

She shook her head, and I wanted to punch the end table again with how fucking infuriating and stubborn and gorgeous she was.

"Santos deserves to know what's going on," she insisted. "But we can leave immediately after. Just lie low until I get back."

"Right," I snapped, my threadbare control snapping like a single strand of hair. "I'll just wait here with all the lights off while you take one last ride on your gladiator rodeo. Brilliant fucking idea."

"I haven't fucked him, Torr! Jesus fucking Christ!" She threw the whiskey glass across the room as she shouted. It bounced and slid across the floor but didn't break. "Not that you'd fucking believe me, but there it is. Satisfied?"

Oh I was, more than I would ever admit. Something possessive and toxic inside me felt immensely pleased that she hadn't gone through with it. Rori's heart followed where her sex life led. I'd seen it happen many times. If she hadn't pounced on this guy, she wasn't falling for him.

Yet.

"I do believe you." I shoved my hands in my pockets, jerking my chin down in a quick nod. "Fine then. Go let him know what's up."

Rori was still fuming, her chest rising and falling with harsh, furious breaths as she glared at me. "This is the last time I'm going to ask you," she said, her voice just on the edge of calm. "Why do you suddenly care about who I'm fucking, when it has never mattered to you before?"

My throat closed up as though my heart had jumped in there to choke off my words and protect itself. "You really don't know?" I forced out.

She swung her hands out to the sides, then let them flop against her legs with a *duh* expression. "Now would be a great time to use your words and actually *talk* to me, Torr."

Oh hell no. This was the last place I wanted to be, putting my heart on the line to Rori fucking Wilder. I didn't do that for anybody, especially not her.

I wanted to scurry off to the gym and lift until I was a puddle of sweat on the floor. Or better yet, bend her over that counter and *show* her how I felt. I wouldn't stop until she was an orgasmic mess, wouldn't that be enough? My love language was nonstop orgasms, but saying it in words was too damn much.

Rori scoffed in response to my silence. "That's what I thought." She then moved coldly past me to the door and left.

24

SANTOS

Two private sessions with guests in one day was always exhausting, mentally and physically. Especially when the day began with one of the guests I hated most, an heiress named Blair who believed the whole world should kneel at her feet. The only thing that made it bearable was knowing my day would end with Aurora.

On both occasions, my time with Rori had passed too fucking quickly. An hour with her felt like five damn minutes. Whereas an hour with Blair felt like a year.

Holding Rori's hand toward the end of our last session felt more intimate than any of the sex I'd had in the last four years. When the time came, I never wanted to let her go.

"How soon can I see you again?" she'd asked immediately.

That question and the eagerness in her voice made my chest swell so much, it felt like I'd swallowed a balloon. "I should be free tomorrow evening," I'd told her. "Book me as soon as you're out of here."

"I will." When our hands separated, it felt like she took a piece of me with her.

My routine was the same this morning—shower, shave, a

spritz of fragrance. But every motion felt like swimming through mud. I didn't want to be here. Hell, I never wanted to be here until *her*. But right then, I would have traded anything to not do this appointment. My lack of choice in this matter had never felt so painfully apparent until now.

I walked out into the room with boulders in my stomach and cement blocks on my feet. My smile at the morning guest felt like the corners of my mouth were being pulled apart by fish hooks. "Good morning, Blair."

"Butcher," she crooned, assuming what must have been a seductive pose, one foot on the floor with the other propped up on the back of the couch. "I've been waiting for you to come split me apart."

The gown Blair wore was some sheer lacy material, leaving nothing to the imagination. Her chest was so augmented, her breasts looked like flotation devices. I knew every cosmetic surgery scar she tried to hide with body paint and fake tanner, because she had come to see me many times before. Blair had two obsessions: looking as physically perfect as possible, and rough, if even dangerous, sex.

There was a time when I almost felt sorry for her. What happened in this woman's life to make her reach for an unobtainable, idealized version of herself, while craving such degradation in the bedroom? She never even wanted aftercare. She only ever wanted me to be as brutal to her on this couch as I was out on the sands. If I'd been allowed to bring my machetes in here, she'd probably be thrilled.

That desire for the rough stuff was shared by nearly all of the guests I serviced, to varying degrees. They wanted the fantasy of the Butcher, to flirt with danger and experience my persona like an amusement park ride. Wild, thrilling, heart-pounding, but ultimately, completely safe.

Only Rori wanted the real me. Santos Antonio Jimenez.

I tried to swallow at Blair's spread open display, but no moisture remained in my throat. "Something to drink before we begin?" I turned to the minibar, blatantly stalling. Fuck, I really didn't want to do this. Not when I had to face Rori right afterward.

Why I felt some strange sense of loyalty to her, I had no idea. We'd spent a total of two hours together, nowhere near enough to form any kind of bond. But damn if those two hours weren't the best time I had in years. Maybe my perspective was all fucked. I'd been in this shithole so long that I latched onto the first pretty woman who talked to me like I was a fellow human being.

But Tezca told me to trust her, and she had a companion god too. No matter how logically I tried to look at it, we had simply been destined to meet. To what end, I didn't know. But right then, every cell in my body revolted at the woman currently lying on the couch, and wished it was Rori instead.

"The only thing I want to drink is your cum," Blair crooned from the couch. "I want you to make me choke on it like last time."

I made some kind of dismissive noise while pretending to be busy at the minibar. She liked it when I was mean to her, so I could keep stalling and denying her a bit longer. My dick was not excited in the least, though. Fuck, I should've popped one of those erection pills this morning. I could not imagine getting through this any other way.

"Hurry, Daddy," she whined. "I need you to fuck me until I bleed."

I had just swallowed a shot of the same whiskey Rori and I had shared yesterday and nearly threw it back up when I heard that. "I'll fuck you when I'm good and ready," I said, adding a hard tone to my voice.

The truth was, the hardcore domination stuff had never

appealed to me. It didn't matter who it was with. I was a brutal, relentless fighter by necessity, not because being violent turned me on. But that was all these people wanted, and I was so beyond fucking sick of playing that act.

Before falling asleep last night, I got turned on by the thought of resting my head in Rori's lap. I imagined her scratching my head like we'd joked about, running those nails over my neck and back.

And I hadn't been joking about being happy to serve her. I wanted to earn her head scratches, her smiles, her approval. Hell, maybe even her love. Because I already knew I could trust her. I *knew* she wouldn't exploit or abuse me like I had been for nearly half my life. And that only made me want to worship her even more.

God, if a woman like that could actually love me? That kind of happiness didn't seem possible.

"Butcher," Blair barked from the couch. "You are wasting my time and my money. I pay for you to use your cock, not stand around with it in your hand."

I whipped around and launched myself at her, making the couch rock from the weight of my impact. Blair wore dark blue contacts today with little swirly golden designs in the irises. Those eyes flashed with fear as I straddled her, bringing one hand to her throat. She moaned, and I squeezed harder, which only made her writhe underneath me. If I felt between her legs, I knew she'd be wet.

"I'll use my cock on you," I growled, rubbing the soft organ with my free hand. "I'll use it in all your filthy holes until you're screaming for me stop, and then I'll fuck you even harder. Is that what you want?"

"Yes, please," she begged. "Destroy me, Butcher. Tear me apart like a filthy whore on the street."

I hate this. I hate this. Holy fucking shit, I hate this.

No amount of touching myself was working, so I racked my brain for ideas. The last thing I wanted to do was touch her with my fingers or mouth. She loved when I shoved her head down on my cock, but I didn't want to do that either, plus then she'd know I wasn't getting hard. We weren't allowed to use toys because the risk of injury to the guests was too high.

God damn it, what the fuck was I going to do?

I released Blair's throat and lifted off of her. Before she could complain, I roughly manhandled her into another position, pressing down on her upper back so that her face and chest were shoved into the couch cushions.

"Oh yes!" she cried out, lifting her hips in the air to rub her ass against me. "Take my ass, Daddy. Shove it in, and fuck me rough."

God, if she would just shut up, I might be able to fantasize about something else to get through this. But that grating voice and those demands that made my skin crawl kept me firmly in the limp zone.

"You're *my* little whore to use." I lifted the sheer, shimmery fabric of her gown over her hips, staring at her bare, wet cunt in an attempt to feel any-fucking-thing below the waist. "Be quiet so the other gladiators don't take you from me."

"Oh, I would love for the others to use me! I want all of them to defile me and stuff me full of cum."

Yeah, right. She'd end up dead if that were to really happen. I wouldn't wish such a fate on anyone.

When Blair arched deeper and pressed back, I stopped her with a hand on her hip to keep her from rubbing on me again. The grab was rough. She mistook it for things getting started and practically trembled with anticipation.

"Ohh yes! Give it to me hard, and make it hurt. I can't wait any longer."

Well, that was definitely not happening. And so much for keeping quiet. The seconds ticked by, and it was becoming increasingly clear that this wouldn't end well for me. I couldn't stall anymore, and no part of me had the stomach to even fake it through this.

Sorry, Rori. I'm going to be in rough shape when you see me.

I stood from the couch and lowered my gaze to the floor. "I'm very sorry, Blair. But I can't perform the duties as requested."

"What?" I heard a rustle of fabric as she most likely moved from her position, and my downcast gaze saw her feet touch the floor. "What do you mean, Butcher?"

"Regrettably, I am unable to perform, ma'am. My sincerest apologies." I was supposed to offer another gladiator to her, but no way would I subject any of the guys to this headfuck.

"What are you talking about? You're a male in your prime, what's wrong with you?"

"I'm afraid I don't know. Maybe my training this morning exerted me too much." I didn't even know why I was making excuses. It was all bullshit that didn't matter.

"Fucking idiot," she huffed. "If you can't do it yourself, I will *make* you perform."

Blair got up from the couch and approached me, making a grab for the front of my pants. My arm shot out on pure instinct, catching her wrist in my grip.

"Don't touch me," I hissed.

She looked at me with surprise at first, then pure loathing as she pulled her arm free. "You don't have the right to refuse me! You are here to do exactly what I want and nothing less. So do as you're told, gladiator, or I'll have you locked in the black box."

I ground my molars. The rotten bitch would threaten me with the sensory deprivation dungeon, the same prison that drove the crazed knight mad for months before they sent him out to be killed by me.

Blair apparently took my silence for compliance, her hands going to the waistband of my pants again. That action, that fucking entitlement, pushed all the threats and consequences from my mind.

Fuck the consequences. I wasn't a sex toy anymore.

I shoved Blair back by her shoulders. "I said don't fucking touch me!"

Her arms windmilled as she fell back on her ass. I'd pushed her harder than I meant to, but she wasn't hurt, just stunned that I kept exercising a right I supposedly didn't have.

"The panic button is under the coffee table. Call them in, fuck it. I don't care. As long as I don't have to fuck you anymore." I started pacing, just waiting for her to give the order to send me to whichever hell she chose.

"What did you say?" Blair asked in a low, malicious voice as she moved slowly, easing herself back up to the couch.

"I don't want to fuck you anymore." I was already dead, most likely, so why stop at half truths? The dam was broken, so I might as well let it all out. "I've never wanted you. I've hated every moment of being with you. So send me to the black box, I don't give a fuck. At least I won't have to touch you ever again."

"I see." She sounded calm, eerily so. Her ego was so overinflated, none of what I said probably hit where it hurt. Though I'd hopefully scratched the surface.

Blair stood from the couch and calmly crossed the room. She went to the doorway I usually came out of and knocked softly. The door opened, and a few minutes of quiet conversation passed. Then she turned and walked across the room to the guest doorway, not glancing at me once as she passed through.

"Butcher." A pitmaster appeared in my doorway and beckoned me forward. "Your session is over."

I went to him, ready to be escorted to the bowels of the colosseum. A sudden, panicked thought flashed through my mind that I must have fucked up seeing Rori tonight. Shit, what would they tell her? As a paying guest, she could demand to see me. But would she?

A sharp pain cut across my jaw, jerking my head to the side. I tasted blood, and realized I'd been too in my head to see the hit coming. Another one crashed into my gut, and it felt like a battering ram swung into my stomach.

I doubled over, and my legs seemed to stop working, so I fell to my knees. My vision swam while I tried to catch a breath. When I looked at the hand that had clutched my stomach, red blood streaked across my palm. I patted my stomach again, wincing at the pain and wetness that was definitely my blood.

I looked up to find three pitmasters standing over me, all of them brandishing fancy brass knuckles with spikes on the ends. Shit.

"Not every day we get to whale on the fuckin' Butcher," said the middle one gleefully, lifting his brass knuckles to admire them more closely.

"Hey!" The left one snapped his fingers in my face, prompting a snarl from me. "Your sandy ass has another guest to serve tonight. Don't fuck it up this time."

"Yeah, stand up. Show us whatcha got," the third one piped up.

I was beyond sick of everyone ordering me around, but I also had too much pride to remain on my knees for these assholes. With no small amount of effort, I rose to my feet. My stomach muscles screamed in protest, spasming from my injury. The spikes didn't go deep from what I could tell, but they hurt like a bitch.

No sooner had I stood to full height than a hit came swinging for my jaw. I dodged it, but then got a crash of metal to my temple that made my skull ring like a bell. I went down again, my vision darkening. More drops of blood fell on the floor, and all I could think about was cleaning it up before Rori stepped in it.

Another jarring blow came to the back of my head, and then darkness swallowed me up.

25

RORI

I paced the opulent room for nearly ten minutes after my appointment was supposed to start, and Santos was still nowhere to be seen. Thoughts raced through my head while I chewed down the nail on my index finger. Did he not want to see me after all? Well, it wasn't like he had a choice, which just heightened my anxiety even more. Maybe he didn't have any open spots today or was with another client. No, Nella managed his schedule and would have said something.

"What the hell?" I grumbled, my feet intent on wearing a hole in the rug. I was so frazzled after seeing Torr, and it made me extra anxious to see Santos. I needed the distraction of those warm eyes and that gorgeous smile, even if it was for the last time.

The door across the room finally creaked open, and my heart leaped at the sound. "You know, it's rude to keep a lady waiting." I spun to face him, grinning, but all humor fell away as my jaw dropped open. "Santos!" I cried, rushing to him. "What happened?"

His face was bruised, swollen, and scratched deeply in several places, like his jaguar had swiped at him, although that was impossible. He also held a hand to his stomach and took small, pained steps into the room. "Sorry to keep you waiting." His voice was quiet, scratchy, defeated. And it broke my heart.

"Come sit down." I took one of his arms. "You can lean on me. I'll get you water."

"I can walk," he said but grimaced as I led him toward the couch.

I let him keep his pride, despite wanting to throw his arm over my shoulder and force him to use me as support. He sat down with a groan, and I rushed to the minibar for water and some cloth napkins. The scratches on his face looked fresh, and some were still bleeding.

Once settled next to him with my supplies, I wet a napkin and reached for his face. "Turn your head, let me see."

He leaned away from me instead, shaking his head. "No. It's not your job to take care of me."

"Right now, it fucking is," I snapped. "Come here, Santos. Please." The last word came out softer, a genuine plea. "I don't like seeing you hurting. Let me help." I leaned forward with the cloth again, and he remained still, so I took my chance.

He allowed me to dab at his jaw and temple for a few silent minutes. "Who did this to you?" I asked, getting up to check the other side of his face.

"Doesn't matter."

"Yes, it does."

"Really, it doesn't." He lifted those dark eyes, which now looked empty and sad, to mine. "It's just what they do to us."

"Why?" I could only imagine the injuries were from staff. If it had been another fighter, they never would have been able to land any hits on him. Santos had only been hurt this badly because he couldn't fight back.

"Because...I refused to do as I was told." He looked at me

with so much pain and unsaid emotion, I couldn't bring myself to look away. "I'm sorry, Rori."

"Sorry?" I lowered the bloodstained napkin and touched the one unmarred spot on his cheek. "You have absolutely nothing to be sorry for. This is not your fault."

"I was so looking forward to seeing you." He looked away, a mirthless smile pulling at his lips. "I'm sorry I had to ruin our time together by being all busted up like this."

"Stop it. You're not ruining anything." I let my head fall to his shoulder. "I'm just worried about you."

"Don't be. I'll be alright." His arm moved behind me like he was going to wrap it around my shoulders, but then he froze with a grimace and a hiss.

I lifted my head, poured more water on the napkin, and straightened up. "Where else?"

"Rori," Santos sighed. "Enough. You don't have to nurse me."

"Yes, I do!" My hands shook, just as my eyes blurred with tears. "I care about you, okay? I can't just act like nothing's wrong when you've been beaten up for no reason. I hate that they do this to you, that you don't have choices, and you're treated like this. So *please,* just let me care about you like you deserve."

"Hey, don't cry." I closed my eyes and felt rough thumb pads sweep tenderly over my cheeks. Santos' voice was soft and so close that I felt his breath over my lips. "Don't cry for me, Aurora. I'm not worth it."

"Yes, you are," I choked out. "You're worth so much more than what they've made you here."

"You barely know me."

"I know enough."

He chuckled lightly at my repetition of his words from yesterday and leaned back, his hands falling away from my face.

I sniffed and opened my eyes, composing myself. "Will you please let me look at your other injuries?"

He sighed, and the deep breath made him wince and touch a hand to his stomach again. "If you insist."

"Shirt off, then. Do you need help?"

"No, I got it." Santos leaned forward, pulling the black linen shirt from his back. He sat back and hesitated once it was over his head, keeping his arms in the sleeves and his stomach covered. "It's really not as bad as it looks."

"Off with it." I went to pull the shirt off one of his arms, and he begrudgingly allowed me. The moment he was uncovered from the waist up, my blood ran cold. "Santos..."

It was definitely as bad as it looked, if not worse. His torso was covered in dark blue and purple bruises overlaid with those same deep scratches and what looked like puncture marks. Small, round lacerations all evenly spaced apart in sets of four. And there were hundreds of them all over his chest, stomach, ribs, arms, and back.

"What are all these from?" It took every ounce of self-control to ask the question calmly when all I wanted to do was scream. "Brass knuckles?"

"Spiked ones, yeah."

"Fuck."

I went to clean a few that still leaked blood, clenching my teeth to keep my jaw from shaking. But the tremors in my hands gave me away, as did the hot, burning tears springing to my eyes again.

"Rori, it's okay." Santos took my hands, the roughness of his palms a soothing texture against my icy rage. "I'll honestly be fine. It's all surface stuff, they can't damage me permanently. I make this place too much money, remember?" I heard, rather than saw, the forced smile in his voice. "I'll be sore for a while, but I promise I'll live. It's what I do best."

"I'll kill them," I heard myself say. Tears fell, and my vision cleared, the sight of his bruised, welted skin solidifying the promise in my mind. He had to be in so much pain. "I'll kill whoever did this to you."

Santos let out a soft huff of breath, barely a laugh. I felt his hand on my cheek, then he was looking at me. The warmth in his eyes had returned, and the smile he wore was genuine, the one that made my heart flip-flop.

"No woman has ever said she'd kill for me before." His thumb touched the corner of my mouth.

"I'm fucking serious." I placed my palm over his hand and laced my fingers through his. "You haven't seen me fight yet, but I can. And for you, I will."

"I believe you, Aurora." He stroked my lower lip with his thumb, eyes rapt where he touched me.

"I don't have a lot of time left here," the words came out in a frantic rush, urgency hitting me like a train. "Torr assaulted some guards, and we're likely to get kicked out soon. But we're not done here, Santos. I won't let you die as a gladiator."

His brow furrowed, mouth flattening. "Kicked out? They'll never let you back in."

"Well, we're not exactly coming to the front door and knocking politely."

That smile returned, although sadder and more subdued than before. "I'm so glad I met you. You're an incredible woman, Aurora."

"You don't even know me," I teased.

"I know enough," he returned, eyes lighting up.

We had gotten so close at some point. I was one outstretched leg away from straddling his lap, and our noses were nearly touching. My lips ached from wanting to kiss him so badly. With the way he kept stroking my mouth, it seemed we had similar ideas.

Neither of us spoke for a while. It felt like a tiny, fraying string held us apart, the final barrier between us threatening to snap at any moment. When it finally did, the two of us crashed together like storm clouds.

We met in the middle, and there was nothing tentative about that kiss. I opened my mouth to him, and his tongue swept in, tasting like desperation, like this first kiss might also be our last. The thought had my tongue caressing his, and I tasted bits of blood. Worried I'd hurt him, I pulled back to sip at his soft, plush lips, but he was having none of that. Santos wrapped an arm around my back and drew me closer, deepening our kisses until there was no space left between us.

I barely needed to move, but kissing him wasn't enough. My leg flew over his lap, and he drew me down with a tender hold around my waist. Our lips never separated as I settled into him, resting my hands on the sides of his neck. I kept my forearms lifted off his chest until he ran a light touch from my wrist to my shoulder.

"You don't have to be careful with me," he murmured, kissing the edge of my jaw.

"I don't want to hurt you more than you already are." My head tilted back, shamelessly offering my neck to his mouth, and he obliged me, running a sensual trail of kisses from my earlobe to my shoulder.

"Imagine how hurt I'll be if I never see you again." Santos kissed the hollow of my throat, moving higher up the front of my neck.

"You will." Our mouths connected in another kiss, and I gave a little tug on his lip with my teeth. "I swear on both the gods protecting us, I'll come back for you."

Santos looked unsure, his eyes flicking away for a moment. "Even if you do, what happens when that guy realizes how perfect you are and wants you for himself?"

I barked out a bitter, pained laugh. "Torr has never shown any interest in me in all the years I've known him. He's not about to start now."

"I'm not so sure about that."

"He knows how I am. How, you know, I was raised with multiple dads. And he's never been a sharer, so it's a moot point."

"Ah, right." Santos leaned back, his expression studious. "You're never going to end up with just one guy, huh?"

I shrugged. "I'm not wired that way, but it hasn't worked out for me so far, so who knows?"

His hold tightened on my waist as he let out a little scoff. "You're fierce, brave, beautiful, and ruthless. You deserve rooms of men."

I laughed a little, leaning forward to kiss him. "I only want one man right now."

This time, I allowed myself to melt against his chest. Santos only wrapped tighter around me, pulling me closer until our chests were flush. He brought one hand to my knee, running a hard grip up my thigh as he pushed my dress up to my waist. His touch continued up and behind me, grabbing my ass in a rough squeeze that made my hips roll forward—and make contact with the stiff erection in front of me.

"I want you, Aurora," he groaned, nipping at my throat again.

"I want you too, Santos." I was needy and hot, fighting the urge to rub against him and soothe the pulsing ache between my legs. "But..."

He was still a gladiator. I would be using him. I didn't want this unless he had the complete free will and inalienable right to say no.

Santos seemed to follow my train of thought and held my

chin between his thumb and forefinger. "That's not what this is. You don't see this as a transaction, right?"

"No, but..."

"*I* want this. For me." He cupped my cheek, kissing me tenderly. "You wanted to do something for me yesterday. Will you give me this?"

I let out a soft laugh of disbelief, rocking my forehead against his. "This is what you want? To be with me?"

"It's all I want."

Another '*you don't even know me*' hovered on the tip of my tongue, but I stopped myself, realizing how serious he was.

And how much I wanted the exact same thing. Right now, while I still had him.

26

RORI

I kissed Santos in reply, sealing the deal for both of us. He returned it with equal fervor, pulling me in with that possessive hand on my ass, and I let myself slowly crash into him.

Santos shoved away all of my dress fabric that was pooling around us, his hands running up my thighs to my hips like he couldn't get enough of me. His cock was long and thick behind his pants, and I wanted to shove away his clothes like he was doing with me. But I forced myself to wait, to run my aching core over him from base to head. My hips lifted and lowered, simulating riding him at a slow, tantalizing pace.

"Mm, should've known you'd be a tease." He grinned, holding my waist to guide my movement.

"Foreplay isn't just for women, you know." I leaned in to kiss his neck and maybe also to kiss some of his bruises. I wasn't fucking joking about killing whoever did this to him.

"I know. It's just..."

I nipped at his earlobe when he trailed off, and a sexy moan rolled out of his throat when I ground harder against his erection. "Just what?"

"I was gonna say it's been a while since I've done this, but that's not exactly true, is it?"

"That wasn't sex. You were being used." I eased back in his lap and pulled at the ties on his linen pants. "I bet you weren't even being pleasured, were you?"

"Mm, no." His dark eyes fell between us to where I'd freed his cock and stroked him. He was so hot and rigid, the thick length of him pulsing against my palm. "Not like this. No one's ever touched me like you."

I had a feeling he was flattering me again just to be sweet, but the words made me smile and flush with heat all the same. I wanted to believe him. And damn it, he deserved to feel good after everything he'd been through.

Sliding backwards off his lap, I held his gaze as my feet hit the floor first, then my knees as I separated his thighs to make room for myself.

"What are you doing, paloma?" His voice was low, eyes hooded behind those dark lashes. His fingers trailed over my arms, my shoulders, and neck. He touched me like he was endlessly in awe of me and stared at me like my beauty was something to marvel at. I knew I wasn't a cave troll or anything, but no one had ever looked at me like *that*.

"Giving you what you want." I kissed one of the bruises on his ribs, just barely brushing it with my lips so as to not pain him. Then I kissed one on his lower stomach. "What you deserve," I added.

"I want to please you too." Santos traced my cheekbone with his thumb. "I want to make you come and hear you say my name as I get you there, over and over."

"You will." I placed a kiss on the deep line in his hip crease, squeezing harder around his cock as I stroked upward. "When I come back for you."

"Aurora," he rasped in frustration.

"Santos," I answered, looking up at him. "I can't be selfish with you. Not right now. Please, can you understand that?"

Before he could answer, I lowered my mouth to him, sliding my lips and tongue over his blunt head until his chin tipped up with a moan.

"I...guess I can live through this," he sighed in answer.

I laughed a little, then dragged a long lick from the sensitive tip to the base of his cock. "Besides, you're injured," I pointed out, licking my way back up. "I want you fully recovered and far away from this place when you fuck me."

"Can't happen soon enough." Santos caressed my neck, pushing my hair out of the way as I savored him with my mouth. "Fuck, you're so beautiful. You feel, uh, so fucking good..."

His praise encouraged me, and I started to suck him in earnest, working the entire length of him with my hand and mouth. In truth, it was all his nonverbal reactions that made me feel like a fucking goddess. His soft moans and hisses of breath. The subtle rolls of his hips to drive deeper into my mouth. The way his grip tightened on my hair or shoulder when he felt espe-cially good.

Too many times I had given blowjobs where it felt like I was slobbering on an inanimate object, not a person experiencing pleasure. It got my anxious spiral rolling, wondering if I was doing it well enough or if the guy actually liked me. With Santos, I had none of those thoughts. His responsiveness was not only reassuring, it turned me the fuck on. I didn't have to touch myself to know my panties were soaked.

My hand went there anyway, partially to soothe my clit that was aching to be touched but also to see his reaction.

Santos' cock jerked against my tongue, his breaths getting even more ragged. "Oh yes, touch yourself for me. I want you to come. Be a little selfish for me, paloma."

It wouldn't take long. I was slick, and my flesh was so sensitive to every rub I made with my fingertips. Santos was getting close too, his grip on me tightening while he stiffened and swelled inside my mouth. I felt his hand reach lower, diving inside the bodice of my dress to find my breasts.

I was moaning too now, wordless and muffled with my mouth stuffed full of him. My orgasm was building hard and fast while I rubbed myself and Santos rolled my nipples with those callused fingers.

"You really want to know why I got beat?" he rasped, his voice tight.

"Mmm!" I took him further down my throat, sealing my lips down his solid length.

"Come for me first." He laughed when my moan turned into a throaty growl of frustration. "Your pleasure is the price for knowledge. Show me how much you like sucking my dick."

Oh Jesus. Not only was he a responsive lover, he could tease and talk dirty too. I couldn't afford to fail at torching this place and freeing all the gladiators. Not when I'd just found the perfect man.

And the part I couldn't get over? He wanted me too.

"Don't stop, just like that," Santos groaned, kneading a breast in one hand while he stroked my neck and face with the other. "You're so perfect, so good to me."

My breath was shortening, the building orgasm coiling tighter in my clit like a compressed spring. Sucking down Santos became a race to see which would come first—me, him, or my need to breathe.

He spilled on my tongue with a ragged groan, hips pistoning to drive his releasing cock through the seal of my lips. His sounds of pleasure, and the salty taste of him, spurred my own orgasm to let loose. The spring uncoiled, stretching free. My legs clamped shut as they shook, trapping my hand against my clit as I swallowed every thick pulse of Santos' release.

I let him fall from my mouth when he grew soft, resting my cheek on his thigh as we looked up at each other. He was so fucking sexy, sitting back on the couch with his knees wide, chest rising and falling as he caught his breath. With his powerful physique, the injuries dotting his skin, and the light sheen of sweat coating him, he looked like a sated god of war.

"Come here, paloma," he rasped, cupping my cheek.

I rose from the floor, accepting his embrace. He turned me sideways, draping my legs across his lap while those powerful arms encircled my waist. Santos kissed me deeply, possessively, holding me tightly in a way that showed that he never wanted to let go.

The tenderness of it nearly made me want to cry. I wasn't used to this either, any kind of cuddling or afterglow following anything sexual. I didn't even realize until right then that he was probably the first guy to initiate this with me.

Maybe this was what I was missing, genuine affection freely given. It was like how my fathers always were with my mother. At least one of them was always touching her just because they loved to be connected to her. Kissing, cuddling, even holding hands, were things I always had to fight for with a guy, and I always initiated.

Santos was acting like I'd already saved him, and this was just a blowjob.

"Don't you have something to tell me?" I whispered, my lips brushing his.

"You're the sexiest fucking thing I've ever seen," he said, kissing me again. "And your mouth, fuck." He touched his thumb to my lip, his smile lazy and sated. "These lips are magical."

"You know, you're very good at using charm to be distract-ing." I almost said, *you remind me of Torr,* but I thought better of it. "But I'm not easily distracted. What were you going to say before?"

"Hm, you'll have to remind me." He kissed my mouth again, then the bridge of my nose. "Because I am very easily distracted, and this gorgeous face hasn't been kissed enough."

"Santos!" I laughed as he moved on to my cheek and my neck. God, why couldn't this last forever? Finally, an adorable, sweet, funny man who was also hot as fuck and wanted me just as badly as I wanted him. Right when I had to leave too, and I could only hope he would still be here when I came back to storm the castle. "You know what I'm talking about. I paid the price for knowledge, so tell me why they did this."

He kissed my shoulder and then rested his forehead there for a moment, barely even a second, when the knock came to the door.

"Time's up. Three minutes to put your clothes back on."

"Fuck," we said in unison.

"I hate this," I whispered, wrapping my arms around his shoulders. "I hate this so much."

"Me too. Rori, listen." Santos pulled back and held me by the shoulders, his face gravely serious. "They're most likely going to put me in isolation after this. As further punishment."

My heart felt like it stopped and then clenched with fear. "Isolation? What does that mean for you?"

"It means..." He inhaled sharply before continuing. "I might not be the same person when you come back. It's like sensory deprivation, real fucked-up psychological shit."

Torture. He meant psychological torture.

My hands found his, linking through his fingers as if to create a type of netting that would never separate us. "Then we've got to get you out *now*."

"That's not possible, paloma. I'm sorry."

I started to rise from the couch, keeping our hands linked.

"Come with me through the guest door. We can run. You can hide in our suite until—"

"There will be at least a dozen pitmasters between there and here," he said. "It'll never work."

"We have to try!" I brought our joined hands to my chest. "I can't lose you when I just found you."

It was a dramatic, probably embarrassing thing to say. But it was how I honestly felt in that moment, and I had always been one to wear my heart on my sleeve.

Santos, thankfully, said nothing of it. He only slowly untangled our hands to hold me against his chest. "Go, and bring the cavalry when you come back," he said, lips against my forehead. "I'll...hold on and do what I can here. I have a friend who might be able to unite the gladiators while I'm isolated."

"That'll help," I admitted. "If we have a united front on the inside while we come from the outside, we can't lose."

"It won't be easy. Gladiators only look out for themselves."

My hands went to his face, and our mouths met in a kiss that had me simultaneously burning and melting from passion. Fuck, it was all I could do to not drag him from that room and start running *now*, but I knew logistically it would be insanely difficult. It would be easier for me and Torr to go, gather support, and come back.

But fuck, it killed me to leave him.

"I'll come back as soon as I can," I promised in a hurried whisper, knowing our time was running out. "You stay strong in there for me, okay? Not just for me but for you. For the life you're going to have after this."

Santos' smile was easy and almost infuriatingly calm. "Don't be scared for me, paloma. Surviving's what I'm best at, remember?"

"Entering in twenty seconds!" called the guards from the door.

Shit, shit, shit. That was no time at all. What could I do besides kiss him some more? So I did just that, and he kissed me back with a bone-crushing embrace.

"Entering now!"

"I refused to fuck a guest," Santos whispered before he was abruptly pulled away from me.

"What?" I was dazed from kissing him, heartbroken at the sight of three guards leading him toward the door. One of them had spiked brass knuckles hanging from a loop on his belt, and it hit me right then. These were the ones that 'punished' him, and he was telling me why.

"Because I only wanted to be with you." Santos' eyes were dark and intense as he was walked across the room.

"Excuse me, gentlemen!" I called out. "Can I ask you three something?"

The three guards paused and all whipped their heads toward me. "Yes, ma'am?"

I smiled sweetly. "I just wanted to see your faces. Thank you for your service."

27

RORI

My bravado ended the moment I stepped out of that room, but my mind latched onto the faces of those guards, burning them into my memory. I headed back to the suite, fighting every impulse to turn around and wrestle Santos free of those men. He needed me. Torr didn't.

I didn't know what to expect when I returned. The chances of Torr being there or not were fifty-fifty in my mind. With a shaky breath, I opened the door to find him stretched out on the longest couch with only a single lamplight illuminating the whole space. Night was creeping in quickly, filling spaces with darkness and shadows.

Torr swung upright as soon as he heard me, pinning me with a hard expression. "You okay?"

No, I wasn't. My heart wanted to crack open at the question, but I kept it together, pulling in another breath, which unfortunately made my nose sniffle. "You ready to go?"

Torr stood, approaching me with long strides. "Have you been crying?" Again, he completely ignored what I said and reached for my face.

I jerked away from his hand, well past my limit with him. "No. Let's just go."

"Rori, what happened?" He would not get out of my way and succeeded in cupping his palm against my cheek. Such a different feel to Santos' hands, and it seemed so incredibly cruel that he'd be affectionate and caring with me now. Too little, too fucking late.

"Stop, Torr." I batted his arm away, taking several steps back to move around him. "You were in such a big fucking hurry to go, so let's *go*."

"Not until you tell me what the fuck happened in there." He grabbed my upper arm, spinning me to face him. His jaw and cheekbones cut harsh lines from the shadows, and my mind flashed back to when he lit my cigarette under the lamplight. "Why are you upset? Did he hurt you?"

"No! Jesus fucking Christ!" I pulled my arm free, swung it back, and stopped myself from using the momentum to punch him. That was not me. Torr was pissing me off beyond all belief, but he was not my enemy. "I blew him, okay?"

Torr froze. I wouldn't have needed a punch to knock him over. My pinky finger would have done the job. "What?"

"I gave him a BJ. Went down on him. Sucked him off." I waved my hands in front of me in a mocking *ta-da* motion. "You're gonna keep harassing me until I tell you, so there it is, Torr. It finally happened, are you happy? And I'm upset because he got his ass kicked for me. I actually fucking like him, and he's gonna get tortured while we're off taking who-knows-how-long to get enough muscle to torch this place."

"Shit. Rori, I—" Torr raked a hand through his hair, looking more flustered and uncomfortable than I'd ever seen him in my life. He usually kept it all locked away in a safe, but right then, he seemed moments away from bursting.

"I'm sorry he went through that. Is *going* through that. I

wasn't going to ask you what you did with him. You're right, it's none of my business. I just...don't like seeing you upset."

"Huh." I turned in the direction of my room so I could change clothes and pack. "That's a first."

"No, it's not."

The forcefulness in Torr's tone made me stop in my tracks and look back at him, confused. "What?"

"I've always...cared about you, Rori. As more than a friend. More than my best friend's sister." His throat bobbed with the force of his swallow. And in the silence that followed, the noise of that swallow seemed to echo in the room.

"Wait...what?" My brain felt like it short-circuited. How long had I been fantasizing about hearing those exact words? That the gorgeous man who everyone wanted felt the same way about me as I did him? It had been so long and, since meeting Santos, I began to let go of that yearning for Torr. Now that he was telling me what I wanted, it was almost nonsensical.

He shifted uncomfortably and cleared his throat. "Look, I'm not good at this emotional stuff, but I'm trying." He licked his lips and inhaled sharply as he looked down at his shoes. "It's true. Like, the real reason I've never been able to commit to anyone is because...I always compare them to you." He looked up, the vulnerability plain on his face. "I always wanted to spend my time with you because...you've always been there for me, and you're just...perfect."

"Are you fucking kidding me?" I understood that he was putting his heart out on the line, probably for the first time in his life, but I was still pissed. "You're telling me you spent years chasing tail all over Four Corners because you didn't have the balls to say, 'Hey Rori, let's go out on a fucking date'? Is that seriously what you're saying right now?"

Torr's mouth hardened. "I wasn't the only one sleeping around, remember? What was I supposed to think when you'd drag two dudes off to a bedroom at a party, huh? You never did your little come-hither thing at me, so why would I try?"

"Don't turn this around on me! I'm not responsible for what comes out of your mouth." I stabbed my index finger at my own chest. "You *knew* I wanted something real, something more than hooking up. You were *there* when I cried about getting dumped. I told you about every single failed relationship and how much it hurt me that they never worked out. And here you are, going from woman to woman, making it very fucking clear that you want nothing lasting. So what was *I* supposed to think, Torr?"

He started shaking his head, looking away from me. "Forget I said anything."

Oh, fuck that. "What? No, *you* opened this can of worms. Let's talk about it." I went around and planted myself in front of him.

"Rori, move," Torr growled.

Oh, how the tables had turned.

"I'm not going anywhere." I spread my feet wide, placing my hands on my hips.

"I don't want to talk about this anymore."

"Too bad." I cocked my head at him. "We've known each other for thirteen years. You never had *one* opportunity to ask me out? Or just, like, kiss me? Just to see if maybe I felt the same way you did?"

"Nah." He shook his head. "It wasn't for lack of opportunity. I just knew it'd never work out."

"Why not? You never even tried!"

He shrugged, the movement jerky and stiff. "Just wasn't a risk I was willing to take."

"I can't fucking believe you, Torr." I pinched the bridge of my nose. "Why are you like this?"

"Like what?"

"Just...so emotionally constipated!" My hands flew up in

frustration. "Did it ever occur to you I might want you back? That if you had just been real with me, I would have said yes? I would have given us a chance, at least."

"No." He swallowed hard, shaking his head again. "No, I couldn't have even asked you out. I was ready to go to the grave having never taken that chance with you."

I was on the verge of tearing out chunks of my hair. "Fucking *why?*" I cried out.

"Because the last people who were supposed to love me left me in the desert to die!"

The silence following his shout created a void in that room, nothing but pure emptiness. And then it slowly filled to the brim with all kinds of realizations.

Torr kept everyone at arm's length, even Daren. He poured all of his energy into lifting weights so that he'd never need anyone but himself to protect him. When others needed protecting, he did so with an onslaught of fists and years of pent-up childhood fury. Despite my family opening their home and arms to him, he always held back, just a little. He was always on the fringe, never fully allowing himself to be part of us. Because family, to him, meant abandonment.

And he never let himself fall in love so that his heart would never be broken again.

"Torr..." His name was a whispered plea on my lips, and then it was me reaching for his face. He stiffened at my touch but thankfully didn't pull away. "Remember this?" I brushed the back of my fingers against his cheek, letting the black diamond gently run across his stubble. "You can still keep this promise. You and I are in this together, okay? You're never going to lose me."

He was quiet for a long time, so long that I wondered if he'd locked everything away again until he said, "How do I know that?" in a choked whisper.

"Trust." My hand slid around to the back of his neck. "You're going to have to unclench your emotional butthole and trust me a little."

I was expecting more of his stoicism but he actually laughed, his forehead lowering to brush mine. "See, this is why you're perfect."

"I'm not." I placed both hands around his neck, letting my nails drag along the tight muscles there. "But I'm here. And..." My throat tightened. It was my turn to lay it all out there. "And I'm yours. If you'll have me."

Torr's hands fell to my waist in a heavy, solid grip. "What about your gladiator?"

"That depends," I mused. "Would you let me keep him?"

His fingers closed into fists, bunching up the fabric of my dress. "Probably. As long as you keep me too."

We drifted closer together in a proximity that was familiar, yet these touches were completely unknown territory. "Never shut me out again," I said, meeting his eyes. "Talk to me, and don't bury what you're feeling. And I promise I'll never let you go. But if you shut me out again, that's it. We're done."

Torr nodded, his arms sliding around my back. "I'll do my best to not fuck it up." One hand returned to my face, his thumb measuring the distance between our lips as he whispered, "I'm sorry about how I acted. Then, now. All of it. Forgive me?"

"Yeah." Our noses touched now, the warmth of his mouth heating mine. "I still need you, Torr." I traced his mouth once before adding, "I still love you."

His kiss tasted like a drug I'd been craving since I was at least sixteen, maybe younger. It was a heady rush that made my knees buckle, but he was thankfully there to catch me. All the years of yearning, wishing, wanting, hit me like a motorcycle at full speed. And the reality was still better than I'd imagined.

Torr held me flush to his chest, an urgent tightness in his

grip that suggested he still had fears about me leaving him. That would take time to alleviate, and I was patient. I'd waited this long for him after all.

We parted for a breath of air, and I dragged my lips across his jaw to his ear. "Not going anywhere," I whispered, untucking his shirt to dive my hands underneath. "You might share me, but you'll always be mine."

"Yours," he groaned, palming my ass with both hands. "I've only ever wanted to be yours."

"You want your name tattooed back there?" I pressed lightly on his chest, making him walk backwards until he hit the couch, then shoved him down to lie on it. "Just say the word, and I'll do it."

I straddled him and together, we got his shirt off. All of the times I'd seen him topless, made excuses to touch him but not too gratuitously, it was laughable now. My hands ran shamelessly over his abs, his sculpted arms and shoulders, smoothing over the flat planes of his chest. He grabbed my wrist, stopping my hand directly over his heart.

"That's where I'm tattooing your name." He grinned. "And I'm gonna have your dad do it."

"Ew, no! Do not bring my dad up right now."

He laughed, then speared his fingers through my hair and closed his fist, bringing me down for a possessive kiss. "Let me try to be sweet," he growled against my lips.

I ground my core against his bulge, pressing into the friction separating us. "Try again without mentioning any of my family members."

"We should fuck on Daren's kitchen table when we get back. I always thought it was the perfect height for that."

"Torr!"

He cackled gleefully, and I had to admit the moment of pure joy lighting up his usually-brooding face was beautiful to see. Even as I squeezed a hand around his throat, glaring at him as hard as I could, I was laughing too.

"I'd kill you if I didn't love you so much." I was smiling too hard to sound threatening, and his grin pressed to mine, hands running up my thighs.

"You already kill me." His teeth scraped my lips as his fingers headed for the space between my legs. "You knock me dead all the fucking time."

"See, now you're being sweet—ah!"

He shoved my panties aside and touched my bare skin, palm and fingers stroking in a thorough, confident exploration of my pussy.

"You're so wet already," he groaned, eyes meeting mine. "Did your other man get you warmed up for me? How nice of him."

Torr stroked two fingers inside me, and I moaned, rocking forward onto his hand. He didn't sound jealous or spiteful, to my surprise. Maybe it was wishful thinking, but he actually sounded...pleased? It was one hell of a turn-on to think of him and Santos working together, that was for damn sure.

Who knows if I'd be able to keep them both, or if they'd even get along well enough to *want* to share me. But those were thoughts and discussions for another time, when everyone was safely out of this infernal place. And when I wasn't on the verge of coming from Torr's fingers hitting the most perfect spot inside me.

"Fuck." He gave no other warning as he grabbed my hip with his free hand, shoving me backwards off his legs as he rolled up. His fingers continued to work inside me, thumb rolling my clit as he brought his legs behind him and continued pressing me back.

"Torr, what—"

He pressed me down flat on the couch, brought one of my

legs over his shoulder, and dove down to seal his mouth over my clit.

"Oh, *fuck!*"

My hips spiked up so hard, I would've worried about him chipping a tooth if he wasn't already attached to me. He grabbed my ass with his free hand, supporting me while I writhed and bucked against his sensual mouth. Holy shit, his lips and tongue...he was doing some kind of light, constant suction over my clit which I'd never felt before, but it was fucking divine. Gone were the days of men just jamming their tongue against it with no finesse. Torr treated oral sex like an art form.

His fingers worked in perfect tandem with his mouth, spread and curled inside me for maximum friction as he hit that same, perfect spot over and over. I was still sensitive from the orgasm I'd given myself earlier and building up to another one fast. My last coherent thought as my head pressed back with a choked cry, was that maybe there was some benefit to Torr being a manwhore after all. He sure as fuck knew how to please.

The orgasm hit me like the most delicious stroke of lightning, amplified by Torr continuing to work me through the peak and descent until I pushed his head away. Grabbing a fistful of his dark hair, I pulled him up for a breathless kiss. My wetness coated his lips and tongue, and I absolutely loved it.

Through messy, desperate kisses, we both pulled apart his belt and undid his pants. I barely had a moment to touch him, to give his heavy length a stroke, before he notched it at my entrance and pressed all the way forward in one fluid thrust.

"Oh...God!" I clasped onto his arms, my breath stolen at the sudden intrusion filling me up.

"Too much?" He pulled back with a knowing smirk, grin spreading wider at my reaction to the slide of him through me. Cocky fucking asshole.

But he was *my* cocky asshole, and I'd make sure he'd never forget it.

"Don't you dare stop." I squeezed around his hips with my legs, drawing him in again as I locked my ankles behind his back.

"Not on your fucking life." He made sure my panties were still adequately pulled aside before thrusting in earnest, abs flexing like a damn porn star.

"You don't have to look so smug." My hands slid around to his back, pulling him down until we were chest-to-chest, and he settled perfectly between my legs.

"I just can't believe this is real." Torr's head went down to the pillow next to me, his nose touching mine. "I'm exactly where I want to be."

I kissed him, wondering how many '*I love you*'s would make him uncomfortable. He wouldn't say it back to me for a while, if ever. But I knew he was showing me, telling me in his own emotionally-constipated way. He was trying, and I had to meet him where he was, plus make him feel safe whenever he took a chance to be vulnerable.

"You're getting good at this being sweet thing." I hugged around him with my whole body, sinking into his delicious thrusts while running my nails up and down his back. "So fucking good," I added, though the compliment had nothing to do with his sweetness. He took long, deep strokes, stretching me wide and ensuring I felt every glorious inch of him. I moaned against his shoulder, taking the occasional biting kiss of that dense muscle whenever he pressed in especially deep.

"Fucking best I ever had," he groaned into my neck, hips crashing into me more forcefully.

I laughed with a small nip to his earlobe. "You don't have to protect my ego."

"I'm not, Rori." His head lifted, eyes blazing into mine as he cradled my neck and shoulders. "You know why you're the best?"

My heart crashing against my ribcage had nothing to do with the sex becoming more vigorous. "No. Why?"

"Because you're fucking *mine*."

He swelled thicker inside me, and I saw stars with every drag of his cock through me. My head pressed back, and he smothered my moans with deep, passionate kisses that told me more than the words '*I love you*' ever could. He angled my hips higher, striking down with powerful thrusts that hit my clit on every impact. I was screaming into his kiss, the pleasure coursing through me like a fiery river.

"Come for me," Torr said in a rough demand. His muscles were locked, tense and bulging as he pounded into me relentlessly. "Give me all your fucking pleasure, Rori. I need it."

The fire burned and consumed me in an explosive release, pulsing through my blood and licking across my skin. Torr spilled more heat inside me with a ragged growl, his body surging as he rode his own pleasure until he carefully lowered himself on top of me.

I was hot, sweaty, and short of breath, but no way was I going to shove him off me. I raked my fingers through his hair, running my nails over his neck and back until he shivered.

In return, Torr traced his index finger over my arm, spelling out three short words.

28

TORRANCE

I woke up on that same couch with a Rori-sized blanket draped on top of me. Her dress was gone, discarded sometime between the second and third round we went last night. My eyelids were still heavy with sleep, the best fucking sleep I'd had in nearly a week. I smoothed my hands up and down a long, naked back, the warmth of her skin lulling me back to dreamland.

"Question for you."

I startled, nearly dropping to the floor. "Jesus, it's creepy when you wake up and immediately start talking." Rori did that sometimes when we both crashed at Daren's house. One minute she was out like a light, the next, she was busting her brother's nuts for running out of eggs or coffee.

"Shush. I'm perfect, remember?" I felt a kiss on my collarbone and the scrape of a short fingernail circling my nipple. "You couldn't stop telling me that last night."

"Mm, perfectly creepy." I locked my arms around her and brushed a kiss against her forehead while I worked on the whole waking-up thing. "What's your question?"

"You were never going to tell me how you felt, back home." I opened my eyes to find her chin propped on my chest, looking straight at me. Her icy contacts were gone and her natural forest green eyes met mine. "I guess I'm just wondering what changed when we got to this place."

Everything.

I had to pause for a deep breath, fighting the urge to clam up and deflect. Rori and I had broken new ground. To be the man she deserved, I had to be honest with her. Especially when she asked difficult questions.

"Back home...I think I took for granted that you'd always be around. Here, I realized I could actually lose you."

Rori frowned. "To what?"

"Your gladiator, for one. I dunno, I just kind of had a gut instinct that something would happen. Shake up the life we were used to back home. I thought pushing you away would make it easier to get over you. But," my hand trailed up her spine to wrap around her shoulders, "it just made me more desperate to keep you."

"You're stuck with my creepy ass, Torr." She returned her cheek to my chest. "I don't know exactly where things are gonna go with Santos, but he's worth saving from this place."

"So's the Hunter. He seems like an alright guy." My thumb stroked back and forth on her shoulder as I thought. "I'm willing to bet most of those gladiators are decent, normal dudes forced into bad situations and not all mass rapists or whatever."

"I'm thinking the same thing." Rori's hand made a fist on top of my chest. "And they're getting them from somewhere, in steady supply. To get killed and abused every day."

I drummed my fingers on her arm. "As much as I love lying here with you, it's almost morning. We should've left hours ago."

"Yeah, let's head out." Rori sat up, and I reluctantly let my arm fall from her shoulders. "One more question," she piped up.

"Yes?" I held her waist, obsessed with the heat of her skin

and the gorgeous lines and shapes her body made. After only imagining touching her for so long, now I could never get enough.

"Why did you really come with me?"

At least that was easy to answer. "Because I don't ever want to be without you."

Rori froze, like that shocked her. Then she leaned down and held my chin as she kissed me. "I know you can't say it to me right now, and I'll never pressure you to do so," she whispered. "But I love you, Torr. I hope you believe me when I say that."

You're the only person I've allowed myself to fall for. I love you so much it fucking scares me.

The words rang out like a bell in my head, but they never reached my throat. I swallowed, cleared my throat, still nope. There was a complete disconnect from my mind to my mouth, and it pissed me off. Rori deserved to have those words said back to her, but I might not be the man to say them. Despite knowing and feeling the depth of those words for her, it felt like my ability to speak them was on the other side of a vast canyon.

The last time I had said them, I was discarded and left completely alone.

"I do believe you," I choked out. "I'm sorry I can't—"

"No, Torr. You have nothing to be sorry for." Rori held my face, smiling gently as she kissed me again. "Know that I love you. Know you're enough, and it'll all be okay."

I held her tightly for a final long kiss, wishing she could absorb everything I felt through my embrace. Not just my love but my gratitude that she accepted me like this, that she was patient and demanded nothing of me but my honesty.

That she was still my best friend.

I swatted her hip as our kiss ended. "Let's go, creep."

She groaned in annoyance as she slid off my lap, rising from the couch. "I don't know which is worse, creep or damsel."

"There's always honey." I watched her hips sway as she walked naked toward her bedroom, then ran up behind her to smack her ass.

"Ah!" Rori darted into the room and playfully glared as she peeked out from the behind door. "Definitely not that. I actually kind of like creep."

"Damsel it is then." I started toward my room, eager to dig out my jeans, boots, and leather jacket. No more of these fancy threads for me.

"Fuck you," Rori called.

Love you too, I wanted to call out in return. But damn, that heart-mouth disconnect tripped me up again. I really needed to work on that. More than anything, I wanted to see her face when I told her I loved her.

No more than five minutes could have passed when an insistent knock came pounding at the door.

"Shit."

Rori and I came out of our rooms at the same time, both dressed in jeans and leather, and looked at each other.

"Can we go out a window?" I asked her.

She ran to check when more hard pounding came to the door. "Mr. and Mrs. Renault! This is Nella, the guest services manager. It is imperative that I speak to you right away."

"No dice." Rori shook her head as she came back from the window. "It's a sheer drop into the canyon, not even any window sills or roofing to stand on. You want to hide? Fight?"

I clenched my fists, working through the scenarios in my head. Hiding was no good, they'd tear the suite apart and likely knew it better than we did. Fighting was also dicey, especially since we had no weapons. Nella had likely arrived with backup, and roughing up more staff than I already had was likely to cause more problems than fewer.

"We will enter the room in thirty seconds if you do not

comply!" Nella's voice called. Damn, she was not fucking around.

I held my hand out to Rori. "I think we need to face the music and see what we're dealing with."

She took my hand with a nod, lacing our fingers together and squeezing. "Together or not at all."

I love you. I brought the back of her palm to my lips and kissed it before we headed to the door together.

Rori unlocked the door with her free hand, standing slightly ahead of me as she swung it open. "Hello, Nella."

The woman was fuming mad. The scowl she always reserved for me was now aimed pointedly at Rori. The six armed guards behind her, though, were expressionless.

"Are you aware of what your husband has done?" Nella asked.

Rori stood a little straighter. "I am."

"That he inserted himself into routine disciplinary action, assaulted and gravely injured *four* of my staff?"

That was a bit of an exaggeration. I only *gravely* injured one guy.

"I'm aware," Rori answered.

"We do everything in our power to see to our guests' entertainment and comfort," Nella said stiffly. "But we have a zero tolerance policy for getting involved in staff duties and harming those who work here. You two are to leave the premises immediately."

"We figured as much." Rori nodded and smiled politely. "We don't want to cause any further trouble and will be on our way."

Nella blinked, and her expression cracked a little, like she wasn't expecting us to be so compliant. "Very well," she said stiffly. "We'll escort you out."

I released a breath, not realizing I'd been holding it as we stepped over the threshold. Nella led the way, while the guard flanked us on either side and marched at our backs. Rori and I kept our hands connected as we walked, the two of us on high alert. People gawked and whispered as we walked past, but they weren't my concern. I was trying to figure what the catch was, which trapdoor someone would open that would shoot us to the middle of the sand pit to be the bait for the next fight.

Once the elevator was in view, I started to relax a little. Maybe a walk of shame was a big deal to these people, or maybe being banished from the most exclusive resort in the world was considered punishment enough. Big whoop. We'd be back. Just not as fucking guests.

Nella stepped onto the large, concrete platform, and Rori and I followed behind her. The elevator was at the top of the canyon, making a slow descent toward us. Rori leaned her temple on my shoulder, and I kissed the side of her head as we waited.

The glass cage was halfway down the canyon wall when Nella turned to face us with an expression of smug, evil glee.

"Take him," she ordered.

My arms were grabbed faster than I could process, and I was yanked backward off the platform, my hand torn from Rori's.

"No, Torr!"

I heard Rori's cry of protest but was forced to the ground and could no longer see her. Metal cuffs slapped over my wrists, locking them behind my back. Well, at least I still had fucking legs and elbows.

I rolled over to my back, kicking out, and got one guy in the nards. He hissed in pain and backed away, cupping himself, but that still wasn't much of a reaction for how hard I got him. He had to be wearing protection, fuck.

Another guy leaned over me, and I headbutted him. The opportunity gave me a split second to roll up to my knees and check on my woman. Rori was fighting like a hellcat against two of the guards, but they both restrained her to the point where she couldn't do much. Nella just stood off to the side, all smug bitch power pose.

That split second was one too long, sadly. A fist cracked into my jaw and sent me back face down into the dirt with no way to block it. I scrambled to get my feet under me again, and hot, crackling pain zipped up through my whole body. Fucking tasers.

"You fucking rotten bitch, call them off!" Rori screamed. "Let him go!"

"Mm, I think not," Nella said. "I think he'd make a fine gladiator, actually."

It took all four of those guards to start dragging me toward the colosseum, and I made sure they fought for every inch they took me away from her. I kept getting punched, tazed, and restrained until my vision went dark and I could no longer hear Rori swearing to kill them all.

* * *

I COULDN'T FIGURE out if the oppressive darkness was due to my surroundings or being unconscious. My body felt solid, so at least that was a plus, even though everything ached like hell.

Trying to get myself oriented, I rolled with a groan to discover I was on a lying on a hard, dusty floor. It smelled musty here, like there was little fresh air to go around. I blinked my eyes, then brought a hand up in front of my face and wiggled my fingers. Nothing but darkness. Shit, had I been blinded?

I brought my hand to my face and felt around. Yeah, it was sore and swollen in places, but my eyeballs were still there. Either something had been done to my eyes or I was truly in the darkest fucking pit on earth.

"Who's there?"

I scrambled upright, searching my inky black surroundings for the disembodied voice. It sounded like a man, but I had a small flash of hope that it was Astarte. "I could ask you the same thing," I answered.

"Who are you? I don't recognize your voice." Definitely a man.

"Once again, I could ask you the same fuckin' thing."

There was a huff of breath, almost like a laugh. "Hang on. I'm going to walk towards you."

"No thanks." I swept my arms around me as I started moving backwards, away from the voice. "How do I know you don't have a weapon?"

"Dude. You think even if I had one, I can see any better than you do?"

"I dunno, man. I don't know where the fuck I am."

There was a long pause. "Are you a gladiator?"

"No. Not yet, anyway."

Another pause. "A guest, then?"

I was really starting to hate that word. "You could say that. Although given where I am, you could say I'm not very welcome anymore."

"Fuck," the guy whispered. "You're him. Did she escape?"

Footsteps rushed at me, and I felt the presence of a big, muscular guy right in my face. "Whoa! Hold on, I'm right here." My hands stretched out to put space between us, and they landed on a wide set of shoulders only inches in front of me.

"Rori. Aurora," the guy said, leaning into my palms. "Did she get out? She said she was getting out. If you're in here, did she make it?"

Oh shit. I knew exactly who this was.

"You're Santos."

I heard a hiss of surprise and then felt two arms swiftly

break the contact of my hands on his shoulders. "How do you know my real name?"

"Rori told me. And...I dunno." I shook my head even though he couldn't see. "We were right at the elevator, and they separated us. I got knocked out before I saw what they did to her."

"Fuck!"

I felt Santos' presence back away and heard the shuffling of pacing steps a moment later. I wanted to do the same, but I knew Rori better than he did and felt the overwhelming sense to reassure him.

"She'll figure something out, man. We won't be in here too long."

"That's what I'm worried about," he grumbled. "If she finds out we're both in here, she'll want to spring us so bad, she won't stop to consider all the pitmasters in the resort coming after her." The pacing stopped. "What did she tell you about me?"

"Well, she likes you. A lot. And...she told me what happened last time she saw you."

The pause that followed was the longest one yet. "Why would she tell you what we did?" He sounded a touch possessive, which I couldn't blame him for, but not angry. It seemed more like he was curious, which made me wonder how much Rori had told him about us.

I took a deep breath. This felt like a horrible idea, considering I would be stuck with him in this pitch black cell for who knew how long. But he was someone Rori cared about, and he deserved to know the truth. If he couldn't handle her being with both of us, well, then he wasn't right for her anyway.

"When she came back from seeing you, we talked and... well, aired out a lot of things that had been unsaid for too long and kind of...turned over a new leaf."

This next pause was brief, and then soft laughter filled the air. It slowly grew louder, unconstrained, and nearly hysterical. "I *knew* it."

"Knew what?"

"That the fool she came here with would finally wise up before she slipped through his fingers."

Okay, I deserved that. "Yeah, you're right," I sighed. "I was that fool, but not anymore."

"And now she's your girl. Congratulations."

"Well, she's yours too."

I didn't have to wait long for a reaction. The gladiator shuffled over to me until his shoes gently bumped into mine. He touched my shoulder and followed down the length of my arm until he found my hand. Then he clasped his hand against mine.

"Guess we might as well get to know each other."

29

RORI

"Torr! Torr! Fucking wake up! Torr!" I struggled hard, fueled by fury, but the armed guards barely budged as they restrained me between them. I could only scream my throat raw as the four other guards dragged Torr's limp body away.

Straight to the colosseum.

When I realized we were in the elevator heading up, I called on every technique my fathers had taught me to get out of a hold. But because there were two of them and we were in an enclosed space, I couldn't get any leverage. I couldn't even kick my feet out because my legs had nowhere to go. My guards each had a leg braced in front of mine with both hands clasped tightly to my arms.

There was no fucking escape.

It still didn't keep me from fighting. Once we reached the top and the glass door opened, they took me a few steps forward, then released me. I spun around, ready to throw punches and kicks so hard they'd need kidney transplants, only to find two gun barrels pointed at my chest.

"Walk away," one of the guards said. "If you start now, you

260

might find someone to pick you up before you die of heat stroke."

"Fuck you," I spat. "I'm not leaving without him."

"You take one step toward this canyon, you're vulture food." The other guard cocked his weapon. "We're giving you this chance to live because you're a woman. But you will never come near here again or breathe a word of this resort. If you do, there will be consequences."

"Like what?"

"Trust us, you don't want to know. The resort owners have the means to enslave you and your whole family."

If there was just one of them with a gun, I could have had a chance to take it from him. But two was too risky. Still, I wanted to laugh in their faces. They had no fucking idea who I knew or what I had at my disposal.

But I wasn't about to show all my cards. I wanted them to underestimate me. And most importantly, I needed a healthy amount of backup to get Torr and Santos out alive.

"Alright." I started to turn away, toward the empty, barren desert. "You won't see me again."

"If we do, we won't give you a second chance."

As much as it prickled my skin to turn my back, I started walking away. Seconds later, I heard the sound of the elevator heading down to the canyon floor.

I looked eastward. The sun would be rising soon, and then I might be in trouble. This was the Great Wasteland, and I had no food, water, or wheels to get me anywhere. Shit, where would I even go? That tavern we stayed at was a good three-hour drive away, and there was no cell reception there. Home was even farther away.

My hands flew over my jacket and jeans pockets in a panicked rush. A huge sigh of relief deflated my lungs when I found my phone. I pulled it out and turned it on. No reception and only 12% battery. Fuck.

I turned it off to conserve the battery and returned it to my pocket to look around again. Where could I go? *Come on, Rori...*

My gaze settled on the brightest part of the sky again—east. That way was Sevier, my Aunt Kyrie's territory. I had some other family there too, probably closer to me if I was estimating correctly. It would still be hours away, but it was closer than home, and I should be able to make phone calls as I got closer.

Resolved, I started walking toward the rising sun.

I had only gone a few hundred yards when a certain dove chose to settle on top of a cactus and coo at me.

Now I really wished I had a gun.

"Oh, fuck you!" I yelled up at the bird. "Huge fucking help you've been, thank you very much! Do me a favor, and just fuck off, alright? I don't need you, Astarte."

Yes, you do, Aurora. The bird shook out its feathers. *Now more than ever, you do.*

"You know what? I'll take my chances, thanks."

I am not a pet you can dismiss, child. Astarte's voice pressed like a tangible weight against my skin. *You cannot perceive all the threads woven into your destiny, but I see them all. And without me, those threads will tangle and choke you like a fly in a spider's web.*

"Yeah, great job keeping me untangled from the shitshow that just happened. Torr and Santos could be dead or tortured, and for what?" I spread my arms out, looking up helplessly to the god. "What the fuck is the point, Astarte?"

Typical human, she scoffed. *Always so short-sighted.*

"Then fuck off and leave me alone!"

The dove flew off, and while I was grateful for the peace, I couldn't shake the sense that Astarte could see everything. My future, my thought process. My decisions and motivations, like she was both inside my head and also zoomed all the way out with a bird's eye view of the map of my life.

Whatever. As long as that deity stayed out of my line of sight and didn't talk to me anymore.

I was pissed, and since I had nothing to shoot or hit, I put all of my anger into walking east. The sun peeked over the mountains in the distance, gradually revealing itself fully. And on I walked.

The sun rose higher, and I kept walking long after feeling the uncomfortable prickle of a sunburn on my nose and cheeks. After some time, I noticed my shadow in front of me, gradually getting longer. My feet had started aching hours ago, the pain fading to numbness now. I didn't even want to think about my hunger and thirst. That would send my mind into a panic, and I didn't want to venture off-course in a futile search for water.

One foot in front of the other. Again. And again. And again.

At some point, the sun started to set directly behind me, and I felt its fiery blaze on my neck. I knew I had to have walked miles, but I couldn't begin to guess how many. I felt myself starting to sway, exhaustion settling in when my pissed-off determination ran out. As the eastern sky began to darken, I didn't know how I was still upright, let alone moving.

And in a few hours, I'd be in trouble with no shelter and no sun to guide my way. I wasn't much of a star navigator.

Shadow's oddly poignant advice came to me at that moment. *You're stronger than you think you are. There will be times when you want to give up, but you won't. You're going to hold on, because you have it in you.*

"I dunno, Dadow." I could only mouth the words through my cracked lips. "I don't know if I have any more in me."

When the ground beneath my feet felt different, I looked down and had to stare for a few moments before my exhausted brain could process the information.

I was standing on a road. A decently well-paved stretch of highway.

Looking up, the reflective highway sign was riddled with bullet holes but still readable. The red stripe across the top said INTERSTATE. The big white numbers underneath that on the blue background read 80.

Somehow, I put the brain cells together to pull out my phone and turn it on. I stared at it so long, my battery dropped down to 10%. It was with a mixture of disbelief and pure exhaustion that I could only stare at the single tiny bar of cell reception.

Eventually, my aching fingers managed to open up my contacts and call one of the few numbers that actually had a chance of finding me before I perished out here. I brought the phone to my ear and prayed the call wouldn't drop.

The phone rang once. Twice. Thrice.

Once there was a click on the line, I didn't wait for a hello. "LJ, it's Rori." My voice was as rough as sandpaper. "I'm in trouble, and I need a big fucking favor."

Of course, my excitable-as-a-golden-retriever cousin talked right over me and didn't hear a thing I said. "Hey, Ror! What's up? Haven't heard from you in a while. What's new?" There was a shuffling and then I heard his voice farther away. "Carter, guess who it is? Our favorite cousin! What? Of course it's Rori! Nah, I don't know where she's at."

"Lark!" I yelled into the phone, but my throat was so dry it came out like a whisper. "Stop talking for a second! I need your help."

He finally went serious and quiet over the phone. "What's going on, Ror? Where are you?"

"Somewhere in old Nevada, about three hours north of Carvers. I'm on the old interstate 80. I'll explain later, but can you head west and pick me up?"

There was a pause, and I had a moment of terror that the call had dropped, but finally LJ spoke up. "Yeah, cuz. Me and Carter can be there in a few hours. You okay? You need food? Water?"

"Please...and thank you."

"Is Daren or anyone with you?"

"No, and don't fucking call him," I rasped. "Or my parents either. I need to handle some shit and don't want them to worry."

There was another long pause on the phone. LJ was three years older than me and somewhat of an older brother figure. It could go either way that he'd insist on tattling to my folks or be down for what I was about to tell him.

"Should we bring guns?" he asked finally.

"Arm yourselves, just in case. But we don't need the whole armory. Yet."

"Yet, huh? Sounds like you're gonna need it later."

"Yeah, I'll also need bikes." I clenched the phone in my hand. "And a whole lot of fucking firepower."

EPILOGUE
HUDSON

I hated women.

There was nothing in this world that I despised more. I hated their manipulation and lies, their abuse and humiliation. Nothing from their mouths could be trusted. I'd never met a man as joyfully sadistic as every single woman I'd met here.

Almost every man I ran across in here had been confused, bewildered. And then soon enough, terrified. But at least they eventually got the sweet release of death.

As for me? I was still here. And every day was hell.

Santos and Devin weren't afraid, though. They made this place almost bearable. We had each other's backs. Even though Santos was weak, always looking for an extra second at the prettier ones, he understood the situation we were in. This hell that had thrown us together and become our lives.

Now Santos and Devin were gone, and I had nothing left. I was pure hate, barely held together by a man's body.

I hated their smug smiles, their laughter and taunts. But what I hated most of all was that my cock still got hard for them.

Sexual pleasure was a long distant memory, growing fainter

by the day. I felt nothing. My body was a machine, responding to stimuli as it slowly broke down from overuse. One day, it would be beyond repair. That was the only thing I looked forward to, when I would be useless and they would finally be rid of me.

I fantasized about killing them, abusing and torturing them in the same way they did to me. What I would give to see fear twist their features, hear their pathetic cries for help, feel the life get squeezed out of them under my hand. How would it feel to turn the tables and release this burning, bitter hatred that churned inside me like a constant, angry sea?

I hated that even malnourished and weak, I could still kill them if I wasn't shackled all the time. I wouldn't even have to find a weapon, my bare hands would be enough. But I couldn't even remember the last time I had free use of my limbs.

These weak, evil creatures didn't care about fairness, didn't care that I'd never dreamed of hurting a woman before they captured me.

They made me into this.

I was an ordinary man once, just trying to get by like everyone else. I made the mistake of accepting a drink a pretty woman bought for me, then woke up here.

I hated them for everything they took from me.

The current one rolled off of me, and I barely noticed. Dissociation was a skill I'd honed well in this place. I didn't have to look at her to know she was on her back, knees to her chest and her hips tilted up as her labored breathing slowed.

"You're going to give me another daughter," she said cheerfully. Like this was some consensual thing, a decision we made together. She was lying in the bed next to me like we were both involved in what just happened. Now *that* was a fucking joke.

I would have vomited if I could still feel anything. Instead I said, "I hope this one makes you bleed to death."

The woman scoffed. "You are so ungrateful. You have the privilege of creating the next generation of Sisters, and you do nothing but stare at the ceiling and complain. You're lucky your body is nice and your seed is strong. Otherwise, you'd be a moon sacrifice or blood bag."

I'd rather be anything than this. Dead would be most preferable.

The woman turned to face me when I didn't answer her. In some distant part of my brain, I recognized that she scooted closer to me. Her hand came to my chest, her head on my shoulder.

"You don't *have* to be chained up, you know," she murmured, brushing her lips over me. "If you would just... accept your role in this. You would be given so much freedom, veneration even. You would be one of the few men respected in our society, the father who gave us life and made us multiply."

Even if I believed her, I was too dead on the inside to find any enticement in her offer. My heart, my will, my resolve—it had all rotted and withered to nothing but ash. I was only waiting for my outside to match the inside.

She sighed, as if disappointed that I didn't respond again, and lifted away from me. The absence of her touch was only a mild relief.

"The next Sister will clean you before she takes you inside her."

She rolled off the bed, and the mattress creaked as she stood up. Clothes rustled. A toilet flushed. A door opened and closed. All background noise, compartmentalized to a distant part of my mind.

Like always, I sent up a prayer that the next woman would be kind enough to smother me with a pillow.

And for the first time, there was an answer.

Your suffering is temporary, Hudson. You have not been forsaken. Hold on.

My head snapped up from the pillow, looking around the barren room. "Who's there?"

I am with you. With Santos and Devin. You are not alone. Vengeance will be had, my dear son. Hold on for me, just a little longer.

The voice was in my head, but it also ran over my skin like a tangible touch. The first and only one I'd welcomed in years. I was either losing my shit for real or my countless prayers were finally being answered.

"Who are you?" I whispered.

A gust of wind howled violently, and my head snapped to the single small window in the room. The night sky was dotted with stars. I could see them even through the tree branches that scraped against the glass like a monster trying to break in.

I am everything their goddess wishes she could be, the voice said. *I am war. I am sorcery and desire. I am vengeance.*

* * *

TO BE CONTINUED IN HARMLESS - VENGEFUL
GODS MC BOOK 2

PRE-ORDER AVAILABLE NOW:
https://books2read.com/VGMC2

* * *

Want to read about Mari's adventure with the Steel Demons MC? Their series is complete and begins with Lawless.

Start reading now: https://books2read.com/SDMC1

LIKE FREE BOOKS?

Sign up for Crystal Ash's newsletter and get two free short stories!
https://books.bookfunnel.com/crystalashprequels

You can also join my Facebook group, The Ash Coven:
https://www.facebook.com/groups/ashcoven

ACKNOWLEDGMENTS

Dear reader,

Thank you for choosing to read Faithless! I hope you enjoyed it and continue on the ride with Rori and her men.

A big thank you to Telisha, the best editor I could ask for, even when you troll me. Thank you Izzy for staying on top of things when my head is all over the place.

This book would not be possible without my amazing Steel Demons MC fans! Thank you for letting me know how much you love this world and these characters. Rori's got big shoes to fill, so let's see what kind of girl our Demons raised. ;)

See you in Harmless!

-Crystal

ALSO BY CRYSTAL ASH

Harem of Freaks: The Complete Series

Say Your Prayers

Steel Demons MC

Lawless

Powerless

Fearless

Painless

Helpless

Heartless

Senseless

Ruthless

Merciless

Endless

Shifted Mates Trilogy

Unholy Trinity: The Complete Series

For a complete list of books by Crystal Ash, visit her Amazon page.

ABOUT THE AUTHOR

Crystal Ash is a USA Today Bestselling Author from California. She loves writing steamy, heart-wrenching romance with tortured heroes, especially if they're in a reverse harem. Crystal's other loves include animals, mythology, and well-crafted alcohol, most of which can also be found in her stories.

When she's not writing, she's probably drinking craft beer with her husband or trying to coax her feral cat into accepting affection.

crystalashbooks.com

facebook.com/Crystal.Ash.Romance

instagram.com/crystalashbooks

amazon.com/author/crystalash

bookbub.com/profile/crystal-ash